THE MYSTERIES OF THE COUCH

Steen grimaced. "Lieutenant, excuse me. I imagine that to you I sound somewhat heartless. Believe me, I have been deeply shaken—the whole psychiatric community has been. Don't you realize how much all of us wish to see Noah's murderer caught? But there are standards, limits. Do you have the slightest sense of the panic that will ensue among all of our patients when the word gets around—and it *will* get around, I assure you— that the police are reading through a psychiatrist's files?"

He turned to Brenda. "You're a psychologist, Dr. Goldstein. You know what goes on in therapy. It is only because people trust that what they say will never go beyond the room that they have the courage to open up. That is the most important thing we analysts have going for us. If that trust is ever destroyed, we might as well hang up our shingles. . . ."

Bantam Books offers the finest in classic and modern American murder mysteries. Ask your bookseller for the books you have missed.

Stuart Palmer

Murder on the Blackboard

Rex Stout

Broken Vase
Death of a Dude
Death Times Three
Fer-de-Lance
The Final Deduction
Gambit
The Rubber Band

Max Allan Collins

The Dark City

William Kienzle

The Rosary Murders

Joseph Louis

Madelaine
The Trouble With Stephanie

M.J. Adamson

Not Till a Hot February
A February Face
Remember March
April When They Woo

Barbara Paul

First Gravedigger
But He Was Already Dead When
 I Got There

P.M. Carlson

Murder Unrenovated
Rehearsal for Murder

Ross Macdonald

The Goodbye Look
Sleeping Beauty
The Name Is Archer
The Drowning Pool
The Underground Man
The Zebra-Striped Hearse
Black Money

Margaret Maron

The Right Jack
Baby Doll Games
Coming Soon: One Coffee With

William Murray

When the Fat Man Sings

Robert Goldsborough

Murder in E Minor
Death on Deadline

Sue Grafton

"A" Is for Alibi
"B" Is for Burglar
"C" Is for Corpse
"D" Is for Deadbeat

R.D. Brown

Hazzard
Villa Head

A.E. Maxwell

Just Another Day in Paradise
The Frog and the Scorpion

Bob Kantner

Back-Door Man
The Harder They Hit

Joseph Telushkin

The Unorthodox Murder of Rabbi Wahl
The Final Analysis of Dr. Stark

Richard Hilary

Snake in the Grasses
Pieces of Cream
Pillow of the Community

Carolyn G. Hart

Design for Murder
Death on Demand
Something Wicked

Lia Matera

Where Lawyers Fear to Tread
A Radical Departure
Smart Money

Robert Crais

The Monkey's Raincoat

Keith Peterson

The Trapdoor

Jim Stinson

Double Exposure

Carolyn Wheat

Where Nobody Dies

THE FINAL ANALYSIS
OF
DR. STARK

Joseph Telushkin

BANTAM BOOKS

TORONTO • NEW YORK • LONDON • SYDNEY • AUCKLAND

THE FINAL ANALYSIS OF DR. STARK
A Bantam Book / July 1988

ISBN 0-553-26695-0

Published simultaneously in the United States and Canada

Bantam Books are published by Bantam Books, a division of Bantam
Doubleday Dell Publishing Group, Inc. Its trademark, consisting
of the words "Bantam Books" and the portrayal of a rooster, is
Registered in U.S. Patent and Trademark Office and in other
countries. Marca Registrada. Bantam Books, 666 Fifth Avenue,
New York, New York 10103

PRINTED IN THE UNITED STATES OF AMERICA

KR   0 9 8 7 6 5 4 3 2 1

*For Shalva and Howard,
and Meir, Nisan, and Sharona Siegel*

Acknowledgments

Four people helped me greatly in editing this book. Daniel Taub worked with me in the very first stages of its writing, and enriched the text with his keen stylistic advice. I trust that his own ventures into mystery writing will soon be reaching a wider audience. Linda Kachani has worked with me on my last three books, and has once again blessed me with numerous wonderful suggestions and original insights. Dvorah Menashe has helped deepen my characters as she has deepened my life, and God willing, we will be spending the rest of it together. And finally, my editor at Bantam, Kate Miciak. In the preface to *The Unorthodox Murder of Rabbi Wahl* I referred to Kate's editorial suggestions as brilliant. In the writing of this book, they were even more brilliant, and my gratitude to her is truly deeper than anything I can express in words.

My good friend, David Brandes, sat with me patiently while I was working out the story line, and offered invaluable plot suggestions. A number of other friends helped me on specific scenes, generously sharing their time and expertise—in particular, Connie Kestenbaum, Efraim Zuroff, Arlene Lepoff, and Michael Agress. I request forgiveness from anyone whose name I have inadvertantly omitted.

I would like to thank the Art Scroll Series for the volume of Chassidic stories retold by the late Rabbi Zevin, which they published several years ago, and which influenced an early scene in this book; Rabbi Maurice Lamm and his book *The Jewish Way in Death and Dying*; and Elie Wiesl, whose lecture on Rabbi Akiva which I heard almost twenty years ago, has remained with me ever since.

Chapter 1

Monday Morning

"But I tell you, he won't leave, Mr. Schonfeld. He just sits there, reading some large book, and whenever I tell him you're too busy to see him, he just smiles up at me and says, 'That's okay, I'll wait.'"

Lester Schonfeld scowled. It just didn't make sense. Rabbi Daniel Winter of Congregation B'nai Zion, where Schonfeld maintained a nominal membership, had shown up at First Beverly Savings two hours earlier—totally unscheduled—and insisted on seeing him. When Schonfeld's secretary, Carol Harper, informed him that the bank president's schedule was filled—not only that, but he had a two o'clock flight to New York—the rabbi had merely smiled pleasantly, and remained in his seat. When she pressed him for the reason for the meeting, he apologized for being secretive, but said he couldn't elaborate.

"It's just impossible for me to see him today," the corpulent executive said with finality, stabbing his forefinger at the stack of folders on his desk. He shook his bald head. "Who does this rabbi think he is, anyway? Doesn't he understand the word no?"

Carol only shrugged helplessly and dug the toe of her elegant black shoe into the carpet.

Schonfeld let out a long, exasperated sigh. "What the hell! Okay, Carol, I'll be back from New York on Sunday. Tell that to Rabbi Winter. Next week, *he can name* the day and the time." Giving her a satisfied smile of dismissal, he turned to the file in front of him.

Carol was back in under a minute. "He says he'll wait."

Schonfeld pulled off his glasses and muttered a curse. He couldn't understand it. From what he'd seen of the rabbi—on his thrice-yearly pilgrimages to the synagogue —Winter had seemed like a reasonable man. And in fact, he knew that First Beverly's biggest depositor, Sam Bornstein, who also happened to be the synagogue's president, considered Winter the greatest thing to hit the rabbinate since Moses.

So what was the rabbi up to? Soliciting a charitable contribution? Fine. Schonfeld would kick in what was expected. Or maybe, he thought, a sardonic smile curling his lips, the young rabbi would try to give him some religion. He had a momentary vision of Winter winding a pair of *tefillin* around his left arm, or hammering a *mezuzah* onto his office doorpost. He pursed his thick lips. But that couldn't be it. If that were the case, Winter would surely have enough savvy not to barge in without warning.

"What do I tell him, Mr. Schonfeld?" Carol asked uncomfortably.

Tell him to get lost is what Schonfeld felt like saying. But his late father's words came back to him—*Never act fresh to a rabbi.*

"Do we have a choice?" Schonfeld said through gritted teeth. "Show the dear rabbi in."

A moment later Schonfeld, smiling broadly, was ushering Daniel Winter to a suede chair.

"I suspect I caught you on a bad day," the young rabbi began earnestly, leaning forward in his seat. "Please accept my apologies."

"Oh, it's nothing," Schonfeld replied loudly. "As soon as my secretary told me it was urgent, I said to her"—and he made a sweeping arc with his arms—" 'Carol, if my rabbi thinks it's important enough for him to come to me, everything else gets put aside.' " That was another lesson his father had taught him—*If you're going to be gracious, be gracious.*

2

The rabbi relaxed into the levered armchair and stroked his firm, square jaw, while Schonfeld waited expectantly.

"So, how's your family, Mr. Schonfeld?" the rabbi finally asked.

"Er-r, fine. The missus just came back last week from one of those UJA missions to Israel. Said next year she'd *schlepp* me along.

"Have you been?"

"Not yet."

"I envy you."

"What!"

"I envy anybody their first trip to Israel."

"Oh!" Schonfeld said with a short laugh. "Good line, Rabbi. But could you please—"

"And the children?" the rabbi continued. "That's Jeremy and . . . Allison, right?"

"Very good, Rabbi." *Who's he kidding,* Schonfeld thought. *Obviously he looked their names up on his Rolodex before he came here.* He paused, but the rabbi's blue eyes were fixed on him with a disconcerting expectancy. Nonplussed, Schonfeld went on reluctantly. "Well, Jeremy's in his last year at Berkeley, and Allison will be starting there next year. Now, Rabbi—"

"What is Jeremy majoring in?"

"Economics," Schonfeld half-snapped, then caught himself. "Rabbi—"

The phone rang. Grateful for the interruption, Schonfeld took the call. For the next three minutes, half his mind was focused on a dollar that was in sharp decline against the Swiss franc, the other half on Daniel Winter. The rabbi had opened a frayed brown book, and appeared deeply engrossed in it. From the right to left movement of the rabbi's eyes, Schonfeld deduced that it was in Hebrew. Rows of tiny print seemed to alternate in crisscross fashion. *What the dickens was going on here?*

He hung up and heaved a huge sigh. "Rabbi, you realize I have the highest regard for you. But the truth is, today is a bit hectic for me. So if you . . ."

Again, the phone.

"Carol," Schonfeld said sharply, scooping up the extension, "hold all calls. Oh!" He shrugged an apology at the rabbi. "Okay, put him through. But after this, hold *everything.*"

His eyes scrutinized Winter throughout the conversation. *Calm guy,* Schonfeld thought. *Wish I could be that calm.* He surreptitiously checked his watch—12:05. He winced. Finally, he finished the call.

"Okay, Rabbi, I've cleared the decks." *I'll give him five minutes. Rabbi or no rabbi.*

But the rabbi was on his feet. "Thank you very much for seeing me, Mr. Schonfeld. All the best." Leaning across the gleaming desk, he gave the startled man a firm handshake and started for the door.

"Rabbi!" Schonfeld's sharp cry stopped the rabbi inside of three steps. "You wanna tell me . . . I mean, could you please tell me why you came here?"

The rabbi turned around, appeared to meditate for a moment, and then answered slowly, "Mr. Schonfeld, I came here to perform a mitzvah."

"A what?"

"A mitzvah," the rabbi repeated gravely. "You know, a commandment. And now that I've performed it, I can go."

"Which mitz . . . commandment?" Schonfeld stammered, curious in spite of himself.

The rabbi motioned to the book in his hand. "In Jewish law it is a commandment to refrain from saying something you know will not be listened to. So, I came here today to fulfill that commandment."

Schonfeld blinked. "Rabbi, why did you come *here?*"

The rabbi responded mildly. "Because if I stay in my office and you stay in yours, can I adequately carry out the commandment? Obviously not. In order to fulfill it properly, one has to go to the office of the man who will not listen, and *there* refrain from speaking to him. And that's precisely what I did."

Schonfeld stood up. His face was flushed, but his fath-

4

er's words still rang in his ears, and he couldn't ignore them. *Never act fresh to a rabbi.* . . . He struggled to make sense of the encounter. "Perhaps, Rabbi," he entreated, "you'll be so kind as to explain to me what the thing is I won't listen to? Who knows, perhaps I will listen?"

The rabbi shook his head. "I'm afraid not."

Schonfeld pressed him further, but the rabbi continued to refuse. The more he refused, the more Schonfeld felt compelled to learn the secret. "Rabbi, you're driving me crazy. Please tell me," he pleaded.

The rabbi was silent, staring pensively at the book in his hand. Frustrated, Schonfeld tugged at the thin tufts of hair at the side of his head. His two o'clock flight was forgotten.

Finally the rabbi looked up. "Mr. Schonfeld, you know Sadie Rosen, don't you?"

Schonfeld shook his head mutely, baffled.

"From the synagogue. You spoke to her on the phone last week. Her husband Max died last year. They were both Holocaust survivors. It seems she's fallen quite behind in her mortgage payments. She showed me a letter on your stationery, signed by you. Your bank's going to repossess her house, Mr. Schonfeld. She'll be out on the street. She's seventy-six years old."

Schonfeld waved his arms, his former hearty tone restored. "Oh, so that's it, Rabbi, you don't understand. It's not like the debt is owed to me personally. I'm an understanding guy, you know that. Personally, I'd give Mrs. . . . er-r . . . Rosen another year's extension in a minute. But it's not me—it's the bank. We have a very strict policy here. She got three warnings, and six months extension. But there's a limit, Rabbi. We have a fiduciary responsibility to our depositors."

The rabbi shook his head; his dark blue eyes were unreadable. "It's exactly as I said all along—that you wouldn't listen."

And with that, he left the room, leaving Schonfeld staring speechlessly at the closed door.

* * *

Brenda Goldstein darted into her office at homicide headquarters and grabbed the ringing phone.

"This is Hilda Bornstein," the caller began in a cozy, honeyed tone. "I just wanted to make sure that you'll be joining us tonight, Ms. Goldstein."

"Yes, of course."

"You should know that you're the only non-Board member we've invited. The rabbi specially requested that you be sent an invitation. It's very, very special for us—and for the rabbi too, I'm sure—that you'll be there. And we're all *so* looking forward to meeting you." Hilda Bornstein paused, then added silkily, "Everybody thinks it's time. The synagogue needs a rebbetzin."

Brenda gave an involuntary gasp, then recovered quickly and finished the conversation. She hung up the phone and sank into her chair, then picked up the silver invitation on her desk.

SAM AND HILDA BORNSTEIN ARE PLEASED TO INVITE YOU TO A RECEPTION AT THEIR HOME, MONDAY EVENING, MAY 4TH, AT 7:30 P.M., IN HONOR OF THE PUBLICATION OF RABBI WINTER'S NEW BOOK, STICKS AND STONES.

What am I in for? she thought. *A whole evening with wealthy, middle-aged synagogue leaders—all trying to decide if I'll make a suitable rebbetzin for Rabbi Daniel Winter and for their congregation—is not my idea of a fun time.*

She played with the idea. A rebbetzin. Rebbetzin Brenda Goldstein Winter.

She almost laughed out loud.

Russell Grant sat down hard on the black leather recliner. Three months earlier, when he had first come to Noah Stark's office, Grant had spent two sessions stretched out on the psychiatrist's long maroon couch, his eyes focused on the ceiling. He hadn't cared for the experience.

The Final Analysis of Dr. Stark

Russell Grant wanted facial reactions, feedback. He was a man who had to know where he stood. Particularly today.

"See the *Times* this morning, Doctor?"

"Just the headlines. Why?"

Grant bent over the right arm of his chair and deftly raised an elegant grey attaché case. He dialed several numbers, popped the case open, and tossed the *Los Angeles Times* onto Stark's desk. "Page eight, first section."

The article was conspicuous at the top of the page. *LA Area Congressman Considering Senate Race.* While Stark silently perused the article, Grant perused him. With his athletic, blond good looks and seemingly unshakable poise, Stark wouldn't make a bad candidate himself, he thought.

"What do you think?" Grant asked with studied casualness when the psychiatrist looked up, half-smiling.

"Not bad, Russell. It makes you sound quite statesmanlike."

Grant did not return the smile. "Notice the name of the guy who wrote it?"

Stark glanced down. "Roger Levin."

"He's one of your boys, isn't he?"

"Meaning?"

You know damn well what I mean, Grant thought savagely. His glare bore straight into Stark's dark, impassive eyes. "He's Jewish, right?"

"Levins usually are," Stark replied dryly.

"Do you know him?"

The psychiatrist shifted his big body, then leaned forward. "You want to tell me what your concerns are?"

"Would you just answer my question?" Grant insisted, his voice rising.

Stark's expression did not change. "I have no intention of being evasive with you, Russell. But I'm far more concerned with how upset you seem to be. And I'm not sure where it's coming from."

"You want to know where it's coming from, *Dr. Stark?* From the fact that you sit there every time we talk, taking all sorts of notes about me, but you never tell me a damn thing about yourself. So answer my question."

"I do know Roger Levin," Stark said. "Not well, but we've met. Now you want to tell me what's on your mind, Russell?"

Grant bounced up impatiently and paced the deep carpet from one wall to the other. He straightened a portrait on Stark's wall. Then he turned to the window and peered out uneasily. His taut, flushed face contained no hint of the wide, easy smile that had catapulted him into public office four years earlier. Abruptly, he pivoted. His eyes were watchful. "Levin came to my house yesterday morning. He was pretty pleasant, as far as reporters go. We spent an hour or so shooting the breeze, discussing my positions, my chances. Then, just at the end—he had already stood up to go—he mentioned some other people whose comments on my candidacy he wanted to get. Like as if he needed them for a follow-up article to this." Grant gestured toward the newspaper still in Stark's hand. "Most of the names didn't mean much. James River—you know, the businessman from up north who's also running in the primary. Then the Democrat who ran against me last time. People like that. But then, Levin mentioned your name. Very casually." Grant's lips tightened. "Said he was thinking of soliciting your reaction to my candidacy."

Stark straightened. "I don't understand. I'm shocked."

"Not as shocked as I was, *Doctor*." Grant moved toward Stark. "I have not told anybody, and I mean *anybody*, about you. And that includes Anne. Oh, she knows I'm seeing a psychiatrist, but I didn't even tell *her* your name." Grant's right hand curled into a tight fist, the knuckles white. "So you better level with me. Who have you told?"

"Nobody, Russell," said Stark, his gaze unflinching.

Don't give me that crap. Grant felt a white-hot fury sweep over him. *Roger Levin is not some goddamned prophet. If he knows I'm seeing you, it's because someone told him.* He felt like backhanding the big psychiatrist right off his chair. But he caught himself. Noah Stark knew more about his life than anyone else. He couldn't afford to alienate him. At least not yet. Grant sat down abruptly and gripped the chair.

The Final Analysis of Dr. Stark

"Doctor, my whole career—what I've worked for all my life—is at stake here. . . . Think *hard.* Are you sure you didn't mention my name, maybe just let on to somebody that you were treating a congressman?"

"You're a prominent man, Congressman, that's true, but I would never mention your name for any reason—not even to build up my own. Now, if you're ready to accept that, and step back a minute, I think you'll realize that there may be other explanations—instead of fantasizing that there is a Jew, and this reporter is a Jew, they must be in cahoots together."

"That's not fair!"

Stark raised an eyebrow. "All I am doing, Russell, is following the logic you used to conclude that I had dropped your name to this reporter."

"Then how did Levin know?" Grant's face had grown alarmingly white.

"I can think of several ways."

"Yeah. Well, tell me one."

The psychiatrist leaned a long arm on the back of his chair and looked meditatively at Grant. "You've been calling me from Washington an average of about once a week for the last three months."

"Uh-huh."

"It's no big trick for someone to spot my number on your phone bill. It would stick out, a forty-five minute call every Tuesday at 6 P.M. All they'd have to do is call up this number. Either I'd answer, or my answering machine would come on—'This is Dr. Noah Stark.' Once they found out what sort of doctor I was, it would be pretty easy to guess you were consulting me professionally."

"The only person who sees my phone bills is my secretary. Roberta Jameson has been with me fifteen years, and I'd trust her with my life. Don't you dare insinuate she's the one who betrayed me." Grant was practically shouting as he leaned over the desk, his face dangerously close to Stark's.

Stark clapped both palms on his desk. "Who says she's the only one who sees your bill?" At the authority in his voice, the congressman drew back. "The postman delivers the mail to your office—he doesn't personally supervise everyone who reads it. I know for a fact that phone bills are one of the first things investigative reporters try to get hold of. It could be anyone. Who knows, maybe some college kid volunteering in your office has a yen to be the next Woodward or Bernstein and called up the *Times*? Maybe, by pure, rotten coincidence, somebody from the paper, maybe even Levin himself, spotted you coming into this office?"

Without answering, Grant reached into his right suit pocket and pulled out a large pair of sunglasses and a small brown mustache. With a shaky hand, he put on the glasses and attached the mustache.

"Do you recognize me now, Doctor?"

Stark's brown eyes widened. "No," he said, very quietly.

"Well, then no reporter would either. I put these on just before I get out of my car, and take them off when I'm inside your outer office."

After a moment of silence, Stark calmly said, "I understand, Russell, that Levin's comments panicked you, and your way of dealing with fear has been to lash out. So maybe we can explore your fears about this whole issue. Why don't we start with what he said about me?"

"What got to me wasn't just what he said, it was the *way* he mentioned you—so innocently, waiting to see my reaction, like a damn vulture. I tried to be cool. 'Excuse me, I don't think I know anyone by that name.' Levin didn't buy it. 'What are you seeing him for?' he asked. Again I denied knowing you. He pushed it a few more times, just so I'd realize he knew I was bullshitting."

"And you're terrified he's going to pursue it?"

"Ever since that Eagleton business with McGovern, every one of these damn reporters has been itching to get his hands on a candidate's shrink. I can't afford to let that happen. One word about the booze, and my money'll dry up quicker than me. My supporters are very straitlaced— nice, hard-working, religious people. I know them, Doctor.

10

They don't want to hear about congressmen or senators going to psychiatrists, and God knows they don't want to hear about me getting drunk and . . . about any whores. I'm not proud of everything I've done, Stark, but if that comes out, I'm finished. Kaput. I'm so crazy with worry, I don't know who to suspect."

Twenty minutes later, Stark escorted a much calmer Grant to the waiting room, and watched as the man slipped on his disguise.

"We've got to stay in touch," Grant said gruffly, holding out his hand. His left arm hung rigidly at his side, the result of a childhood hunting accident. Cautious politician that he was, Grant went to great lengths to ensure that few of the electorate ever saw his handicap. Stark took the proffered hand, then watched Grant start down the hallway. He turned back to his office, sat down at his desk, and activated his answering machine. "It's Cheryl . . ." came the sparkling voice. As the message was about to conclude, the front door pushed abruptly open. Surprised, Stark started out of his chair just as Grant reentered.

"I forgot the article, Doctor." He strode over to Stark's desk, retrieved his newspaper, and nodded a mute farewell. Grant was at the threshold—and Stark's hand was instinctively reaching for the machine—when the second message on the tape began. "This is Roger Levin . . ." The congressman pivoted at the same instant Stark's finger pressed the stop button.

"Put that back on, Doctor!" Grant rasped. When Stark made no move to obey, Grant repeated his command brusquely, slamming the door behind him.

Without comment, Stark pushed the play button.

"I need to speak to you about an important matter," the message continued relentlessly. "By now, I'm sure you know what it is. How's tomorrow night at eight? Please call me as soon as possible. 555-3541."

Grant's handsome face flushed.

"That meeting must not take place," he said. There was no mistaking the threat in his voice.

"Of course not," Stark said soothingly.

"Don't soft-soap me, Doctor. I'm warning you. I don't want you talking to that reporter. *Am I making myself clear?*"

Grant moved forward menacingly, then seemed to think better of it. Abruptly, he turned on his heel and left.

Daniel Winter had a late luncheon meeting with three members of the synagogue's Finance Committee—"There's a 100,000 dollar shortfall in the budget, and we're relying on you to become a little more aggressive in the fund-raising angle, Rabbi," treasurer Irving Shnall had challenged—then returned to his office, a little after three.

He greeted his secretary with a weary grin. "Any message?"

Pat Hastings held out an envelope. "A messenger from First Beverly brought this over."

He tore open the missive.

> *Dear Rabbi*, the handwritten note read. *I'm paying Sadie Rosen's mortgage for next year out of my own pocket. One year. After that, she's on her own.*
> *Satisfied?*
> *Looking forward to not seeing you soon. I can't afford any more of your visits.*
> *Lester N. Schonfeld*

Daniel gave a single exultant whoop of joy.

Chapter 2

Monday Evening

Sam Bornstein signalled the crowd to quiet down. The portly president of Congregation B'nai Zion, a fat cigar clamped between his teeth, surveyed his living room, overflowing with the synagogue's assembled Board of Directors and their spouses. *Must be fifty-five, sixty people here,* he calculated with a satisfied smile—*who knows, maybe the rabbi's developing a fan club.* Then again, he thought, maybe people just like to be invited to Sam Bornstein's house: to wander in the statue garden, *ooh* and *ah* over the Picasso in the living room, and sip contentedly from the long-stemmed glasses constantly freshened by the two tuxedoed waiters. *So what brought them here tonight,* Bornstein wondered, *Rabbi Winter or me?*

He glanced over at the young rabbi, whose blue eyes were focused exclusively on his girlfriend. *Girlfriend,* Bornstein almost snorted aloud, his gaze shifting automatically to the pretty woman at Daniel Winter's side. Since when do rabbis have girlfriends? Back in Poland, when he was growing up, all the rabbis, as soon as they left the Yeshiva—if not before—were quickly married, with lots of children. Not the sort of men who ran around with tall redheads with piercing green eyes. But as Bornstein continued scanning the room and saw how many eyes were directed where his had just been, he knew that he had finally uncovered the reason for tonight's large turnout. It had nothing to do with his statue garden or his Picasso. Or the fancy drinks and the elegant waiters. Or, for that matter, with Daniel Winter's speech. The star attraction tonight was definitely Brenda Goldstein.

"Don't you dare walk away," Brenda hissed to Daniel through the broad smile that obscured the fact that her teeth were clenched. Her hand gripped his elbow. "Keep talking to me."

"Bill Tabak just walked in," Daniel explained. "I've really got to say hello."

"Sit down," Brenda pleaded, her smile unwavering.

Puzzled, the rabbi obeyed. "Brenda," he whispered, "what's going on?"

"Can't you see?"

"Frankly, no."

"Then you're the only person in this room who can't. I am being scrutinized, *Rabbi* Winter. Like a bug under a microscope. And it's a hell of a lot easier to take when you're sitting next to me. That way I look at you, we talk, and they watch—who cares? But when you walk away, I have the choice of either staring into my lap, or smiling like an idiot at fifty strangers, all examining me for any imperfections."

Daniel touched her hand. "So let them examine. You look absolutely beautiful."

Brenda flushed. The black silk evening dress she wore was stunning against her red hair, drawn back to the side with an almond comb. A touch of silvery eye shadow emphasized the brilliance of her green eyes.

"You really think so? You're not just saying that?"

"You look gorgeous. Every man in this room, I suspect, is envious of me."

"And the women?"

"Envious of *you*."

For the first time that night, Brenda's smile was genuine. "I look *that* good?"

"Not that. Envious of you for being with *me*."

Brenda laughed, drawing back her fist to give him a

playful punch. Then she thought better of it. Who knows how fifty witnesses would interpret *that?*

"Friends," Sam Bornstein began as he took a final puff on his cigar. A faint Polish accent colored his pronunciation. "We're all here tonight to honor our rabbi on the publication of his new book, *Sticks and Stones: On the Ethics of Speech.*" Bornstein cleared his throat loudly as the pungent smoke wafted across the room. "Now, before you start worrying that anybody's going to be hitting you for money, you should know that I personally bought a copy for everyone here. And the rabbi promises me he's going to inscribe each one."

Wilbur Kantor, past president of the synagogue, gave a short laugh, and bent to whisper something to his wife. "You watch your step over there, Wilbur, or the rabbi might just inscribe what he *really* thinks of you," Bornstein rasped. There were snorts of laughter, which Wilbur and Daniel joined in. Kantor's stormy relationship with the rabbi was known to all.

"So, without further ado, I'd like to ask our rabbi to say a few words."

There was a sharp burst of applause as Daniel moved to the brilliantly lit front of the room. He greeted the crowd, then waited for the noise to subside.

"According to the Bible," he began when the room had grown hushed, "God created the world with *words*. Right at the beginning of the Torah, what does it say? 'And God said, Let there be light, and there was light.' Well, one theme dominates my book—that human beings, like God, also create with words."

"Isn't that being a little too poetic, Rabbi?" Wilbur Kantor called out from the second row.

"Not at all," Daniel answered, unruffled. "Of course we create with words. All of us in this room have had the experience of reading a novel and being so moved by the fate of a character that we felt love, hate, anger. Sometimes we cried. Even though the character who so moved us never existed. All that happened was that a writer took a blank piece of paper, put words on it, and created a human being who became totally real. . . . It's because words are so powerful, because words can lead to love, but also to hatred and terrible pain, that Judaism teaches that we must be extremely careful how we use them. For example . . ."

Mel Waxman tapped Sam Bornstein on the shoulder with a stubby forefinger. "Look what the wind blew in," he whispered, gesturing with his thumb to the hall beyond the immense living room. The president turned to see the tall figure of Noah Stark. At Stark's side stood a slender brunette. Bornstein barely suppressed a groan. *Stark has no business being here*, he thought angrily. He had half a mind to go tell him that. He fidgeted a moment longer, then stood up. As unobtrusively as he could, he squeezed out of his row, nodded apologetically to Daniel, and went out to the hall, where Stark and his companion were talking softly, awaiting the end of Daniel's speech.

"Sam. Good to see you," Stark said warmly, stepping forward to pump Bornstein's hand before the president could open his mouth. "I'd like you to meet Jennifer Steen. Jennifer, Sam Bornstein, our host."

"A pleasure, Miss Steen," Bornstein said uncomfortably. His eyes flicked over the brunette, then shifted back immediately to Stark. He cleared his throat. "Dr. Stark, I don't want to be insulting, but you've put me in an awkward position. This meeting was restricted to the Board. If other members of the congregation should hear that non-Board members came, they would be annoyed with me. And justifiably so."

Puzzlement spread over Noah Stark's handsome face. In the living room, an explosion of clapping signaled the conclusion of Daniel's talk. "But I was invited, Sam."

"By who?"

"Your daughter."

"Cheryl?" Automatically, Bornstein's eyes sought out his daughter, who was restlessly pacing at the back of the living room.

"We spoke this morning, and I happened to ask her if she'd seen Daniel recently. She told me that he'd be speak-

The Final Analysis of Dr. Stark

ing here tonight, and she was sure nobody would mind if I came. I'm sorry, Sam, didn't she tell you?"

"Cheryl doesn't tell me anything," Bornstein growled.

"In that case, I'm very sorry, but nonetheless . . ."

But his last words were directed at Noah Stark's back. Stark was already guiding Jennifer Steen into the living room.

Inside, Daniel acknowledged the enthusiastic applause. He grinned widely as Brenda signaled him a thumbs-up, and then swiftly worked his way, self-consciously acknowl- edging compliments, through the crowded room toward Noah Stark.

"Noah," he said excitedly, stretching out his hand. Ignoring it, Stark grabbed Daniel in a bear hug.

"Where have you been hiding?" Daniel asked when he finally broke away.

"Busy times, paisan, busy times." Stark turned dra- matically to the girl at his right. "Daniel, there is somebody I very much want you to meet. Rabbi Winter, meet Jennifer Steen."

Daniel smiled at the young woman, whose perfectly curved figure was tightly draped in a sleeveless violet gown. Then his grin broadened as he saw the large diamond ring on the fourth finger of her left hand. "Does that mean what I think it does?"

"Just happened tonight." Stark's eyes shone with boy- ish eagerness. "Did it the right way. We went first to Jen- nie's father, then I told her we had to come here. To my rabbi."

This time it was Daniel who locked Stark in a hug.

"May I tell them?" Daniel asked, motioning with his head to the crowd. At Stark's nod, he called, "Ladies and gentlemen, I have an announcement to make." The gath- ering quickly hushed, as curious faces turned toward them. "Many of you here know Noah Stark—" During the last two years, Stark had indeed become one of the most active members of the congregation. Jerry Winston, head of the nominating committee, was already touting Noah as a future

Board member. "Well, I have some wonderful news. Dr. Stark has just informed me that he became engaged this evening to Ms. Jennifer . . ."

"Steen," Jennifer whispered, one arm linked through her fiancé's.

"Jennifer Steen," Daniel called out, his face reddening slightly.

Loud cries of "mazal tov!" resounded from all corners of the room. Jennifer blushed becomingly.

"Are you related to Jerome Steen?" Helene Winston called out excitedly.

"He's my father," Jennifer answered, her voice low and husky.

"You see, I'm marrying the boss's daughter," Stark joked. Seeing puzzled expressions, he explained, "Dr. Steen supervised my psychiatric residency."

Over on one of the side couches, sandwiched in between two members of Daniel's congregation, Brenda Goldstein nodded, impressed. Jerome Steen was a prominent name in LA psychiatric circles. Semiretired now, Steen was a founding member of the Dittmyer Center for Psychoanalysis and Psychotherapy, one of the most prestigious institutions in California. Rumor had it that he took on very few residents.

The two waiters, directed by a moody-looking Sam Bornstein, started circulating with fresh trays of drinks. Daniel scooped up a glass of the fizzling champagne and raised it high.

"L'chaim!" his voice rang out. His eyes met Brenda's across the room. "To the happy couple!"

"I suspect the rumors are true." Stark crossed his long legs comfortably. He and Daniel were alone, seated on one of the long velvet couches at the side of the room. A trio of admirers of Jerome Steen, led by a beaming Helene Winston, had kidnapped Jennifer, and were eagerly interrogating her by the glass doors which led out to Sam Bornstein's lawn and statue garden.

"What rumors?" asked Daniel.

The Final Analysis of Dr. Stark

"Oh, that you've also met a great lady."

Daniel laughed. "How can you tell?"

"Because I've never seen you with every hair in place, your tie actually a perfect match for your suit, and snappy Italian shoes. Somebody's been teaching you how to dress, my friend, and I hear it's a she."

Daniel grinned, his eyes drawn to Stark's own tailor-made grey suit and red silk tie. It was rare to get a compliment on clothing from Stark.

"Okay, Sherlock, there's somebody I'd like *you* to meet."

Rising, Daniel led Stark over to Brenda, who was happy to slip away from the impromptu lecture Sam Bornstein was giving to the cluster of admirers gathered in front of his Picasso.

"Brenda, I'd like you to meet Noah Stark. Renaissance man. Psychiatrist. Athlete. And most importantly, good friend."

Brenda and Stark looked at each other. Each tried to make their analysis appear casual. From Daniel's description, Brenda had expected the striking good looks, and the elegance, but what struck her now was just how big Stark was. He towered over even Daniel's near six-foot height. And it was clear that every inch was muscle. Rare to see a doctor, particularly a psychiatrist, in such superb shape.

"So good to meet you," Brenda said easily, finding herself looking upward into Noah's genial face. "Daniel's told me a lot about you."

"Some of it positive, I hope."

"Most of it," she said, returning his engaging smile. "Tell me something, Doctor. With eight hours a day behind a desk, listening to patients, how do you stay in such good shape?"

"You're addressing," Daniel said with mock grandeur, "the last Jewish quarterback at U.C.L.A."

"My P.R. man," Stark laughed, giving Daniel an affectionate thump on the shoulder. "Anyway, I still work out two, three times a week. But to be honest, Brenda, I suspect most of the people here, particularly the men, think you're in a lot better shape than I am. . . . Paisan," he said admiringly, shifting his gaze to Daniel, "where have you been hiding this gorgeous woman?"

"Your paisan's a pretty unusual guy," Brenda intervened, but her cheeks had colored slightly. "When someone stole a very precious watch from my daughter on a synagogue outing, he was quicker than the police in getting it back. We've been friends ever since."

"And you," Daniel asked the psychiatrist, "how long have you known Jennifer?"

"Seven years."

Brenda poked Daniel gently in the ribs. "I hope your paisan over here," she said teasingly to Stark, "is a bit quicker about making up his mind."

Stark barked with laughter and leaned on the curved wooden mantelpiece behind him. "Actually, Jennie and I only started dating a month ago. You see, I'd known her all that time because of her father. But there was never anything between us."

"So what happened?"

Stark grinned. "I always knew Jennie was very special. But I never thought of her romantically, you know, because after all, her father's my training analyst. You understand how it is, Brenda—I was probably too much in awe of him. Then, about a month ago, we ran into each other at a wedding. Jennie was there professionally. She's a photographer, you see. We hadn't seen each other in, I don't know, probably a year. Maybe more. And something just clicked. I know it sounds absurd, but I find it hard to describe love any better than that. Something clicked. I'm happy when I'm with her."

"Good enough definition of love." Brenda smiled. The rich lighting emphasized the smattering of golden freckles on her nose. "Your first marriage?"

"I've been divorced . . . let me see, my son Adam is nine, so that makes it six years."

"And in that time," Daniel grinned, "he went out with two thousand women. All of whom fell madly in love with him."

20

"What was it exactly you were looking for?" Brenda asked.

"You know what Noah always believed was the most important trait in a woman?" Daniel answered mischievously. "Whatever trait the woman he was going out with was missing."

Noah roared with laughter and pounded Daniel on the back.

"He's my rebbe," he declared to Brenda, one arm still draped around Daniel. "Calls God's wrath down on me when I'm being a bad boy. I hope you don't let him prejudice you against me."

"Don't worry," Brenda assured him. "Daniel only teases people he loves."

"Oh, and does he tease you?"

"Hey, this is getting pretty heavy fast," Daniel hastily interjected. He cupped his hand behind his left ear. "I think I hear a telephone ringing for you over there, Noah."

"As a matter of fact, it's for you, *Rabbi*. Why don't you take it, or better yet, go rescue Jennie?" He pointed to a small clique across the room who were reacting with enthusiasm to something his fiancee was saying. "On the other hand, she seems to be doing okay. But meanwhile, I think I'm entitled to a few minutes alone with Brenda— to get to know her a little—without you interrupting every twenty seconds."

Daniel caught Brenda's eye. She nodded reassuringly.

"Maybe that call really was for me," Daniel said with a small smile.

He ambled over to the elaborate buffet, arranged on a table which stretched almost the width of the huge room, scooped up a chocolate-covered strawberry, mumbled a blessing, and devoured it greedily. Seconds later, a waiter approached him.

"Would you like a drink, sir . . . excuse me, Rabbi?"

Do you mean rabbis aren't first? Daniel was tempted to say, then stopped himself. The young man seemed nervous enough as it was. "Do you have a club soda?" he asked instead.

"Certainly, Rabbi."

Waiting for his drink, Daniel picked up another chocolate strawberry, then glanced behind him. Noah and Brenda were gone from their place in front of the mantelpiece. Turning, he caught sight of Noah guiding Brenda's slim figure through a side door into Sam Bornstein's library, all the while glad-handing his way through the crowd. Surprising how many people stopped the psychiatrist with greetings along the way. Some of them must be seeing him professionally, Daniel thought. I wonder who.

"Uh-oh." Phil Stein turned to Bill Tabak, his long-time bridge partner, a wink creasing his heavy, jowled face. "The rabbi better watch his step."

"What do you mean?"

"Look who's making time with his girlfriend."

Tabak turned to watch the figures of Noah Stark and Brenda Goldstein retreat into the library. He turned back to Stein, head cocked wryly sideways.

"You're a troublemaker, Phil. First of all, Stark just announced his engagement. And besides, the rabbi and Stark are like this," he added, crossing two fingers.

"Well, if the rabbi trusts any shrink that much, he should have his own head examined."

"Since when are you so down on psychiatrists?"

"Since Bonnie started shelling out two hundred dollars a week of my money so that I can have the privilege of being yelled at for repressing her."

Tabak's huge frame shook with laughter. "Oh, so that's it."

"Besides, shrinks can't take care of their own lives. Have you ever met a shrink's kid who was *normal*? Forget kids, have you ever met a psychiatrist who wasn't a screwball?"

Sam Bornstein grasped Daniel's hand enthusiastically —and painfully.

The Final Analysis of Dr. Stark

"Excellent, Rabbi. Every word you said, on the money."

"Thanks, Sam." Sam's cigar smoke was making Daniel's eyes smart.

"And Brenda. That girl's a gem. And beautiful too. My Hilda said she only hopes your children have her looks and your brains."

"Thank her for the compliment," Daniel said wryly, surprised that Hilda Bornstein knew of Isadora Duncan's proposal to George Bernard Shaw: "With my body and your brains, what a wondrous child we could have." One thing Daniel was sure of: Shaw's riposte to the beautiful dancer—"Yes, but what if it had *my* body and *your* brains?"—did not apply to Brenda. A psychologist with the LAPD homicide division, Brenda had one of the most insightful and challenging minds he had ever encountered. That was a good part of what made her so exciting.

"So, are mazal tovs in order for you two also?" Bornstein pressed, his homely face creased in a knowing smile.

"Brenda's fantastic. We're still trying to figure out if I'm good enough for her."

Bornstein's bark of laughter reverberated. "Okay, Rabbi. I can take a hint. I won't give you a hard time. I'll let the ladies here do that. . . . Besides," he said, stooping his bald head slightly and lowering his voice, "I want to talk to you about something else."

Daniel looked up sharply.

"Your friend, Dr. Stark," Bornstein continued. "I'm not happy he came tonight. This evening was only supposed to be for the Board."

"Oh, come on, Sam. To tell you the truth, I'm very moved that he came. He's here because he wanted to introduce me to Jennifer. You see, we hadn't seen each other in a long time. Come on, Sam," he urged as Bornstein scowled, "it is truly not worth making a big deal about."

The other man shook his head grimly. "It's not just that. It's Cheryl too."

Daniel's eyes panned the room for Bornstein's daughter. But there was no sign of her. "What's the problem, Sam?"

"You know, we started her with Stark at your suggestion."

"Of course. And my impression is that she's doing a lot better."

"I wish he'd say that. He has her in now four times a week instead of two. At one hundred and twenty dollars an hour. I can afford it, Rabbi, that's not the issue, but I don't like it. Also—" Bornstein stopped abruptly, his protruding brown eyes focused over Daniel's shoulder. "Enough for now," he muttered, "he's coming over." A few seconds later, Noah came up, Brenda alongside him.

"Well, Rabbi," Bornstein boomed with a heartiness which made Daniel wince, "as I was saying, you were positively terrific tonight. I think everything's going to change now for the better—your relationship with the Board, the growth of the congregation," he waved his hands, "everything." Nodding at Stark and Brenda, he started away, then turned. "By the way, don't forget Thursday night."

Daniel looked puzzled.

"The Remnant meeting," Bornstein scolded. "I promised everyone you'd be there."

"Of course." Daniel nodded. The Remnant was a Los Angeles group of Holocaust survivors. Their annual dinner this Thursday was in honor of Sam and Hilda Bornstein. Months ago, Bornstein had extracted an oath from Daniel that he wouldn't miss it. "I'll be there, Sam. Don't worry."

Bornstein grinned, then his eyes flickered over Stark's face and his expression grew troubled. Without replying, he moved away.

Stark's eyes followed him. "Was he talking to you about me?" The room was almost deserted now. Most of the guests had wandered into the garden outside. The air drifting in through the open glass doors was hot and sticky.

"What makes you say that?"

"His guilty look when I came over. I'm a psychiatrist, Daniel, I notice these things. Besides, he said, 'as I was saying,' but when Brenda and I were coming over, he wasn't saying anything at all. . . . So what's the story, was he talking about me?"

"It was nothing," Daniel said, waving it aside. "You know, just a little upset that you busted into a Board function. Even if it was to announce your engagement. But then again," Daniel grinned, "you always did have a flair for the dramatic."

"That's all he said?" Stark persisted.

Daniel sighed. "What's going on, Noah? Sam Bornstein is the first president of this congregation who's really liked me. And I like him. If I could make peace between you, I'd love to. But I don't want to get stuck in the middle of some pointless squabble."

"Bornstein's become increasingly hostile to me, Daniel. He doesn't want to recognize that his daughter has problems."

"I thought Cheryl was getting better."

"She is. But very, very gradually. These things don't happen overnight. It's a long process."

Daniel gnawed at his lip. "Listen, I need to speak to you about Cheryl." He turned to Brenda with an apologetic shrug. "I'm really sorry, Brenda. But I must speak to Noah alone for a couple of minutes."

She stared at him wordlessly, her eyes searching his. Then she turned to Stark. He shrugged. "Of course," she said very precisely, then quickly moved away.

"Noah, I'm worried about Cheryl," Daniel said, his eyes moodily following Brenda's retreating figure.

"You're not the only one."

"Oh, not in the way you are. Psychologically, my impression is that she's doing a lot better. But . . ."

"But what?"

"She used to be so active in the synagogue. Now, I don't think I've seen her at services in . . . I don't know, months. Also, she used to meet with me a lot. Now, even when I leave a message, she doesn't get back to me. It worries me."

"So what are you thinking?"

"I want to get her involved again. The Young Adults Group is sponsoring a singles event next month. I'm planning to ask her to chair it."

Joseph Telushkin

"I wouldn't do that, Daniel. *Believe me*, she's not ready for that sort of pressure."

"I don't know, Noah, I just—"

"Well, I *do* know. It's my business to know. So please listen to me, Daniel. Cheryl Bornstein is not involved in the synagogue, and doesn't speak to you much for a damn good reason. Because Sam Bornstein is president. And it's a damn good thing she isn't involved. Cheryl needs to develop her own identity. Away from her father, and from the synagogue. *Trust me, Daniel.* I'm not speaking to you as a friend, but as Cheryl Bornstein's psychiatrist. Don't ask her to chair that event."

Daniel drew his hand through his thick black hair and frowned. "Okay," he said wearily. "Forget it. Maybe it was a dumb idea." He looked around. "We'd better get back to Brenda and Jennifer."

"In a minute," Stark said softly. He gave a quick look over his shoulder, then reached inside the breast pocket of his jacket. "There's another reason I came here tonight." He pulled out a long manila envelope. "I need you to look after this for a few days. Don't worry, it's nothing dangerous. Just some papers I can't afford to lose. Just put them in a careful place, and I'll pick them up from you soon."

Daniel nodded thoughtfully; during their years of friendship he had grown accustomed to Stark's flair for the mysterious. Absently, he stuffed the envelope in his pocket, and started off after Brenda. Stark's low, deep voice restrained him.

"One more thing, Daniel. I hear rumors. All the time. I'm worried about you."

"About what?"

"About your position here. Some of the heavy hitters, I understand, want you out."

"Who did you hear that from?"

"Never ask a psychiatrist a question like that. Believe me, I hear."

"Anything in particular I should watch out for?"

"Not a thing. A *he*. Your good friend, Mr. Bornstein."

26

The Final Analysis of Dr. Stark

Daniel's face registered his shocked disbelief. The evening, with all its gaiety, had suddenly turned sour.

"Danny boy," Stark resumed gently, clapping a hand on Daniel's shoulder. "We gotta get together and talk. It's been too long.

"How's early next week for you?"

"Sooner than that."

"How soon?"

"Very . . . Tomorrow's Tuesday, and I only have patients in the morning. Then, in the afternoon, I have to take care of a few things. Would five o'clock tomorrow be good for you?"

"Where?"

"My office, okay?"

Daniel nodded.

"Good. It'll give me a chance to show off some of Jennie's pictures to you. My whole office is decorated with them." He embraced Daniel again. "And don't worry, paisan. I promise you. Everything's going to be all right."

So why, Daniel brooded as he left with Brenda ten minutes later, *didn't he feel all right at all?*

Chapter 3

Tuesday Morning

Noah Stark pushed open the heavy door, suppressed a yawn, then strode through his waiting room into his office. He could think of a million places he'd rather be, starting with Jennie Steen's arms, and moving on to other portions of her anatomy. But he had little choice. The correspondence on his desk had reached the danger level—two inches. Inevitably, during those rare hours he devoted to paperwork, Stark wondered if he should hire a secretary. Actually, he'd had one, Denise Weil, for five years. But a year earlier, on the day she entered her ninth month of pregnancy, Denise had left. Stark had promised to keep her job available until she was ready to return. At first, he figured he'd hire an office temp. But as the weeks went by, he concluded that a secretary was an unnecessary luxury. What did his practice consist of—one patient an hour, seven, eight times a day; billings that took him two hours at the end of every month? So when Denise phoned after the birth of her son to tell him she had decided not to return, he was actually relieved.

He pulled up the shades. Checking his reflection in the windowpane, he tugged at his silk tie until he was satisfied that it was perfectly centered. Then, resignedly, he sat down in his soft, black swivel chair, and started his morning routine. All pencils were sharpened, felt-tip pens properly capped, papers on his desk filed in the grey cabinets along the wall. He looked up, and his eyes lighted on his favorite of Jennie's photographs, a framed black-and-white print which hung over the couch. A young man in a poncho bent over an elderly bedridden woman. Jennie had told him the story behind the picture—how the man had traveled fifty miles on horseback from his rural village to a hospital in Mexico City to bring back an antibiotic for his sick mother. He marveled at how Jennie had captured the pain and gentility in the man's eyes. Amazing, too, were the things some of his patients had seen in the picture. One had concocted an elaborate scenario detailing how the man was preparing to strangle the woman. Another had settled on murder by dagger. And one older woman took one look and refused to lie on the couch for the entire session. People never ceased to amaze him.

Noah turned away from the photograph and reached for his answering machine. He examined the thin spool of tape that had accumulated on the left and played his daily game. How many calls had come in since last night? He made his calculation, rewound the tape, and called out in a low voice, "Three."

"This is Jonah," a harsh voice barked as if in response. Stark groaned. The tension level with his brother had risen to an ominous high this past month. "I need to hear from you, Noah. Today—tomorrow at the latest. And I'm not taking no for an answer." Wearily, Stark scrawled Jonah's name on the small pad in front of him. *Jonah doesn't want to take no for an answer,* he thought; but then again, maybe the time had come for his older brother to learn how.

Seconds later, a strident fifteen-second buzz started its trill. The caller had hung up without leaving a message. *Who the hell is that?* he wondered. *A woman, I bet.* For reasons Stark was intensely curious to figure out, women seemed infinitely more likely than men to panic when confronted with a recorded message. Over the years, he had tried different strategies to cut down the percentage of hang-ups, even resorting once to a naked plea—"Please say something, I feel rejected when you don't tell me who you are." But even jokes didn't help. Apparently, the fear of electronics ran very deep. Two more torturous buzzes followed, then a silence, and Stark clicked off the machine, wondering in exasperation if one person had phoned three times, or if three different machine phobics had already checked in since he left the office last night.

He turned to the top letter on his pile. It was a request from a Dr. Abraham Horn of Sacramento for information about a former patient, now in treatment with him. Stark was into the second page of his handwritten reply when a knock sounded on the outer door.

"Come in," he called out, pressing a buzzer.

Seconds later, a pair of bulging teenage muscles, preceded by a large brown cardboard box, stepped in. When Stark saw the words *Van Gogh's* on the boy's blue sweatshirt, his face glowed.

"It finally arrived, doc." The delivery boy from LA's most exclusive gallery set the package down gently on the cream-colored carpet as Stark pushed back his chair and ran to his side. Whistling cheerfully, the boy pried the box open, then the pair started easing the sculpture out.

"You can let go, doc, it's not so heavy," the snub-nosed young man assured him. Stark obeyed, then exclaimed as the bronze statue started to topple out of the boy's grasp. With a muttered curse, he jumped over and steadied it.

"It needs two pairs of hands," the psychiatrist said sharply. Lovingly, he lifted the gleaming sculpture out of the young man's arms and deposited it with infinite care on the end table behind the couch. His eyes gloated over the words on the statue's base—*Jacques Lipchitz, La Joie De Vivre, 1927.*

After the delivery boy left, Stark put away his correspondence, swiveled his chair, and spent the next twenty minutes letting his eyes roam contentedly over the gleaming replica, drinking in the bold curves and angles of the abstract creation, a dancing figure with an instrument. "Absolutely brilliant," he murmured, "a perfect copy." *To hell with Jonah*, he decided, leaning back in his chair. *Nothing's going to put me in a bad mood today.*

The Final Analysis of Dr. Stark

* * *

The intercom sounded. "It's Marjorie Weiss on the line," Pat Hastings told Daniel. "Do you want to take it?"

"Are you asking if I *want* to or if I'm *going* to?"

"Okay," Pat laughed. "I'll put her through."

Daniel always had a certain dread when Marjorie Weiss, the sisterhood president, telephoned. And invariably the dread was followed by guilt. Marjorie was, after all, a sweet woman, one who devoted countless hours to synagogue work. Unfortunately, this devotion came at a price. For Marjorie Weiss liked to talk. Liked to? *Loved* to. Daniel could still vividly recall one dreary Tuesday morning spent listening to Marjorie outline the relative benefits of chopped liver versus grapefruit for the opening course of a sisterhood luncheon. He had never realized that the subject contained the potential for twenty-five minutes of analysis. Sam Bornstein had once mentioned that Marjorie's husband went to sleep every night promptly at nine. Daniel thought he understood why.

"I've been trying to reach you for three days, Rabbi."

"You got my message, didn't you?"

"But you didn't call when I told you to." Indeed, Daniel had timed his call to make sure he got her answering machine. More guilt.

"Anyway, Marjorie, I've compiled a list of some very special people as possible speakers for this year's annual luncheon. Do you want me to read it off to you, or should I just drop it in the mail?"

Say mail, he prayed.

"Forget it, Rabbi. I have wonderful news. We don't need your list . . . you know Donna Tobb, don't you?"

"Of course." Donna and Mike Tobb were long-standing members of the congregation.

"Well, Joan Reider happens to be Donna's first cousin. And she's agreed to speak for free. Isn't that wonderful? Just imagine, Rabbi, the crowd we'll draw."

Daniel stared at the typed page in front of him, his mind racing. He was sure he knew virtually every prominent name in Jewish life. But *Joan Reider?* Had she, unbeknownst to him, come out with some important new book? Been elected president of some major Jewish organization? He decided to play it safe.

"Which Joan Reider is that, Marjorie?"

The woman laughed gaily. "Oh, Rabbi, you're such a kidder. . . . Anyway, can you believe it, *Joan Reider* coming to our shul?"

Game time is over, he realized with a sinking heart. "Marjorie, I suspect I'm asking a very ignorant question. But who is Joan Reider?"

"Oh, you rabbis," Marjorie bubbled. "You're so smart, but you just live in your own little world. . . . For your information, Joan Reider is on the news every night at six. She is also the most popular Hollywood gossip columnist in the country today . . . I'm sure you've seen her."

Vague associations of an overflowing head of platinum curls, a nasal voice, and little tidbits of innuendo delivered in a semisneer came to him. Daniel suppressed a groan. "You're not serious, Marjorie, are you?"

"Serious? Would I be this excited if I wasn't? Joan's a good Jewish girl, Rabbi. Her cousin tells me she feels very deeply about it. She told Donna she'd be honored to accept our award."

"Award!"

"That's how we're getting her here for free. The sisterhood is making Joan Reider Congregation B'nai Zion's Woman of the Year."

"This is absurd," Daniel said, fighting down a rising exasperation. "You know who I had down on my list? Dana Kidder, the author of that new novel on Israel. And Professor Zak, from Brandeis. I thought he could speak on intermarriage and alienation. I was even thinking of the Israeli consul here in Los—"

"And you know what, Rabbi?" Marjorie interrupted. "We'd get one hundred women, one hundred and fifty tops. And they'd be the same women who'd come even if we had no speaker at all. With Joan Reider, the sky's the limit. Who knows, maybe six, seven hundred women will come?

Don't you see, these are women who might never set foot in the synagogue otherwise. Doesn't that count for something?"

"And if we turned the sanctuary into a casino for a night, a thousand people might come to the synagogue."

"That's unfair, Rabbi."

"Why?"

"Because Joan's speech is going to be every bit as Jewish as those other people you were suggesting."

"Really. What's her topic?"

Marjorie's response was triumphant. "Guess Who's Jewish in Hollywood That You Never Suspected."

Andrew Perl stepped into Noah Stark's office and seated himself on the long maroon couch, his tiny eyes never leaving the psychiatrist's face.

"I'm not lying down. Did you notice that, Doctor?" he said, his voice dangerously soft.

"I noticed," Stark said dryly, suppressing a smile. Perl tugged at his perfectly trimmed goatee. "You wanna know why?"

"I suspect you're going to tell me, Andrew."

"You're damn right I'm gonna tell you. I saw you coming out of the West LA Country Club Sunday night with Goodman."

"Hmm."

"Don't give me that *hmm* shit!" The words rapped out like shots. "I wanna know what you told him."

Stark's expression did not change. "I'm more interested, Andrew, in what you think I told him."

Spots of color appeared on Perl's gaunt cheeks. "No, Doctor. Today, it's gonna be you on the couch. I'm gonna ask the questions, and I want answers." His pale eyes glinted.

Stark exhaled slowly, his mind probing to find some way, some technique to defuse his patient's smoldering rage. The diminutive, fastidiously dressed executive had been in therapy with him for the last six months. The request for his treatment had come from an unusual source —John Goodman, founder of West Coast Realty, and Andrew Perl's employer and cousin. Six months ago, during a surprise investigation of the company's books, Goodman's accountant had made the discovery that Perl had embezzled over $15,000 from the firm. The accountant had wanted to go on searching, to see how deep the thievery extended. Goodman stopped him. He wasn't sure he wanted to know. He paid Andrew Perl $80,000 a year to be his vice-president, and he believed him to be worth every penny of it. For Goodman, it was truly the principle of the thing, not the loss of money, that most rankled. That was why he had decided to confront Perl before taking any action. At first, his cousin had reacted calmly, stubbornly denying the accusations. Then he became obstreperous, threatening Goodman with a suit for slander, and then with a punch in the nose. Goodman, a few years older than Perl but a good six inches taller, ignored the threats. He locked his office door and confronted Perl with the evidence.

"The longer you deny it, Andy," he said, "the more you're going to make me think this has been going on a long time. And that can be checked. If not by us, then by the police. You catch my meaning?"

Andrew Perl collapsed like a punctured balloon. Sobbing, he told Goodman a confused tale of gambling debts and loan sharks, swore it had never happened before, and vowed it would never happen again.

John Goodman did not go to the police. He also did not fire Perl. Instead, he telephoned Noah Stark. A long-time member of Congregation B'nai Zion's Board of Directors, Goodman had heard glowing reports from other Board members about the brilliant Dr. Stark. And the few times he had spoken to the psychiatrist, he had been impressed. Stark used none of that incomprehensible jargon that Goodman associated with therapists, none of that "resistances, passive-aggressive" psychobabble. Stark's sharp, common-sensical insights were always direct and astute. So when Perl left his office that day, Goodman had called Stark and asked that he meet the man.

"If you don't, Doctor, I'll have to fire him."

"Stop with the violins," Stark had joked. "Have your cousin come in, and we'll see what happens."

"Thanks so much. He's broke now as it is, so I'll be responsible for all fees, of course."

Stark had been seeing Perl three times a week. At first, Perl had been reluctant to open up. "Shrinks are for crazies," he maintained, and he had sat through several sessions obstinately refusing to speak. But gradually, coaxed by the psychiatrist's patient prodding, he started revealing himself. During the course of the therapy, he had become open, even warm, and quite willing to acknowledge his own self destructiveness. There was a real sincerity and charm to the man, Stark thought—it was easy to see why Goodman didn't want to lose him. But in the past few weeks, new, disturbing sides of Perl had emerged at their sessions. Worst of all, he was gambling again. Heavily. And losing. Both at the poker table and in stock options. And once again, he was dipping into the till. Was it surprising, then, that having seen his psychiatrist together with the very man from whom he'd been stealing, Perl had charged in this morning so aggressively?

"John Goodman is an old friend, Andrew. You know that, it's through him that we met," Stark told the ashen-faced executive firmly. "There's no reason for you to be worried if I spend a social evening with him."

"What did you tell him?"

"Andrew, how many times have I told you, what goes on in this office is between you, me, and the walls? It's not just me you're relying on, it's the ethics of my profession."

"Don't lie to me!"

Stark pursed his lips. Perl was dangerously close to losing control.

"I went to the library yesterday," Perl continued, his reedy voice betraying his anxiety. "I figured I'd better check this confidentiality crap out. . . . It seems, Doctor, there was a case in Berkeley a few years back. A patient told his shrink he would kill his girlfriend for leaving him. The doctor didn't tell the girl or her family about the threat.

Well, two months later, he murdered her. Her parents sued the shrink. And won." His small, hard eyes bore into Stark's. "I'm right, aren't I?"

"You're right," Noah answered wearily. "You're not planning to murder anyone, I hope?"

"Don't joke with me, Doctor. John's your friend, he's paying the bills around here, and I, like a damn fool, let on that I've been borrowing some of his money. Now, what did you tell him about me?"

"Nothing!"

"I don't believe you!"

"Why not?"

"Because yesterday morning my dear Cousin John summoned me into his office. All nice and friendly. Very courteous. The way he's been acting with me these last few months. But then every few minutes he'd throw in a sharp little question. Just when I was off guard. Let me tell you something—it didn't make me feel good. At all. I shot right out of there and went straight to the library."

"Andrew, I'm very sorry you feel that way," Stark said in the even, controlled voice that few patients could resist. "But if you would, permit me to suggest that the reason you're not feeling good has nothing to do with anything I might have said to John Goodman, and has absolutely nothing to do with any questions he asked you yesterday. The real problem is that you're feeling guilty. You know that what you're doing is wrong. And because it's so clear to you that you're acting dishonestly, you imagine it's equally clear to everyone else. I assure you, Andrew, if you felt good about yourself, John's questions would have seemed perfectly normal."

Andrew Perl leaped up from the couch. His fist crashed down on the psychiatrist's desk, sending Stark's pencil holder flying.

"You're so good with words! You sit there and you smirk, and spit out your fancy explanations. And somehow, at the end, it's always me who comes out in the wrong. So let me warn you about something, *Doctor* Stark. If I go down, I'm not going down alone. If you betray me, there's no telling what I might do." Perl laughed. The sound was brittle. "After all, I'm crazy, aren't I?"

Daniel Winter punched out the number of the LAPD homicide division.

"Dr. Brenda Goldstein, please."

Doris Touhey, Brenda's secretary, came on the line.

"Hi, Rabbi. I'm sorry, but Brenda's not in."

"Do you know when she'll be back?"

"Hardtosay." As always, Daniel found himself paying exaggerated attention when Doris spoke. It was not that there was great profundity in the girl's words, it was just that her incessant gum-chewing made a lot of them come out garbled. "She went out with Lieutenant Cerezzi, oh, about an hour ago. A rape-homicide, one of those mutilation killings, I think." Doris's voice was cheerful.

"Oy!" Daniel shuddered. He had known Brenda three months now, but the reality of what she dealt with on a daily basis still shook him profoundly.

"Any message, Rabbi?"

"Tell her I'll be by tonight at eight."

"Thatsit?"

What else should I tell Doris? he wondered. That last night, after they left the Bornsteins', Brenda had acted oddly distant? He was tempted to ask the secretary about Brenda's mood this morning, but stifled the impulse. The author of *Sticks and Stones* had better things to do than encourage Doris to gossip about her boss. All the same, Brenda's abrupt change of mood last night had puzzled him. There was only one thing he was sure of, it had something to do with Noah. But what? Last night, when he had mentioned the psychiatrist in the car, Brenda had been evasive.

"He's a great guy, isn't he?"

"He's very charming," she answered, her words spaced with cool precision. "One of the most charming men I've ever met."

"And bright too!"

"Uh-huh. He's not stupid, Daniel. Then again, I'd be shocked if any friend of yours was."

Evasive, he thought again unhappily. So uncharacteristic of Brenda. She normally bubbled over with her enthusiasms and her angers. Always so direct. It was one of the things he loved about her. So how to explain last night? Was it that she disliked Noah? Or maybe that she did like him, too much? He bit his lip, ashamed. That's crazy. No, it was something else, something about Noah that had deeply bothered her. Her comment about his great charm was revealing. He remembered Brenda once saying to him how charming her ex-husband was—and she hadn't meant it as a compliment.

Well, if that was the problem, it could be easily solved. Noah Stark was charming, true enough, but his warmth was unquestionably genuine. Let her just get to know him a little better.

"Anything else?" Doris Touhey prodded. He could hear her unwrapping a fresh stick of gum.

A puckish smile creased Daniel's mouth. He picked up a Bible and quickly located the verse he was seeking. "Tell Brenda to suspend judgment—I still stand by *Genesis* 6:9."

Doris Touhey carefully noted the message.

With swift, furious steps, the young woman strode over to the table behind Stark's couch. Her deep blue eyes flamed as she ran a delicate finger along the onyx base of Stark's new statue.

"So cultured," Cheryl Bornstein said. Sarcasm dripped from her voice. "Always with beautiful new art. The most expensive, I'm sure. And such taste. But you don't fool me, Noah Stark. Culture or no culture, you're a goddamned liar. . . . You're going to pay for what you did."

"Cheryl, please—"

"I'm not taking this lying down," she cut him off, as her trembling hands locked around the statue's neck. Her wide, sensitive mouth, smudged with shimmering red lipstick, twisted into a mirthless smile. She shook back her golden hair and met Stark's impassive gaze. "You're a cold, selfish man," she breathed. Without warning, she scooped up her purse, catching the makeup that was spilling out from the sides, and whirled towards the door. "Don't think I'm going to be quiet about this!"

Stark winced as the outer door slammed. Wearily, he ran his palm over his forehead and felt the sweat there. He had gambled, he had tried a shock tactic with Cheryl. And he'd lost. Now he sat brooding, wondering how vindictive she would be, how much damage she was capable of.

He stared at the photographic portrait on the wall to his right, between the rows of diplomas and Jennie's beautiful black-and-white studies of children and their toys. The piercing smoke-gray eyes of his own teacher, Jerome Steen, stared back at him. Steen was no saint. Who knew that better than he? But he was smart, the most perceptive psychiatrist Stark had ever known. How would Steen handle this? He remembered a sermon Daniel had once given about the difference between an intelligent man and a wise one. An intelligent man, the rabbi had said, gets out of difficulties that a wise man never gets into. Noah Stark remained at his desk, pensive. He felt very unwise.

A delicate feminine fist rapped lightly on the glass pane. "Come in," Andrew Perl responded.

Rhoda Dean stepped in, but just barely. "The chief wants to see you," West Coast Realty's blond executive secretary announced in a peculiarly grim voice.

Perl stiffened. He nodded curtly at Dean, watched her back out of the room, then moved quickly to the executive washroom, where he stood in front of the long mirror. For long minutes, he held an arm outstretched, willing himself to keep his hand steady. Part of him—most of him really —longed to head straight out the front door to the elevators. But that would solve nothing. Besides, maybe it really was all in his imagination. Perl forced himself to breathe slowly, each breath held slightly longer than the last.

Then, without hesitating, he marched straight from the men's room into Goodman's luxurious office, pushing open the door without bothering to knock. It took only one look. His stomach tightened. John Goodman sat behind his massive desk, head bowed, open ledger books covering every available inch of the blotter. Beside him, the bespectacled company accountant was leaning forward, stabbing at a line of figures with a mechanical pencil.

Goodman looked up. His gray eyes held no trace of their usual warmth.

"Andrew," he said, "I suppose you know why I called you in here."

At precisely 5:00 P.M., Daniel entered 1350 Westwood Avenue, the ultramodern office building where Noah Stark practiced. He wove through the crowd streaming toward the doors, got into an empty elevator, and pressed nine. He walked through the long, narrow corridor and tapped twice on Stark's door. No answer. He tried the heavy steel knob, and it gave. *Thoughtful of Noah to leave it open*, he thought.

"Noah?" he called out as he walked into the tiny, thickly carpeted waiting room.

No response.

Daniel picked up a *Los Angeles* magazine from the coffee table and, sighing, sat down on one of the soft, black armchairs. He skimmed through a long piece on the upcoming mayoralty race, and was halfway through an article about price wars on Rodeo Drive when he looked at his watch. 5:21.

He was annoyed. This was not the first time Noah had been late. His lateness, in fact, was so habitual that the last few times they'd met, Daniel had insisted it be at a bookstore. That way, he explained, at least he'd have something to do while waiting, instead of standing on a corner fuming. The more logical technique, to come late himself, had backfired the one time he'd tried it. Noah had arrived on time—and had never let him forget it.

But this time Stark's tardiness really rankled. Daniel had rushed through his last two appointments because Noah had sounded so damned mysterious, so insistent that they meet. He rummaged inside his jacket pocket for a pen and paper. He'd write a note and go. Next time, let Noah come

The Final Analysis of Dr. Stark

to his office. He groaned. His brief search had yielded only a pen. He walked over to the desk. No paper. There must be some in Noah's office. He pushed the door open and headed straight for the desk. In one fluid movement, concentrating on his mission, he saw a pad, reached for it, and eased himself into the high-backed swivel chair.

Then he looked up, and the color seeped from his face. He started to cough, a hacking sound, harsh in the stillness. For a wild moment he was sure he would vomit. Finally, the coughing stopped. He started to rise, but his legs were rubber. He fell straight back.

With fingers that would not stop shaking, he picked up the phone and dialed the number he had learned so well these past three months. On the third ring the call was answered.

"I'd like . . ."—and his voice had never sounded so foreign to his ears"—"I want to report a murder."

Chapter 4

Tuesday Evening

He was still sitting in Noah's chair, staring at the photos on the wall, when two officers—a man and a woman—came through the door. As Daniel turned toward them, the first thing he saw was the woman's drawn gun.

Feeling absurdly as if he were watching a scene from a movie, he watched the massive black policeman move to the couch. The man let out a long whistle. "Jesus, these guys weren't fooling."

A man's body lay on the couch, right arm dangling over the side, the face broken and bloody. The top button of the stained blue shirt was open, and the bloodstained tie was loose. Only one eye could be seen, grotesquely focused on the ceiling. Broken fragments of bone protruded from the shattered skull.

The big cop gently touched the bloody eyeball with his fingertip. The eye stayed open. Automatically, he lifted up the wrist and felt for the pulse, but it was a pointless gesture. He let the hand drop.

Keeping one eye on her partner's actions, the petite Chicano woman circled around behind Daniel, darted a glance at the hands concealed beneath the desk, then, convinced that they were empty, cautiously returned her gun to its holster.

"Officers Pelayo and King of the twenty-ninth pre-

The Final Analysis of Dr. Stark

cinct," she announced. "You're the one who called in to report this?"

Daniel nodded. He didn't yet trust himself to speak.

"Do you know who the dead man is?"

"Stark. Noah Stark. Dr. Noah Stark."

"What kind of doctor?"

"Psychiatrist."

The two officers exchanged a glance. Pelayo nudged her chin toward Daniel. "What's your name, please?"

"Daniel Winter."

"Are you a patient of Dr. Stark?"

Numbly, Daniel shook his head.

King's voice was crisp. "Do you want to tell us, then, what you were doing in his office?"

Daniel gazed blankly at his two interrogators. A moment ticked by before he realized the implication behind the question. Then, as his outrage mounted at their undisguised suspicion, he swallowed, and suddenly found his voice. Succinctly, he told them about the five o'clock appointment, his attempt to find paper on Noah's desk, and his subsequent discovery. King and Pelayo watched him impassively.

"Anybody here?" a voice boomed. Seconds later, Lieutenant Joe Cerezzi's burly figure stood in the doorway. His dark eyes took in both the corpse and the figures around the desk in one shrewd glance. Then he moved straight to Daniel, and bent down on one knee.

"Are you all right, Rabbi?"

King's brown eyes widened.

"I'm going to be all right, Lieutenant," Daniel said. He carefully averted his eyes from the couch. "I'm . . . just shaken. You see, Noah . . . was a very close friend."

"I'm sorry, Rabbi," Cerezzi said softly. "You know, maybe you should come with me." A moment later, he deposited Daniel on the chair in Stark's outer office. "No reason to stay in there and torture yourself, Daniel. Just call out if you want anything."

Dazed, Daniel fingered the *Los Angeles* magazine he

had been reading earlier, desperately trying not to hear the exchanges inside. After three unsuccessful attempts to focus on the journal, he dumped it, and then found himself staring up into Noah's office, at a point just over the psychiatrist's desk. The spot was dominated by a framed photograph of Noah, long rifle in hand, sandy hair blowing. He had never seen the picture before, and with a painful start he realized it must have been one of the Jennifer Steen photographs that Noah had told him about so proudly.

The shattering scream of police sirens startled him out of his chair. From inside, Cerezzi called out brusquely, "About time!"

Seconds later, four people entered. One of the men threw Daniel a puzzled, sidelong glance, then followed the others inside. A young Oriental cop nodded a mute greeting to Cerezzi, then opened up his satchel and withdrew several pairs of plastic gloves. Silently, he handed them around to his own team, then to Cerezzi and the two officers. Daniel turned away.

A few minutes later, Cerezzi stepped back into the waiting room. "Brenda should be here soon," he said.

"You told her?"

"When you called in the murder, the desk sergeant recognized your name and buzzed my office. That's why I got here so quickly. I left word that they reach Brenda as soon as possible."

"Thanks," Daniel said gratefully. He and Cerezzi had met three months earlier, during the investigation into the murder of Rabbi Myra Wahl. A cordial relationship had quickly developed between the two men, based at first on respect, later on genuine affection. The fact that Cerezzi was Brenda's boss ensured that the two men continued to see each other often. Daniel found himself at homicide headquarters at least once a week, and had fallen into the habit of dropping by the lieutenant's office briefly, just to say hello. Now, still shocked and unnerved by his discovery, he found himself unexpectedly touched by Cerezzi's concern.

"I can see how bad it is for you, Daniel. . . . I'm sorry.

And I really wish I could stay out here with you. But I gotta go back inside for a few minutes."

Bending forward in his chair, Daniel could see Cerezzi pulling open Noah's desk drawers, scanning some manila folders, frowning, and then canvassing the desktop. Suddenly, the room started to blur. He could still hear the tumult inside, yet he became aware of a high-pitched ringing sound in his ear. The sound became sharper, until he felt as if he had a siren in his skull. Cerezzi's voice pierced the sound.

"Rabbi, could you come here for a minute, please?"

Daniel forced himself to his feet. Cerezzi motioned him forward, but Daniel's eyes were directed—with mounting horror—elsewhere. Over at the couch, one of the men was forcing Stark's limp fingers, one after another, onto an ink pad, then pressing them down. Daniel's stomach lurched.

"Don't look, Daniel," Cerezzi was curt, moving to interpose his large frame between Daniel and the activities of the lab men. "You're not doing yourself any favor." He pointed to the sheet he held in his hands. It was a listing of names and phone numbers. "Is that Stark's handwriting?"

Daniel peered at the neat script. "I think so . . . Yes, I'm pretty sure it is." Behind him, a camera flashed, casting shadows over Cerezzi's face.

"Good," the big police lieutenant encouraged. "Any of the names mean anything to you?"

". . . Jonah is probably Noah's brother."

"Very good." The lieutenant made a quick notation in his hip-pocket pad. "What about the others?"

Daniel inspected the list. A Ron, Pam, and Dennis. "I don't recognize anyone here. They must be patients."

Cerezzi stepped over to the answering machine and pressed the rewind button. "There's a message on here, Daniel, that I'd appreciate your listening to."

"Lieutenant, I don't know anything about Noah's practice."

"I think this one's personal," Cerezzi said, pressing the play button.

"This is not for me," a husky female voice began. "I'm

calling for Adam. He's not too good at making phone calls just yet, but he's fine at asking questions. Like why you didn't come to see him last night. I lied for you. I told him I was sure there was a good reason. And I'm sure there was. Like two dazzling legs and tits. I know you'll pick this up after your next session. I better hear from you, Noah, or I just might drop in at your office and make a scandal. I mean it this time. I'm really fed up."

The message ended with an abrupt banging of the receiver. Cerezzi clicked the machine off. "From the look on your face, Daniel, I gather you know the caller."

"Well, I only met her once. But it must be Arlette. Noah's ex-wife."

"Ex-wife," Cerezzi repeated, pensively. "Then Adam, I suppose, is his son?"

Daniel bit his lip until he tasted blood. "He's only nine."

Cerezzi waited a minute. "Look, Daniel, is it all right if I ask you a few more questions? I know the timing is terrible, but it'll take five minutes, max. But if you don't want to, just say the word."

Daniel nodded mutely and mechanically followed Cerezzi back to the mercifully hushed waiting room. This time, Cerezzi sat down on the sofa opposite him.

"How long was Dr. Stark divorced?"

"Six years, I think."

"Messy?"

Daniel flinched at the hopeful note in the detective's voice. "More on her part than on his, from what I understand. Noah didn't talk about it much."

"How long were they married?"

"About five years."

"Did he have a girlfriend now? Any big relationships?"

"He just got . . . engaged last night."

"To whom?" Cerezzi asked, suddenly very interested.

"Jennifer Steen." Daniel filled Cerezzi in on the evening at Bornstein's, while the lieutenant scribbled notes.

"Tell me, Daniel, were you Stark's rabbi?"

"You could say that."

"People often tell their clergymen things they don't tell anyone else. Did Stark ever speak to you about any enemies, maybe a patient or former patient, anybody who might have threatened him?"

Sam Bornstein's angry comments of the previous night flashed through Daniel's mind. He lingered over Cerezzi's question a moment before answering. "No," he said at last.

But Cerezzi had scented his hesitation. "You're sure of that?"

"I honestly don't know of anything, Lieutenant."

"What about money? Was he rich?"

"I don't know what Noah had."

"Well, for starters, did he give much money to your synagogue?"

"He recently announced a ten thousand dollar pledge to erect a stained glass window in memory of his parents."

Cerezzi smiled sardonically. "And you don't know whether he was rich?"

"Well—"

"Daniel, nobody gives away his last ten thousand dollars. The guy had money. Did he ever speak to you about a will, by any chance?"

Daniel leaned back. "As a matter of fact, he did. Last winter, he almost killed himself skiing at Vail. When he got back, he decided to draw something up." He asked me about it, said he wanted some Jewish input."

"What did you tell him?"

"What I guess anybody would have told him—you don't have to be a rabbi for that. That he should make sure to take care of Adam. Then figure out whoever else really mattered to him, and might need money. And leave ten percent to charity."

"People in their thirties," Cerezzi said, "often talk about making wills, but don't do it. Do you know if he went ahead with it?"

"Yes, he did. A few weeks later—it was a Friday night—we were at the synagogue. Noah brought over his lawyer, Tom Kahn. Told Kahn I should get a commission on whatever fee he charged." Daniel smiled faintly at the recollection, while Cerezzi marked the lawyer's name down. "We joked around. I suppose talking about a will made us anxious."

Cerezzi waited for more, but Daniel was silent.

Willie King came in from the hallway. The black officer carried a big cardboard box. Stark's name was scribbled prominently on the side. "I think we're on to something," he said, passing the box to Cerezzi.

"What was in this?"

"You're looking at the wrong side," said King. Cerezzi turned the box over, and Daniel read the words embossed over the emblem: VAN GOGH'S SCULPTURES AND REPRODUCTIONS—A CLASSIC NAME IN THE CALIFORNIA ART WORLD SINCE 1945.

"So?"

"Do you notice any statues in this office, Lieutenant?"

"Nope. Where'd you find it?"

"Next door. There's a little room there with a service elevator."

"Anything there aside from the box?"

King shook his head. "A couple of empty garbage cans. A Coke bottle."

Cerezzi's finger traced the *Van Gogh's* logo. "I'm starting to get an idea," he said to King. "Let's step back in there."

Daniel started to follow.

"You don't have to come," Cerezzi said, turning.

"I want to hear your idea," Daniel answered.

The lieutenant shrugged. Experience had taught him how stubborn Daniel could be.

Inside, the photographer was still snapping pictures of the room from different angles, while another man was replacing instruments in a black bag.

"Something strike you as odd about this murder?" Cerezzi asked, his eyes shifting to the couch.

King frowned. Pelayo, who'd been standing by the

The Final Analysis of Dr. Stark

fingerprint technician, joined them, her coal-black eyes intense.

"You mean the way he was murdered? No gun or knife, just smashed on the head?"

"Maybe, but that's not what I was getting at."

"Stark didn't seem to put up any struggle," King said. "Strange, a big guy like him. Almost as if he was just lying there, waiting to get his head bashed in."

"Uh-huh," Cerezzi turned to Daniel, still standing tentatively at the door. "Anything seem strange to you, Rabbi?"

"The couch," Daniel said, very quietly.

"Yes?"

"Patients in analysis lie faceup on the couch. . . . Just like Noah's lying now. There's something deliberate, very sadistic and vicious, about the way the killer placed him there, like Noah was now the patient."

"That's just what I was thinking, Rabbi. The moment I heard he was a shrink, that's what intrigued me. A psychiatrist on the couch!" Cerezzi started to chuckle, then, seeing the stricken expression on Daniel's face, stopped abruptly.

Twenty minutes later, just as the forensic team was leaving, Brenda Goldstein rushed in. She ran over to Daniel and hugged him tightly.

Over her shoulder, Daniel caught Officer Pelayo's intense, oddly hostile stare.

"Are you all right?"

"No," he replied. "I'll live, don't worry, but I'm not all right."

Brenda took his hand and clasped it between hers. It was at that moment that she saw the body. She gasped, and her grip on Daniel's hand tightened.

Cerezzi's deep voice broke the stillness.

"You're the expert here, Brenda. What can you tell us about the significance of a couch in psychological treatment?"

49

She stared down again at the body. When she spoke, her voice was quietly professional, and she had released Daniel's hand.

"In classical psychoanalysis, the patient lies on his back, free-associating whatever comes into his mind. He never looks at the analyst."

"Why is that?"

"It goes back to Freud. Freud didn't want the psychoanalyst's facial expressions or body language to influence anything the patient said. For example, a patient might say something simply to please the analyst, or, for that matter, to antagonize him. Freud claimed that if the patients just laid back and said whatever came into their heads, eventually they'd start expressing their feelings about the analyst. But since they didn't really know anything about the analyst, you could assume that what they were really doing was projecting their feelings about others."

"Sounds like a roundabout way of getting into somebody's guts."

"There's another theory as to the origin of the couch," Brenda said, smiling faintly at Cerezzi's skepticism. "Freud also used to say that he couldn't stand people staring at him for eight solid hours. That's why he preferred to have them looking at the ceiling."

Cerezzi pointed to the leather recliner in front of the desk.

"What did Stark need this for then?"

"I'm not sure, Lieutenant. I'm a psychologist, not an analyst." Her green eyes shifted from the couch to the chair. "I can hazard a guess, though. You see, it used to be a binding rule among analysts that patients had to be on the couch. In recent years, though, a lot of analysts started questioning the wisdom of that rule. They argued that it made it impossible for some patients to speak naturally. So now, many analysts use different procedures with different patients. Whatever works."

"So you assume Stark had both sorts of patients?"

"He did," Daniel broke in, very softly. All eyes

The Final Analysis of Dr. Stark

turned to him—Brenda's quizzically, Cerezzi's with a new intensity.

"You know that for sure, Rabbi?" Cerezzi asked.

"Yes."

"How?"

Daniel swallowed, and looked from Cerezzi to Brenda.

"You see, Noah Stark used to be my psychiatrist."

Chapter 5

Tuesday Night

Gladys Perl put the last of the dirty dishes in the sink, then put a fresh place setting on the table. The roast was reheating in the oven. She glanced at the clock. 7.55. She turned on the radio. At least she could catch the news while she waited for Andy to come home. The Perls usually dined at 6:30. The girls were, after all, only nine and eleven, and Gladys liked to have them in bed before nine. But Andy had phoned, and told her not to hold dinner for him. She knew Paula and Jill would be disappointed—dinner was a family ritual—but she also knew better than to insist. There had been a savagery in Andy's voice, a frightening note that Gladys had not heard in the first thirteen years of their marriage—but one that had become increasingly common these past months. When he finally stormed in, just as the news began, there was no polite hello, no cursory kiss.

"Dinner ready?" he barked, throwing his jacket on the chair.

Gladys nodded dumbly, and pushed a strand of dyed blonde hair off her face. She caught a whiff of alcohol, and was glad that the children were in their rooms. His drinking was something else that had not been there during the first thirteen years. But now, it seemed anything was possible.

As she served the slightly burned roast, the news-caster's voice sliced through their strained silence.

"You want to turn that crap off?" Andy yelled, twisting a paper napkin in his fingers.

"Of course, darling," Gladys soothed. Her hand swiftly moved to the button. The voice stopped her.

"Noah Stark, a local psychiatrist—"

"Turn it up!" Andrew rapped.

"—was found brutally murdered late this afternoon in his Westwood office."

Gladys Peri's hand flew to her mouth. Andrew fingered his blond goatee; his eyes glittered feverishly.

"First reports, released by the LAPD, indicate that Stark's head was crushed by a heavy, blunt instrument. There is no further information at this time. Lieutenant Joseph Cervazzi, of the homicide division, asks that anyone who saw Stark today, including patients, contact his office immediately. The number—"

"Should I get a pencil, Andrew?"

"Shit up."

"—in the 213 area code is—"

Andrew Peri reached over and slammed the button down.

"My God, that's the man you've been seeing, isn't it?"

"No," he said harshly, refusing to meet her eyes. "I'm sure it's another Stark practicing psychiatry in Westwood."

"Didn't you have a session with him this morning?"

Andrew laughed sourly. "No, I just told you that so you wouldn't give me a hard time. Actually, I was screwing a gorgeous hooker at the Malibu Inn."

Gladys Peri was close to tears. "Stop it, Andrew. This isn't a joke. Are you going to call the police? Maybe you know something—"

"*Are you out of your ever-loving mind?* And put myself smack in the middle of a goddamn murder investigation? What's the matter, you have a sudden desire to see my picture on TV?"

"And if the police trace you?" she asked softly.

"So what do you suggest I do?"

"Go to them. They must have a list of Stark's patients.

It'll be a lot better if you go to them before they come to you."

"There is nothing I could tell them that matters. I saw Stark at nine this morning. He was killed in the late afternoon."

"How do you know that?"

"They just said so."

"Andrew," Gladys said, her thin voice almost breaking with anxiety, "all they said was his body was discovered late this afternoon."

"Well, all I know is that he wasn't dead this morning at nine. And I'm sure there were plenty of nuts he saw after me."

There was a silence, broken by a loud hum from the refrigerator. Gladys drew a long, tremulous breath. "Andy, I think you should go to the police."

"And I think you should cut up that damn roast and button up."

He saw the determined set of her thin, frail jaw, and slammed his fork down against the table. "Ok, damnit! I'll go to the goddamn cops. . . . Satisfied?"

She walked in back of him and put her arms around his rigid shoulders. "It's the right thing to do, honey."

"Right thing, my ass," Perl said bitterly. "I didn't do anything, but fat chance the cops will believe that."

He shook her hands off his shoulders, walked over to the refrigerator, and pulled out a cold beer. "You know," he said, popping the can open, "when you think about it, it's not so surprising that a shrink gets bumped off. They ask too many damn questions for their own good, or for anybody else's. . . . You think I'm sorry he's dead? I got along without Noah Stark before I met him, and I'll get along without him now."

A sudden smile twisted Andrew Perl's mouth. He seemed pleased at his witty reworking of the 1950s song. Throwing his head back, he took a long swig of beer.

Gladys Perl did not share in his joke. Her hands clutched the back of the empty chair. Suddenly, she was very afraid.

The Final Analysis of Dr. Stark

* * *

"How come you never told me that Noah had been your therapist?"

Daniel had originally intended to take Brenda out for a fancy meal that night, and then to the newest Woody Allen film. Instead, they now found themselves cross-legged on the wooden floor of his living room, sharing a pizza. Neither had had the inclination to change out of their work clothes. Daniel was still in white shirt and tie, Brenda in white silk sweater and black pants.

"I was self-conscious. You know Sam Goldwyn's line, 'Anybody who goes to a psychiatrist ought to have his head examined'? That's the sort of house I grew up in. My parents felt everybody should be able to take care of their own problems. And the truth is, that philosophy pretty much worked for me. Until my wife died. Those first months without Rebecca, I just wanted to make sure I had no time alone. I worked harder and harder. Somehow I had enough sense to realize I had to get out of New York. To go somewhere where every damn street, every park, every theater, didn't remind me of something she and I had done together. I jumped when the offer came from B'nai Zion. I figured LA was exactly what I needed. Something totally new. But coming here, of course, created its own problems. I didn't know *anybody,* so suddenly I was spending an awful lot of time alone. A few months after I started as rabbi, I organized a weekend at the synagogue for Jewish singles. Now that I was single myself, I could see how alienating it was for singles that synagogues are so exclusively family-oriented. Sisterhood programs all week, men's clubs on Sundays, and a million activities connected to the school. But nothing for singles." He paused. "Perhaps, part of me was hoping I'd meet someone at the weekend. Well, I did."

"Oh?" Brenda said coolly, pretending to choose another slice of pizza.

He laughed and bent over to stroke her cheek. "It wasn't a woman. It was Noah. He sat next to me at every meal that weekend, and we just hit it off. A member of the congregation, An—" He hesitated. "A patient of his, an older woman who liked me a lot, had suggested that he come. Meet some nice Jewish girls and learn something about Judaism. I was happy to hear that. I liked the idea of a psychiatrist who would listen to a patient's advice. I also found Noah enormously bright. And that was very reassuring. You see, after Rebecca died, someone suggested I speak to a therapist. But I was skeptical."

"Of what?"

"I feel like an idiot saying this—it sounds so conceited. I thought I would be brighter than the therapist, and so he wouldn't be able to see through me. You know, I imagined I would sort of patter along, showing how everything in my life was really fine, and string him along. . . . Then, that weekend, Noah and I took a long walk. I just found myself talking and talking. That in itself was strange for me. When I meet someone I can tell a few stories about myself, make a few introspective comments—you know, give the impression that I'm very open. But beneath that first layer, I don't find it easy to let people in deeper."

"I know, Daniel." Brenda's voice was soft. "You're always so afraid to let me see you in a bad mood. As if you never had the right to complain or be angry. As if you were afraid it would make me stop caring for you."

"It's crazy, Brenda." He played with the stem on his watch. "I care about you so much. But even so, I find it hard sometimes to talk." He looked up at her. "All day, I sit in my office. People come in, pour out their troubles, and I try to help. And invariably they tell me how easy I am to talk to. So why do I find it so hard to talk?"

Brenda's green eyes were bright. "I know the feeling." She wanted to go on, to tell him about the loneliness she had known the years she had been a psychologist, giving feedback and getting none, going to work in the morning with her own problems and coming home that evening with eight hours of other people's problems as well. She wanted to tell him all that. But this was not the time. Ever since she had met Daniel, she had waited for this moment, when he could trust her enough to show his vulnerability.

The Final Analysis of Dr. Stark

She hugged her knees and bent forward. "Go on."

"Well, I started seeing Noah as a patient. And right away, he saw through all my defenses and anger. Oh, was I angry! I never would have admitted it, of course. I was too busy being the martyr. I had lost my wife, but I went straight on, not missing a beat. Teaching Talmud, preparing bar and bat mitzvah students, counseling, as if nothing had changed. Inside, though, I was seething. It sounds childish, I suppose, but I was furious at God. Rebecca was twenty-nine. We'd been married only three years. It was so unfair. I told myself I was angry for *her*, for the waste. She never even had a chance to be a mother. . . . Noah was the first person I ever expressed all my anger to. It's funny. My faith is strong now, in certain ways maybe even stronger than before, but if somebody had overheard my sessions back in Noah's office, one thing they would have been sure of. That was no rabbi inside with him."

"Oh, I'm not so sure of that."

"How so?"

"Seems to me you have a lot about God to get angry at Him."

Daniel smiled gravely. "Anyway, a lot of people think therapy can destroy your faith. But with me, it only helped. And a lot of that was due to Noah. He was fantastic for me. The first time I went to see him, I was so defensive, sitting there with my arms folded in front of my chest. I wasn't going to let anybody in. And he worked with me. Five sessions later I was teasing him." Daniel smiled. "You saw the way Noah dressed, so formal, shirt always up to here."—Daniel drew the lapels of his shirt tightly around his neck—"and I said to him, 'Don't you ever relax?' And Noah said, 'Oh, if I was stretched across that cozy couch like you are, I'd also lay back and relax.' You know why I could speak to Noah like that? I always felt he was my friend."

Brenda arched a brow. "That's exactly what a therapist is not supposed to be."

"I know all that stuff about how therapists are supposed to keep their distance from patients. And, I suppose, in principle it's right. But Noah always made me feel that our relationship was not just professional. That's what made it so much easier for me to be open. You know, just talking it through with him made me realize a lot about myself. It wasn't that I was just angry at God, of course. I was petrified. Afraid the loneliness would never end."

He stopped and abruptly pulled himself up on the sofa behind him. Then, stretching out his hand, he pulled Brenda up beside him. His arm rested around her, and for awhile they sat in an easy silence. He put his lips in her thick, wavy hair, loving the scent, like fresh apples. He playfully nuzzled his nose on her cheek, making soft, growling noises. His arm tightened around her head, as in a mock wrestling match. Brenda chuckled, welcoming the relief, and threw fast, short jabs to his chest, like a boxer warming up in a gym.

"That's what I call a tough copper," Daniel mused.

She looked up at him, and there was a glint in her eyes. "Jessica's staying over at a friend's tonight. . . . That means I can stay here."

He sighed. "I love you, Brenda. A lot. And I wish you could. But we've been over this. And you know it's not so simple. I'm a religious Jew. It can only be with my wife. Which you know I want you to be."

She pulled back. "We've only known each other three months. I do love you, Daniel. You know that. But three months is not enough time to be certain—"

"But I'm certain."

"Maybe that's because your marriage was a good one. Mine was a horror. I suppose that's why the whole subject makes me so nervous. Please don't press me. I can't help it. I need more time."

"I understand." He stroked her gleaming hair. "And I had no intention of pressing you. I just wanted to explain why as much as I want it, I can't let you stay over."

She looked at him uncomprehendingly. Behind him was a wall lined with religious books. Her eyes wandered over the gilded covers, the volumes on Jewish law. Once again, with a pang, she realized how foreign much of his

The Final Analysis of Dr. Stark

world still was to her. "I can understand and accept the other things, Daniel—Shabbat, keeping kosher. But this makes no sense at all. A piece of paper's not going to make a difference. . . . This is the twentieth century."

"But for me it's also the fifty-eighth." He smiled weakly and shrugged his shoulders. "I live in two centuries."

Brenda stood. Two angry spots flamed over her high cheekbones.

Just before ten, two minutes of news summaries interrupted the Dodgers game. At a bar at LAX Airport, waiting for the 10:45 red-eye to Washington, Congressman Russell Grant sat, nursing his third double scotch. He welcomed the dimness of the bar. He didn't have to smile at anyone. No one knew him, the sunglasses and mustache guaranteed that. And no one, no nosy reporters, would bother him on the plane. He looked up groggily from his glass, surprised to see a handsome, well-dressed man in suit and tie on the screen, in place of Tommy Lasorda. "Police reported discovering the body of psychiatrist Noah Stark late . . .

Grant sobered quickly. The account was brief. "Apparently," the commentator concluded, "the police have no solid leads at this time. They request that anyone who had recent contact with Dr. Stark contact them immediately."

"Sure thing!" Grant mumbled into his glass. He signaled the waiter for another scotch.

Chapter 6

Wednesday Morning

"Mortimer Green, Rabbi." A dutifully mournful telephone voice performed perfunctory introductions. "Service coordinator with Hauser Mortuary." The somber voice *ahemed* and then droned on. "A Lieutenant Cerezzi of the Los Angeles Police Department just called to inform me that the . . . ah, autopsy has been completed, and the late Dr. Stark will be arriving here within the hour. Ms. Leslie Stark, sister of the deceased, asked that I confirm with you the two o'clock service."

Why don't you just say funeral, Daniel thought irritably, the words trembling on the tip of his tongue. "Thank you," he forced himself to say instead, well aware that Mortimer Green was only the innocent target of the much larger fury he had been feeling since the previous day. "Will the clothing Noah was wearing be arriving along with his body?"

"I couldn't say, Rabbi. I would guess, however, that, in a case . . . like this, the authorities will keep the garments of the deceased. Why do you ask?"

"I want those clothes buried with him, and during the funeral I want some of them placed on the casket."

Green's sharp intake of breath was audible. "I hardly think, Rabbi, that would be appropriate. I've had the privilege of serving with Hauser Mortuary for twenty-five years. In that time, I've supervised over six thousand services, and I've never heard of such a thing. I'm quite certain that

60

many mourners would find the idea exceedingly distaste-ful." Daniel didn't reply. Green coughed meaningfully. "Is the bereaved family aware of what you're planning?"

"I'll speak to them."

"In any case," Green went on, his professional tone now buried under an inch of ice, "I think it extremely unlikely that the authorities will release those garments to you."

"I intend to take care of that." Daniel's tone clearly implied that it was none of Green's business. "In the mean-time, thank you for your cooperation, Mr. Green."

He hung up without waiting for a response and im-mediately dialed Cerezzi's number.

"Hello, Rabbi." The lieutenant's greeting was warm, but Daniel picked up the undertone of exhaustion in his voice. Cerezzi hadn't slept much since Stark's murder had been reported the previous afternoon. "I had the autopsy done right away, like you asked, so the funeral won't be delayed."

"Thank you very much, Lieutenant. By the way, what did you do with Noah's clothes?"

"You mean the ones he was wearing when he was killed?"

"Yes."

"We kept them here, of course. In the lab."

"Do you need them?"

"We certainly want to go over each item very carefully. There are a battery of tests the lab boys are still running them through. See if any fibers from the assailant's clothes might somehow have brushed onto Dr. Stark's. Check for other blood types. Things like that. Why, what's on your mind?"

"I'd like you to cut off a large section of the shirt, a section that has blood on it. I want it displayed at the funeral, then buried with Noah."

"Is this a religious issue, Rabbi?"

"Yes."

Cerezzi cleared his throat. "I can't promise you any-thing, Rabbi, but I'll see what I can do. . . ."

Thanking him and hanging up, Daniel returned to the oversized volume he had been studying at his desk. He reviewed once again the ruling in the *Shulkhan Arukh*, the Code of Jewish Law, legislated 400 years earlier by Rabbi Joseph Karo. "If a Jew is found murdered, let him be buried as he was found, without a shroud, and without even his shoes being removed." The bold print of Karo's text was surrounded by eleven commentaries, proposing a variety of explanations for the ruling. Daniel had been delving into them since early that morning. Now, he read them over yet again. Since the Torah equates blood with life, one said, the blood must be buried along with the life. Another commentator, writing in a different volume on Daniel's shelf, noted that as Jews are required to cover even the blood of slaughtered animals with earth, how much more so must they take heed to bury the blood of a human being. But, in the last analysis, these were not the arguments that convinced Daniel. It was the simple eloquence, rather, of two commentators known by their abbreviations—the *Shakh* and the *Taz*—to which he found himself drawn. When a Jew is murdered, these seventeenth century scholars had written, "we bury him as we found him, to provoke in people fury and the desire to avenge."

He remembered an article he had read a few weeks earlier in the *Times*. More than twenty-five percent of those who commit murder never get caught, the LA Chief of Police was quoted as saying. And, he thought angrily, even for those murderers who *are* caught, what then? The California special—a life sentence translatable to parole in seven to thirteen years? Or maybe an insanity plea—in which case the murderer, sane enough to make every effort to cover his tracks, might be able to escape punishment entirely.

He slammed his fist down on his old wooden desk. *Mortimer Green finds me offensive? That's his problem. Noah's death isn't going to be sanitized. I want everybody to see what happens when a person's murdered.* He banged his fist down again, painfully. *My friend,* he swore, *I'll see your death avenged.*

The Final Analysis of Dr. Stark

* * *

As the first officers on the scene, Willie King and Maria Pelayo had requested to be assigned to the ongoing investigation into Noah Stark's murder. Now, as they entered Cerezzi's office five minutes early for their 11:00 A.M. meeting, King strode briskly forward, while Pelayo followed closely behind, gnawing at her lip. King slumped into a chair. Pelayo remained standing. Cerezzi's eyes flicked over them impassively.

"Thank you, Lieutenant," the young policewoman said impulsively.

Cerezzi pulled his feet off his desk and sat up. He scowled. "For what?"

"I'm just a rookie; I know you could have requested someone more senior."

"I would have," Cerezzi growled, "but I'm in such a pain in the ass to work for, everyone else would have turned me down."

King grinned. After a moment, deciding Cerezzi was teasing, Pelayo managed a faint smile.

What Cerezzi didn't tell them was that he had indeed spoken last night with Captain Donald Lass of the twenty-ninth, expressing his reservations about Maria Pelayo, a twenty-four-year-old with less than a year on the force. Lass had been insistent. Six months earlier, he told Cerezzi, Pelayo had graduated the police academy second in her class. "Give her a chance," Lass urged. "This might be her first homicide investigation, but she's sharp as a whip, and great with people.

"This isn't a social event," Cerezzi snapped. As the public outcry over the psychiatrist's death grew, he couldn't afford to be wet-nursing a rookie and they both knew it.

Lass was undaunted by Cerezzi's tone. "She has two other things going for her, Joe. A lot of common sense, which we both know is damned uncommon, and a hell of a partner. King's solid as a rock. Three departmental commendations in the last two years. I want to see him promoted. This case is perfect for him . . . and *he'll* be good for you," Cerezzi's superior added reassuringly.

"Okay, Captain, you win," he finally told Lass. "But on one condition."

"Yeah?"

"King and Pelayo have one week to prove themselves. If it doesn't pan out, we yank 'em."

Now, as Cerezzi inspected the two officers, he had to grudgingly admit he liked what he saw. In Pelayo's case, it was her eyes that gripped him, dark and shrewd, belying her shy, tentative manner. As for King, the man exuded power, from the bulging muscles on his arms to the massive thighs that strained the seams of his uniform. They might make a good team.

"I don't think you three met formally yesterday," Cerezzi said, nodding at Brenda as she entered. "Dr. Goldstein is a clinical psychologist assigned to homicide. Particularly because the victim was a psychiatrist, I've asked her to work very closely with us on this case.

"Now," he said, tapping his desk, "let's hear what you two found out this morning at *Van Gogh's*."

King pulled out a small pad. "Ernie Koll's the name of the kid who went to Stark's office yesterday. He's a delivery boy for *Van Gogh's*. Worked there the last six months."

"What time did he arrive at Stark's?"

"A little before nine A.M. yesterday."

"And what exactly did he deliver?"

King squinted at his notes. "A small statue called . . . er . . . Le Joy de Veevre."

Brenda suppressed an exclamation of surprise. " 'La Joie de Vivre'?"

"Yeah, that sounds right."

"You know it?" Cerezzi asked, cocking an eyebrow. The woman was an apparently endless source of information.

"It's a Jacques Lipchitz sculpture," she answered, with the passionate assurance of an art devotee. "I assume that what Stark bought was a replica?"

"Uh-huh," King answered. "That's what the kid said. Apparently, the original is gigantic and kept in some foreign

The Final Analysis of Dr. Stark

museum. Stark's copy was a rare one, though. According to Koll, it weighed about twenty pounds.

"Did they have another copy in the store?" Cerezzi patted his pocket for a cigarette, then remembered he wouldn't find one there. He was trying to quit, and this first week of abstinence was pure agony. Intercepting Brenda's amused look, he irritably popped a mint in his mouth.

"No."

"Any picture of it?"

"We asked, Lieutenant. Nothing."

"The original's at the Israel Museum in Jerusalem," Brenda said. "I must have spent a good few hours once looking at it."

"You want to describe it?"

She squinted, visualizing the monumental black sculpture boldly silhouetted against the dazzling Jerusalem sky. "It's a dancing man holding a large musical instrument. It's an abstract, of course, so the figures don't really look exactly like a man and an instrument."

"Great," Cerezzi groaned, snapping the mint in two between his teeth.

"Oh, but with practice you can recognize them, Lieutenant. What's really remarkable, though, is the illusion the piece gives of motion. You see, Lipchitz sculpted—"

Cerezzi held up a palm. "Brenda, what we need here is not an art appreciation class. What we need to know is how you could smash somebody's skull in with the damn thing."

"Sorry," she murmured, the light suddenly gone from her voice. "I guess you'd hold it by the figures and smash down with the base."

Cerezzi turned abruptly to the two officers. "You have a sense now of what we're looking for? Good. Then start over at Stark's building. Given that it weighed twenty pounds and would be conspicuous as hell to carry, the statue was probably dumped in the building. I'm guessing the murderer just stepped out of Stark's office into the service elevator—that would make it pretty damned unlikely he'd run into anyone. I want you to check everything, the garage and garbage cans in particular. Then go on to the surrounding blocks. And check with the people at the Sanitation Department about the garbage carted away from Westwood last night and this morning."

Pelayo's lip quivered. "This case," she said, "is starting to stink."

Everyone but Cerezzi laughed. He pulled another mint out of the pack and crunched it grimly.

"If only we could find that statue," Pelayo went on, eager to make amends, "who knows, I wouldn't be surprised if we found fingerprints."

"Most murderers," Cerezzi rasped, "have enough sense not to leave their fingerprints on the weapon."

"Even in a case like this?" Pelayo asked.

"What do you mean?"

"From what I understand, Lieutenant—and I realize," she faltered, "that most of my knowledge comes right out of textbooks—homicides like this one, you know, with blunt instruments, are a special category. A statue like the one we think was used to kill Stark isn't the weapon of a premeditated killer, it's the weapon of a person suddenly aroused. Somebody who just grabs the nearest thing at hand and strikes out with it. That's what I meant when I said the murderer might not have thought about fingerprints."

"Not bad reasoning," Cerezzi grudgingly allowed. "Except for one thing. Any murderer who was thinking clearly enough to lug that twenty-pound statue out of there, wouldn't be likely to forget about fingerprints."

Pelayo's olive skin flushed.

"But still and all," Cerezzi resumed, "most of what you said I can go along with. Most specifically, that we're probably dealing with an impulse killing. The statue, the excessive violence. Skolnick—"

"The medical examiner," Brenda whispered to Pelayo, catching her puzzled glance.

"—tells me some of the blows were delivered after Stark was dead. All this suggests a killer out of control. But obviously," he nodded at Pelayo, "any fingerprints we find will be manna from heaven. Unfortunately, TV and the movies have done too good a job. Even unpremeditated killers usually think fast enough to wipe their prints off a weapon."

"Even crazies?" asked King.

"Unfortunately," Brenda responded, disappointed, as usual, at the naive view some of her colleagues still had of psychology, "there's no shortage of mentally disturbed killers who take plenty of precautions to make sure they're not caught—from Jack the Ripper to the Son of Sam. The fact that somebody is disturbed in some areas doesn't mean they can't act with complete sanity in others. Besides, plenty of people who are seeing psychiatrists, particularly those in analysis, aren't what you might think of as crazy. Most of them are people like us, reeling under the force of some problem. Tell me," she said, looking meditatively at King, "have you ever been so upset that you didn't want to get up in the morning?"

"Who hasn't?"

"Well, then you're a perfect candidate for analysis, except that you might not have the three or four hundred dollars a week to spare for it."

"Ouch," the black officer said with a sheepish grin.

Cerezzi looked impatiently at the agenda on his desk. "Let's move on. . . . You remember the thing that struck me most was the couch. . . . That the murder was committed on the couch."

"That's exactly the point, Lieutenant," Brenda said with a snap of her fingers. "I kept thinking about that all last night. It's as if some disgruntled patient was saying to Stark, 'You sit over there in your chair like God Almighty Himself, while I lie here spilling out my guts.'" She stood up and her voice rose dramatically. "So now *you're* gonna lie here, and I'm gonna spill out your guts. Today, I'm playing God. . . .'" She paused, her cheeks gradually becoming the color of her red hair.

"Maybe," Cerezzi conceded, reaching for a cigarette, then frowning. "But there's one question you haven't answered, Doctor. We know Stark was killed on the couch—

Skolnick says the body wasn't moved. The pattern of blood stains proves that. So how did our killer get him on the couch?"

"Maybe he ordered Stark to lie down?" King ventured.

"You mean with a gun?"

"Why not?"

Cerezzi raised an eyebrow. "Anything's possible, but if the killer had ordered Stark to the couch with a gun, he would have shot him. And if he didn't, then the moment he put down the gun to lift up the statue, Stark would have fought him off. He was a big guy."

"Couldn't he have been just taking a nap?" Pelayo asked.

"In that case, he would certainly have locked the door first. Which means that Stark had to have admitted whoever iced him." He rapped the desk. "Furthermore, as carefully as we have canvassed that office, we still haven't found any appointment book; you know, listing the patients, when they—"

"Does that mean," Pelayo broke in, "we don't know who the doctor's patients actually were?"

Cerezzi lifted a manila folder from his desk. "We got these. Stark's records on each of his patients." He scowled. "Problem is, we've got hundreds of them, most of them probably not even current. Shrinks,"—he caught Brenda's frown—"*psychiatrists* don't see that many people at one time. We need that book to know who he was seeing *now*. But it's more than that. That damn appointment book might be at the root of the whole thing. *Why* is it missing? Five to one because the murderer took it. But why? To hide this last appointment? Or what?" He stopped. "Oh, and one last thing. We got nine responses to the message we put out."

"Great." Pelayo's pretty face brightened.

"Unfortunately," said Cerezzi, dismissing her optimism, "only three of them saw Stark yesterday. Businessman named Andrew Perl at nine. A girl named Cheryl Bornstein at ten. And finally, the shrink, er, psychiatrist had a psychiatrist. A retired guy, I gather. Guy named Dr.

68

The Final Analysis of Dr. Stark

Jerome Steen says he had a session with Stark between 12:30 and 1:15. At Stark's office. In the meantime, no one's come near owning up to seeing Stark between 2:30 and 4:15, which are the outer limits suggested by Skolnick for the murder.

"Where do we go from here?"

"Home," Cerezzi answered firmly in the voice of a man used to giving orders. "Everybody change into the most conservative outfit you've got. We're all going to a funeral."

The large sign dominating the front window of the Sunset Pharmacy proclaimed in bold letters: *All photos ready within twenty-four hours, or you don't pay.* But the short, wiry man now anxiously pushing his way through the revolving doors had not come in search of any bargains. He headed straight for the back counter, the stub ready in his hand. The clerk fished inside a drawer for a minute, humming merrily, then pulled out a thick envelope. The man paid her and raced outside, the manila envelope still unopened.

One look at its contents, however, and the tension drained from his face. The man studied the photograph grimly. Emerging from an office building, in between two people, was the unmistakable image of a tall, middle-aged man, his face hidden by dark sunglasses and a curved mustache. Roger Levin's drawn face twisted into a thin-lipped smile. *Let's see the great Congressman Grant wriggle out of this one.*

Chapter 7

For the fourth time in ten minutes, Daniel checked his watch. In one hour he would be standing up to speak at Noah Stark's funeral—and all he had in front of him was a blank sheet of paper. *If I don't come up with something soon,* he thought despairingly, *the only thing I'll have to offer the hundreds of mourners will be tears.* Noah deserved them, he knew. But he also deserved more.

As he anxiously panned the tall bookcases which covered almost every inch of available wall space, his eyes suddenly stopped on one leatherbound volume. He jumped up and pulled it down. A moment later, he found what he wanted. "The Daily Prayer of a Physician" was an old Jewish text, attributed by some to the most famous Jewish doctor of all, the twelfth century physician Moses Maimonides. In it, the author enunciated the lofty ideals intended for doctors to follow: "In the sufferer let me see only the human being. . . . Preserve the strength of my body and soul so that they will always be ready to cheerfully help rich and poor, good and bad, enemy . . ."—Daniel's face went grim—"and friend . . ."

He read straight through to the end. On the page opposite, the editor of the volume had printed "The Oath of Hippocrates"—the ancient pledge most doctors still took upon graduation. He read through that document, too, his eyes moving back and forth between the words of the an-

The Final Analysis of Dr. Stark

cient Greek doctor and the Jewish prayer. Still standing, he grabbed a notecard from the bookshelf, pressed it against the page, and furiously started making notes.

The silver-haired man withdrew a handkerchief from his grey suit pocket and blew. "Hay fever," Dr. Jerome Steen explained with delicate courtesy. "These last few days have been impossible."

Brenda nodded understandingly. The smog level had reached a peak lately. Joe Cerezzi could sympathize too— his wife was also a sufferer. "As you were saying, Doctor," he prompted.

Steen methodically refolded the handkerchief and returned it to his pocket. He looked up from behind thick gray glasses. "The president of the Dittmyer Center for Psychoanalysis and Psychotherapy has asked me to represent the" Center in the investigation of Dr. Noah Stark's murder—

Cerezzi sighed and leaned an arm over his chair. "That's what you said over the phone, Doctor. I still don't follow what this has to do with the LAPD."

"Lieutenant, let me first make a confession." Steen smiled wryly. "Excuse me; those are probably the wrong words to say to a policeman. What I wish to explain to you, though, is that I myself am feeling a bit of a conflict of interests. You see, Noah Stark had just become engaged to my daughter. . ."

Brenda nodded, her eyes sympathetic. "We know, Doctor."

"But even this is not the entire extent of my involvement here. Years before Jennie ever became involved with Noah, I was already very close to him. I was his training analyst, you see."

"Anyone training to become a psychoanalyst has to go through analysis himself," Brenda explained to Cerezzi. "The doctor who does that analysis is called the training analyst."

"So, given my connections with Noah," Steen resumed, with a nod at Brenda, "you can understand that I feel as intensely as you do about apprehending his killer. On the other hand, I am also the chairman of the Center's Committee on Ethics. And this is the role I was asked to represent here today. . . . Now, correct me if I am wrong, but it was President Caplan's understanding that your people confiscated all of Dr. Stark's files."

"I wouldn't exactly use that term." Cerezzi was curt. "We—"

"You may not be aware of this," Steen cut in, "but everything in those files is privileged information."

"This is a homicide investigation, Doctor. And in a murder investigation, the police have every right to examine anything that could help yield the murderer's identity."

"But you—"

"Without those files, Doctor, how the hell are we even supposed to know who Stark was treating?"

"Are you telling me, Lieutenant, that you didn't bother checking his appointment book?"

Brenda decided it was time to intercede. "The appointment book is missing."

Steen blinked, thoughtfully assessing Cerezzi and Brenda through his thick glasses. "In that case, I can understand your problem a little better. Unfortunately, however, it does not fundamentally alter the Center's position. I truly wish I could be of more assistance to you, but the Center must have those files back."

"Tell Dr. Caplan they'll get them," Cerezzi said. Steen's stern expression relaxed a fraction. "*After* the murderer is found."

"Lieutenant," Steen asked, with a weary sigh, "how many files are there?"

"Over three hundred."

"Then what good can they possibly do you? You cannot investigate three hundred people. Besides, many of those people—most of them I'm sure—weren't even seeing Noah anymore."

"So what?" Cerezzi said impatiently. "Who says the murderer was one of Stark's current patients?"

The Final Analysis of Dr. Stark

"Dr. Steen," Brenda interjected with a conciliatory smile, "surely you must understand that we have to investigate every possibility. It might not turn out to be a patient at all."

"That is not the issue," protested Steen. "I am not denying that the person you seek might be a patient. I am even willing to say there is a good chance he or she is. But you are talking about one patient out of three hundred. Even if one of them is the killer, the other two hundred ninety-nine are not." He paused. "Noah was my protégé, the most gifted student I ever had. I loved him. But the very thought of a policeman interviewing a psychiatrist's patients, asking all sorts of intimate, accusing questions," —Steen grimaced—"the very thought, Lieutenant, makes me shudder.

"And the very thought of not catching Noah Stark's killer makes *me* shudder.

"Lieutenant, excuse me. I imagine that to you I sound somewhat heartless. Believe me, I have been deeply shaken—the whole psychiatric community has been. Don't you realize how much all of us wish to see Noah's murderer caught? But there are standards, limits. Do you have the slightest sense of the panic that will ensue among all of our patients when the word gets around—and it *will* get around, I assure you—that police are reading through a psychiatrist's files? We want Noah's killer caught. And punished. But there has to be a better way. What do you do in all the murder cases where you do not have a psychiatrist's files?" He shook his head, his gray eyes sorrowful. "I cannot see sacrificing hundreds of innocent people to get at one guilty one."

Steen met Cerezzi's furious gaze squarely. "Noah Stark, Lieutenant, would have said the same thing." He turned to Brenda. "You're a psychologist, Dr. Goldstein. You know what goes on in therapy. It is only because people trust that what they say will never go beyond the room that they have the courage to open up. That is the most important thing we analysts have working for us. If that trust is ever destroyed, we might as well hang up our shingles." He shrugged delicately.

"Let me suggest something, Dr. Steen." Brenda felt compelled to find a solution—she could easily imagine herself, three years earlier when she was still in practice, sitting in Steen's chair and explaining to some skeptical police officer why he couldn't have the files. "You know Dr. Stark's methodology better than anyone else. In fact, I'm sure you'd also understand his notes ten times faster than I would. What if the two of us sit down together with the files? We could narrow down those patients who should be looked at more closely. And then the department would undertake to investigate their movements on the day of the murder. I give you my word that at no time would any of the people under investigation have the slightest idea that their files had been read. . . . Now, is that something you could agree to?"

Steen scrutinized her impassively. "It's a possibility. At least I could then reassure my colleagues that the Center will have some input. But I must speak about this first with Dr. Caplan. Then we will give you our decision."

"Fine."

"Can you give me your word that you won't go through the files until then?"

Brenda's eyes sought Cerezzi's.

"When are you going to get back to us?" the lieutenant demanded of Steen.

"As quickly as possible. Certainly by tomorrow morning."

Cerezzi rapped his desk thoughtfully. Then he nodded his reluctant assent.

The psychiatrist rose.

"Just one more thing, Doctor. For how long were you Dr. Stark's training analyst?"

Steen eased back down and canted his face thoughtfully toward the ceiling. "Six years . . . give or take a few months."

Cerezzi whistled softly. "You must have known him better than anyone. . . . And you realize, of course, that you might well have been one of the last people to see him alive yesterday."

The Final Analysis of Dr. Stark

Steen shivered. "Yes, I've thought about that."

"Your sessions, I understand, took place at his office. That's a bit unusual, isn't it?"

"Until two years ago, when I gave up most of my practice, we met at my office. It was only since then that we met at his. I have very few other patients at the moment. And once Noah became engaged to my daughter, I was, of course, planning to terminate my treatment of him."

"Anything special come up in yesterday's session?"

"No."

"Would you tell me if it had?"

"If it had relevance."

"Don't you believe the police department should be the judge of that?"

"Lieutenant, I've practiced psychiatry for forty years. I trust my judgment."

"Did Dr. Stark discuss his cases with you, or solicit your advice?"

"He did. Listen, Lieutenant, you seem to forget that I'm on your side. Still, I do not see these questions . . ."

Cerezzi waved away the objection. "Okay, okay." A sudden wave of violent sneezing engulfed the psychiatrist, and he dug deep into his suit pocket, extracting two fresh handkerchiefs. Cerezzi waited till Steen composed himself.

"Were you happy about Stark's engagement to your daughter?"

"I was very pleased, of course. Noah was not only a fine doctor, I believe he would have been very devoted to my daughter. He was not perfect, but then again, neither am I. Or, for that matter," Steen said, his face crinkling into a brief smile, "as hard as it is for me to admit, is Jennie. My daughter loved him very much." Steen paused. "Her happiness is what matters most to me."

"And can you give us an accounting, Dr. Steen, of your whereabouts Tuesday afternoon?"

"I returned home from Noah's a little after 1:30. I spent the rest of the day trying to complete an article for the next issue of *Psychiatric Review*."

"Did you see any other patients that afternoon?"

"No. As I indicated before, I am more or less retired."

"Did you leave your house at all between two and four-thirty, see anyone?"

Steen brushed his hand against his cheek. "Not that I can recall. . . . No, definitely not."

"Receive any calls?"

"Not that I can . . . No, I don't believe so."

"One last question. Knowing Stark as intimately as you did—as you yourself put it, he was not perfect—can you think of anything, some skeleton in his closet, something that might have come to your attention as head of the Ethics Committee, anything that would help us find the person who murdered your daughter's fiance?"

"With all due respect, Lieutenant," Steen said crisply, rising and adjusting his thick glasses, "that is most assuredly confidential information."

Chapter 8

Wednesday Afternoon

Hauser Mortuary was a name familiar to most non-Jews in Los Angeles. This curious fact had nothing to do with a sudden burst of gentile curiosity about Judaism, or about dead Jews. It did, however, have a great deal to do with the Los Angeles transit system. On the front of virtually every bench along LA's bus routes were affixed notices, *HAUSER MORTUARY CARES.* To anyone looking out the window of a moving vehicle, those three reassuring words were about all that could be discerned. If, however, some-one was waiting for a bus, there was ample opportunity to learn the mortuary's phone number—*Just remember 213-KADDISH*—and that Aaron Hauser was the man to contact to secure the most beautiful resting place for those you love.

Hauser's aggressive advertising was hardly restricted to public benches. Shortly after Daniel's arrival in Los Angeles three years before, he had visited the mortuary to attend the funeral of a friend's father. The service was a lengthy one, made considerably lengthier by the officiating rabbi's unshakable conviction that every noun demanded two synonymous adjectives: "this tender and compassionate man . . . this scholarly and educated soul . . . this warm and loving father." About ten minutes into the hagiography, the young man seated next to Daniel, an incongruous smile on his face, passed him a pamphlet, a copy of which was tucked into the compartment in front of their seats. Spread over the front cover were two words: *WISDOM IS* . . . Puzzled by his neighbor's cheerful expression, Daniel looked at the pamphlet, trying to guess which quotations about wisdom would appear inside. When he opened it, however, he quickly learned that, at Hauser Mortuary, wisdom had a very special meaning. "Wisdom is . . ." the inside page piously declared, "not waiting until your loved one dies before you look for a plot."

Even now, Daniel remembered how he'd spent the rest of that service alternately biting his lip and digging painfully into his thumb with another finger. Anything, anything to keep from laughing.

"Which service are you here for?" the uniformed guard asked now, as Daniel drove down the ramp and through the ornate black gates.

"Noah Stark."

The guard consulted the clipboard in his hand, then pointed. "Second building over on the left."

A small cluster of automobiles was parked at the entrance to the low building. Daniel smiled when he saw Brenda's.

The smile was erased, however, when he entered the auditorium. Hollow shrieks of hysteria, more animal than human, echoed off the cold, brick walls. In the gloom, it took Daniel's eyes a moment to focus. When they did, he saw that the screams came from a thin young woman standing before the simple pine coffin. As he watched, she made a sudden move to force it open, but the elderly man at her side—his face oddly familiar—succeeded in holding it down. Daniel raced over.

"Excuse me," he said, "I'm Rabbi Winter. Can I help?"

As the woman raised her tear-stained face, he realized with shock that he was looking at Jennifer Steen. She bore little resemblance to the superbly groomed woman he had met two nights earlier at Sam Bornstein's. Her makeup ran in jagged patterns down her face, and deep hollows marked her once-beautiful eyes. Her thick auburn hair was snarled.

The Final Analysis of Dr. Stark

Now, despite Daniel's introduction, she made no gesture of acknowledgment. Instead, she made another lunge for the coffin.

"It is not wise, darling," the older man urged her firmly, pressing against the coffin's handle. Daniel recognized the face now, from the picture hanging in Noah's office. This was Dr. Jerome Steen. "Just remember him as he was."

"Noah," she moaned, burying her face in her hands. "I want to see you again." She dropped her hands and fixed a wild gaze on her father. "Can't you understand that?"

"Of course I understand, darling, but . . ."

"You kept Mama's coffin open!"

The bespectacled man took out a handkerchief from his pocket and ran it over his perspiring brow. He looked beseechingly at Daniel.

"Jennifer," Daniel said gently, stepping forward.

Her eyes regarded him dully. "I want Noah's coffin open," she whimpered. "I never got to kiss him good-bye."

Daniel shuddered. He sensed the girl's need; how could he not? Hadn't he wanted to see Rebecca one last time? But the Jewish principle, the absolute separation of life from death, made even more sense to him. It explained why meat, the symbol of death, could not be eaten with milk, the symbol of life. And it explained why Jewish law forbade beautifying a lifeless corpse and then putting it on display. Nothing was to be done that denied the reality of death—no cosmetics, no fancy clothes, no elaborately pillowed and satined coffins. This attitude, he knew, caused considerable annoyance to many morticians—after all, they were often praised for their ability to make the dead look lifelike. That's why they took such pride in having an open coffin. But what was the point? He remembered one of his teachers at the seminary attacking this American custom. "When you open up the coffin, what you're seeing is not the man, but his ghost. And it's a mockery to parade before this painted and propped-up ghost, saying 'Good-bye.' " Daniel's own experience as a rabbi only confirmed his teacher's observation. He still winced at the memory of the time he had to physically drag away an old woman who had raised her dead son's head and was frantically hugging it to her chest.

"Jennifer," he urged, very gently. "Listen to me. I saw what Noah looked like after he was killed. I promise you, you don't want to see him."

The girl looked off into the distance. Her father withdrew a clean handkerchief and passed it to her. Her sobs gradually subsided. She dabbed briefly at her eyes, then passed the handkerchief back.

"Did he suffer?" she demanded.

"The police believe he was killed by the first blow," Daniel said quietly.

Jennifer nodded. Her shoulders sank. The tempestuous outburst seemed to have drained her. She stood uncertainly a moment longer, then moved away, head bent. The silver-haired man started to follow.

She shook her head. "I want to be by myself, Dad."

He nodded, and slowly walked back to Daniel's side.

"Thank you, Rabbi," he said, extending a hand. "I am Jerome Steen."

Pleased to meet you, Daniel almost began, then bit his lip. How inappropriate the most ordinary phrases sounded today.

"I think she will be okay." Steen's eyes carefully monitored Jennifer's retreating figure. His hands were clasped behind his back, his spine was perfectly erect. Daniel could not help admiring the man's composure.

"It'll take a while," Daniel said. Funerals, he thought, bring out their own special brand of banality.

Steen regarded him gravely. "Rabbi Winter, I understand that you and I will be the only speakers at the service. I'm feeling quite tense today. Would it be all right with you if I spoke first?"

"Of course, Doctor. By the way, about how long do you think you'll be speaking?"

The elderly man slipped a printed sheet from his pocket and briefly scanned it. "Oh, seven, eight minutes."

Daniel's throat went dry. "Can I see that . . . sheet, please, Dr. Steen?"

"It is nothing," Steen said, passing it over. "The Oath of Hippocrates. That is an oath all physicians take."

"I know." Daniel returned the sheet. His stomach muscles tightened into a knot.

"I am going to base my comments about Noah on it," Steen went on composedly.

"Very interesting," Daniel managed to stammer, then abruptly excused himself.

He had arrived at the mortuary early, figuring he'd seek out Noah's brother and sister, and some of the other mourners. Instead, he sought out Mortimer Green, and was escorted to a quiet study. He had thirty-five minutes in which to compose a new eulogy.

Medical Examiner Sol Skolnick's glasses slid precariously down his uneven nose, and his large brown eyes bore down intently on Joe Cerezzi. He tugged hard on his beard.

"Are you crazy?" he demanded for the second time.

"Crazy folks wouldn't think they were, would they, Sol? So if I said I was, it would only prove to you that I was probably sane."

Skolnick laughed. "Look, Joe, this has been a helluva long day. I've been here since four in the morning. And now I feel like I'm having a nightmare. So let's just start this meeting all over. Why don't you go out for a minute, come back in, and we'll take it from there?"

Joe Cerezzi lifted his eyes heavenward but complied. He stepped outside and knocked.

"Come in," Medical Examiner Sol Skolnick invited cordially. "Ah, good to see you, Lieutenant. What can I do for you?"

"I want some of Noah Stark's clothes. In particular, something bloodied."

"Uh-huh," Skolnick replied in an exaggeratedly even tone. "And what do you need it for, Lieutenant?"

"To display at the funeral."

Skolnick's even temper finally cracked. "Are you *crazy*?"

Cerezzi walked over to the window and stared out. He understood Skolnick's position. After all, it was no different from his own.

Skolnick picked up a half-smoked cigar from his ashtray and, taking his time, lit it. Cerezzi winced. His hands ached for a cigarette. Skolnick blew out a winding smoke ring and leaned back in his chair. "Lieutenant, I've been a Jew for fifty-five years. I've been to umpteen Jewish funerals. And I never saw or heard of such a thing. Are you sure this rabbi isn't nuts?"

"Thank God you're not a psychiatrist. You'd be locking people away left and right. . . . Now what's the story, Sol —can you give me something?"

"Are you cr—" Skolnick started, then stopped. "It's evidence, every millimeter of it."

Again Cerezzi walked over to the window. Daniel Winter was a friend, and that counted for something. He swung round. "What if I brought the clothes back after the funeral?"

"I thought you said this lunatic rabbi wanted to bury them."

"I think displaying them is the main thing. Symbolism, you know. Come on, Sol," he coaxed. "Let me have it."

"You understand it's all on your head," said Skolnick, crushing his cigar into an ashtray.

Cerezzi nodded. Skolnick regarded his face for a moment, withdrew his Mount Blanc from his shirt pocket, and grudgingly signed the requisition form. He shoved it across the desk.

"You know something, Joe," he said, as Cerezzi grabbed it up and opened the door. The lieutenant turned.

"You're—"

"Crazy," Cerezzi finished, his face breaking into a big grin, as he slammed the door behind him.

The Final Analysis of Dr. Stark

* * *

"I am speaking here today as a colleague, a teacher, a friend—and, in a certain sense, I even feel as a parent."

Jerome Steen paused, looking out over the solemn faces. In the front row, Leslie, Stark's sister, looked up at him quizzically.

"For one thing," the elderly man continued, "Noah had just become engaged to my daughter, Jennifer. I happily anticipated the day he would become my son-in-law. But even before that, it was Noah himself who once suggested the parent role to me." Steen glanced down at the sheet of paper on the podium. "He once brought to my attention the opening lines of the Hippocratic oath, in which the physician swears, 'to hold him who has taught me this art as equal to my parents' . . .

In a chair on stage, in back of Steen, Daniel sat, following along in the copy of the text he himself had brought.

For a few minutes, Steen recalled different incidents involving Stark, tying each one in with yet another trait from the Oath of Hippocrates. At one point, the psychiatrist sought out Cerezzi's face at the back of the audience and looked steadily at him, then read in a clear voice: "'What ever I may see or hear in the course of the treatment or even outside of the treatment in regard to the life of men . . . I will keep to myself, holding such things shameful to be spoken about.'

"Noah had a right to expect more," the doctor continued, his voice shaking with emotion. He glanced again at the two-thousand-year-old words. "'If I fulfill this oath and do not violate it, may it be granted to me to enjoy life and art, being honored with fame among all men for all time to come. . . .'" He removed his glasses and pressed his forefinger and thumb over his strained eyes. A moment later he tried to resume, but a wave of sneezing swept over him, and, with a gesture of defeat, he moved back to his seat. Daniel regarded the text in his hands, seeking the conclusion of the sentence Steen had begun. *If I transgress this oath and swear falsely, may the opposite of all this be my lot.*

A cold knot formed in his stomach.

Maria Pelayo had conscientiously recorded thirty-three license plates—even before the service began—when she caught sight of the cream-colored van pulling into the mortuary lot. An elegant blonde, clad entirely in black, stepped out, her face concealed behind a pair of large black sunglasses. Pelayo's eyes charted the new arrival. The woman moved gracefully toward the cluster of people near the hall entrance waiting to sign the guest book. She joined the line, nodding a greeting to one or two in the group. Then, seemingly impatient, she left the line and drifted inside. Discreetly, instincts tingling, Pelayo followed.

The woman moved up to the coffin and stood by it silently, her palm pressed against the casket's lid panel. Her lips seemed to be moving. Next, she headed for the family room. The policewoman considered following her, then decided against it—Cerezzi had been very specific about her assignment, and she was far too junior to start improvising. *If I could at least speak with him,* she thought, her eyes desperately darting around the auditorium and back out onto the lot. No luck. Finally, she shrugged her shoulders—*it doesn't look like that lady's running anywhere,* she consoled herself—went back outside, and succeeded in recording seventy-four more license plates before the service started.

It was then that she caught sight of Cerezzi. He was standing at the back of the auditorium—all seats were now filled—eyes scanning the crowd, as Jerome Steen delivered his eulogy.

She slipped into the hall. "Lieutenant," she whispered, edging over to him and tugging gently at his black suit. An annoyed chorus of "shhs" hissed out at her.

Instantly, Cerezzi turned around and, with a sharp jerk of his head, motioned her outside.

"That was not the best place to call me lieutenant," he snapped. "Now what the hell is so important?"

The Final Analysis of Dr. Stark

Pelayo bit down on the rush of apology and drew him to the plate glass windows enclosing the auditorium. "That blonde over there with the sunglasses, two seats over from Dr. Goldstein; do you know who she is?"

Cerezzi peered inside. "Arlette Stark, Stark's ex-wife. She was pointed out to me in the family room. Why?"

"I thought you might be interested," Pelayo announced nonchalantly, "to see the car she arrived in." Cerezzi's eyes followed her raised finger—and then widened.

Two words, painted in rich burgundy, were emblazoned on the side of the van parked in the middle of the lot. VAN GOGH'S.

"There's an old proverb," Daniel began, looking around the crowded auditorium. "'You can't tell the size of a tree until it's been cut down.' Only now that Noah Stark is dead can we begin to measure the stature of this man . . . There were many, many layers to Noah. Anyone who ever saw him with his son Adam knows what a loving father he was. But he was much more than that. He was a healer. Anyone who was ever treated by this wise and compassionate doctor can affirm that. And Noah was a friend . . . my friend."

Daniel elaborated on the traits that made Stark so special, most particularly what he called "Noah's third ear, his ability to answer not only the questions people asked, but those they didn't ask as well."

A moment later he finished, his voice so low that only a few people at the front could decipher the mumbled, "*Yehai nafsho keshura*—may his soul be bound up in the bond of eternal life." He started to move away from the podium when he caught sight of a baffled expression on Joe Cerezzi's face. Daniel's eyes darkened, and he turned sharply back.

"One last thought," he began, his hands tightening on the microphone, his eyes sweeping the faces raised to him. "Several days ago, an article in the *Times* reported the random shooting death of a sixteen-year-old boy here in Los Angeles. The police arrested the sniper, and afterward, the boy's father, a religious Christian, announced that he forgave the murderer. My friends, what that father did is not the Jewish way. No one has the *right* to forgive a murder committed against another. No one has a *right* to forgive a murder at all. When God confronted Cain after the murder of Abel, He didn't forgive him. He shouted, 'Your brother's blood cries out to me from the ground!' " In a sudden motion Daniel bent forward under the podium and lifted out the bloodied shirt he had concealed there earlier. Gasps rose from the audience. He held it high.

"This blood cries out too." His voice rasped in the stunned silence. "This blood too!"

Russell Grant gazed out the window of his inner office at Dawn Bentley and Greg Owen, the two university students who had worked as volunteers in his office these past months. True enough, with Stark dead, he felt a lot less vulnerable to Levin. On the other hand, the thought that one of these two might be in cahoots with that reporter didn't fill him with a sense of security. Bad enough to have the media circling around like piranha—worse yet to have an inside spy filling them in on where you liked to go swimming. He was hunched forward, resting on his right elbow, wondering which of the two students was the most likely candidate for the Ethel and Julius Rosenberg Spy Award, when his secretary, Roberta Jameson, returned from lunch. She headed straight for his office, limping slightly —the result of recent hip surgery.

"Russell," she said with surprise, "I thought you'd still be at the Committee meeting."

Grant made a downward motion with his thumb. "Waste of time. Anything happening here?"

Jameson put a hand up to her gray hair. "The usual. Three constituents visiting D.C. wanted to see you."

"Important people?"

"I don't think so. Tourists. I told them you were wrapped up in sessions all day and gave them signed pictures. They went away happy."

"Right." Grant smiled gratefully.

The Final Analysis of Dr. Stark

"Remember, at 4:15 you're meeting with that visiting high school class, Cashman High School," she said, drawing out each syllable. "You got it fixed in your mind?"

Two years earlier, at a high school commencement, Grant had ringingly referred to "the great football team of Midland's High, the pride of all California"—and had been astonished by the stony silence that greeted his patriotic peroration. "Midland's High, the pride of all California," he repeated glowingly. A line like that, he knew, usually brought a crowd to its feet. Now, like the only one to stand up was a pink-faced, overweight principal, who scurried over to Grant's rescue. "This is West Orange High School, Congressman," he said in a high-pitched stage whisper that must have carried to at least half the auditorium. Ever since that infamous night, Rhoda was under strict instructions to go through this drill with Grant before any speech.

Grant nodded. "Got it . . . Midland's High," he said, his mouth a straight, serious line. "The pride of all California."

Roberta's hand flew to her mouth, then she saw Grant's famous grin.

"Oh, you are a devil," she giggled. Her eyes returned to her notepad. "Your wife told me to remind you that you're having guests tonight—so be home by seven. And that reporter, Levin, called."

Grant's palms went clammy. His smile froze. "What did he want?" he asked, all the fun gone from his voice.

"Something about a picture . . . That was a nice article he—"

"What picture?" Terrifying images of hotel and motel rooms throughout California suddenly flooded Grant's imagination.

"Some picture of you. I suppose he wants to run it in an article. Tried to make it sound like it was a big deal."

Who the hell is this son-of-a-bitch Levin, Grant wondered savagely, *a reporter or a damn blackmailer?*

"Should I try and get him?" she asked.

"No, Rhoda, just give me the number."

"It's no bother. I'll do it—"

"Just give me the number, please," he said, somehow managing to keep his voice even. "I'll take care of it myself." He waited until she left, then dialed. At 4:00 P.M., 5:00 P.M., 6:00 P.M., and 7:00 P.M. he got Levin's answering machine. Each time he left no message. By the time he arrived home at 7:30, a half-hour late for dinner, Russell Grant was a very frightened man.

Jonah and Leslie Stark, Noah's brother and sister, stood beside Daniel on the lush slope of the cemetery, the raw grave gaping at their feet. The hot sun beat down on their heads. Beside the grave, on the grass-covered earth, lay the plain pine coffin.

Daniel withdrew a small pair of scissors from his suit pocket and held them out toward Jonah.

"Time for the kria," he said. *Kria*, the Hebrew word for tearing, was a distinctive aspect of Jewish mourning. Unlike many Jewish traditions, this one could be traced all the way back to the Bible. When Jacob saw Joseph's coat of many colors drenched with what he thought was his son's blood, he tore his garments. David, too, tore his clothes when he heard of King Saul's death, and Job, whose mourning seemed perpetual, also stood up and rent his clothing. But now, as Daniel motioned to Jonah to raise his jacket, the tall, dark man who, except for his height, bore little resemblance to his brother regarded him blankly.

Leslie tugged at her brother's arm. "Come on, Jonah," she said impatiently, "the rabbi has to make a cut."

"But this is my best suit."

"Damn it, Jonah. We talked all about this last night. What's the matter with you?"

Jonah stared at her, but said nothing.

"Are you ready, Mr. Stark?" Daniel asked.

Sourly, the big man nodded. Daniel lifted the lapel of Jonah's dark suit jacket and made a small incision.

"Well, at least it won't show," Jonah said, inspecting the damage.

The Final Analysis of Dr. Stark

Daniel handed the scissors to Leslie, who quickly made a small cut in the collar of her gray blouse.

"Is that all right, Rabbi?" she asked, shading her red, swollen eyes from the fierce sun and looking up at Daniel.

Daniel nodded. Jewish law was quite specific on the nature of the tear. When mourning for a parent, one had to tear the garment on the left side, over the heart, and the tear had to run for at least three inches. For siblings, any tear, even one that did not show, was permissible.

Now Jennifer Steen stepped forward. Noah's fiancée had regained her composure since Daniel had last seen her, but her face was ravaged with pain. She took Leslie's hand in hers, and kissed her on the cheek. For a moment the two women clung to each other. Then Jennifer turned toward the open grave and ripped violently at the shoulder of her black silk blouse. The material came away in her hand. She stood there, unmoving, her left shoulder exposed.

Daniel quickly motioned to the six pallbearers, who started lowering the casket into the grave. The only other sound was a jubilant bird overhead and an occasional muffled sob. Finally, the casket thumped hard against the earth.

"Oh, my God!" Jennifer shrieked, and bent over as if to follow it. Jerome Steen came up behind her, once again trying to restrain her. "Noah!" she cried, breaking away violently from her father's arms. "Noah! I love you!"

The mourners around the grave awkwardly tried not to stare, as Brenda pushed through the crowd and knelt beside the grief-stricken young woman. She put an arm around Jennifer's shoulders and cradled her for several long minutes. Slowly, the hoarse cries melted into sobs. Then, with Jennifer's head resting on Brenda's shoulder, the two rose, and slowly moved away from the graveside.

A large mound of earth stood by the grave. Three shovels protruded from it. Daniel withdrew one shovel, then dug into the mound. A stone came up with the earth in the shovel's blade, and when he released it over the hole, it knocked with a hollow sound against the casket. He motioned Jonah to join him. Noah's brother stubbornly shook his head and held his place. Two of the pallbearers grabbed shovels and began to dig. Dirt pelted the casket. Daniel replaced his shovel in the mound and waited while Leslie stepped forward and withdrew it, tears streaming down her pallid face. Soon a silent crowd gathered around the diminishing mound, waiting their turn to perform what Jewish law considered the final, and most difficult, act of kindness to the dead. Only when the casket was fully covered by earth did Daniel ask the diggers to stop.

He chanted the *El Maleh Rakhamin*, the memorial prayer asking "God, who is full of compassion," to bind the soul of the dead to eternal life. Then he stepped over to Jonah and Leslie.

"Now the Kaddish," he said.

Again, Jonah shook his head. His eyes seemed focused somewhere in the distance.

"Mr. Stark, I don't understand what's troubling you, but you must say the Kaddish."

Icy gray eyes gazed back at Daniel. "I don't have to do anything."

Daniel turned helplessly to Leslie.

She grasped her brother's arm. "Jonah, I'll never speak to you again. I swear it."

After what seemed like an interminable wait, Jonah yanked the sheet from the rabbi's hand and turned fiercely to his sister. "For you, Leslie. Not for him."

Daniel shivered, then passed another sheet to Leslie. "*Yitgadal*," he prompted, and a second later, the two joined in, their eyes on the English transliteration.

"*Ve-Yamleekh malkhutei*," they recited, stumbling through the Hebrew, "May He establish His kingdom soon, in our lifetime. And let us say: Amen."

Daniel surveyed the crowd, who joined in with a fervent "Amen!" Arlette Stark, he noticed, was silent. Her face expressed no emotion, nor did she seem to hear the mourners' response.

The Final Analysis of Dr. Stark

"*Oseh shalom*—May He who makes peace in heaven, make peace for us on earth. And for all Israel. And let us say: Amen."

A loud chorus of amens followed. Even Cerezzi, looking stiff and awkward in a dark suit, joined in.

Daniel gestured for everyone to break into two lines, so that the mourners could pass between them. As Jonah and Leslie started down the path, people called out their condolences with the traditional formula. "*Hamakom*, may God comfort you among the mourners for Zion and Jerusalem."

Daniel, too, recited the formula, but automatically. His mind was elsewhere. Already, as his eyes followed the retreating figure of Noah's older brother, one thought preoccupied him. What had Jonah Stark been doing yesterday afternoon between two-thirty and four?

Daniel arrived home from the cemetery shortly after four. Exhausted, he quickly slipped out of his black suit—the "funeral suit," as they had called it at the Yeshiva—and headed for the shower. Jewish custom dictated that one wash one's hands after leaving a cemetery, but for Daniel the encounter with death always demanded a more total immersion. Today he let the hot water pound full force onto his shoulders, but the tightness in them didn't ease. His mind remained preoccupied. With Jonah Stark. But also with something else. And damned if he could figure it out. He was forgetting something, he was sure of it, but what?

Eureka came two minutes later. Oblivious to the thick lather of shampoo covering his black hair and the wet footsteps he was leaving on the carpet, Daniel bounded out of the shower, and headed straight for the bottom left drawer of his bedroom dresser. He jerked the drawer out with such force that it went skidding onto the floor. On his knees, Daniel rummaged through his underwear—the soap and water dripping down—to his bankbooks and his passport. Then he found it—the thick envelope Noah had pressed into his pocket at Sam Bornstein's house two evenings ago. Anxiously, his wet fingers tore open the envelope.

A quick glance at the contents, and he was back on his feet, heading for the telephone.

For the second time in twenty-four hours, he punched out the same seven numbers.

"Lt. Joe Cerezzi, please. It's urgent."

Chapter 9

Wednesday Evening

Brenda Goldstein sat at Joe Cerezzi's desk, poring over the sheets he passed her.

"So what do you make of it?" he asked, bending his large frame over her shoulder.

She frowned. "I have a funny hunch, Joe."

"Good. I could use it, funny or no."

She jumped up and moved to the door. "But first, I've got to check something in my office."

"Brenda!"

"I'll be back right away."

Cerezzi paced. For the past hour, since Daniel Winter had brought the files in, the lieutenant had felt a tension in the pit of his stomach. The Stark case was finally moving. After a swift glance at the contents of the envelope, he had summoned Brenda. Maybe, being a psychologist, she'd have a clue as to what it all meant—why Stark had asked Daniel Winter to safeguard Xerox copies of two patients' files.

"Shit," Cerezzi muttered impatiently, waiting for Brenda to return, as he looked again at the name on top of the first file. Russell Grant. He knew the name well. In the past two congressional elections, the Policemen's Benevolent Association had actively supported Grant's candidacy. "Elect Russell Grant," Association President David White had urged, "and give law-abiding people a friend in Congress." Grant had so liked the endorsement that he had it printed up on shopping bags and distributed all over the district. What was more, Cerezzi knew, the congressman was currently being touted for the Senate.

For just a few seconds after he had managed to hurry Daniel out of his office, he had stared at Grant's file, brooding on the agreement he had made with Jerome Steen that morning—not to read the patients' files until the psychiatrist got back to him. Bullshit, he had finally decided. There was no argument Steen could come up with that could convince him these files were irrelevant. And anyway, he thought, with a sardonic twist of his lip, they came from Daniel's house, not Stark's office. Therefore, they weren't part of the agreement. He opened the file.

Not a lot of psychiatric jargon, he immediately noted with relief—and for a doctor, the handwriting was pretty legible. *Russell Grant. Saw me interviewed on the Ray Walker Show. Asked him if he didn't want somewhat more reliable recommendation. He told me he trusted his instincts, and didn't want anybody, stressed word three times, to know he was seeing a head doctor. At that point, he told me he was a congressman. Patient seemed disappointed, hurt even, that I didn't know who he was. Demanded guarantee our meetings would remain secret. Gave him standard speech.*

Apparently, it was the first encounter with Grant that had most intrigued Stark, because after that the notes became much sketchier. *Heavy drinking* was written in a red pen after the next session, and circled. *Not yet a complete alcoholic dependency, but close—history of alcoholic abuse in family, father.* A few sessions later, there was again a complete account, apparently an incident in which a man, most likely a pimp moonlighting as a blackmailer, had taken compromising photographs of Grant with a call girl, and the congressman had had to pay five thousand dollars in hush money. Cerezzi's jaw clamped. He was annoyed at the congressman, and yet at the same time embarrassed for him. He was also embarrassed to be reading and knowing all this—God knows, there was no shortage of incidents in his own life he wouldn't care for anyone else to know about.

The Final Analysis of Dr. Stark

Finally he turned to the other file—Anna Gorman. The first entry was dated just over three months earlier. Asked her how she came to me, said she had heard about me a few months ago from Sam Bornstein. Cerezzi frowned, and he riffled through the papers on his desk until he found Cheryl Bornstein's name. He pulled out a Beverly Hills phone book and checked Sam Bornstein. Same address as Cheryl. Cerezzi made a notation on a pad and turned back to the file. *Extraordinary,* Stark had written, *Extraordinary revelations! Martin Reisman, Dr. G. Simon, Hannah Weller, Bierman.* The first name was underlined. *Patient said it was all brought out by that picture. Tried to calm her down, convince her that everything she was telling me had nothing to do with her reality now. Started her on Valium. I am very excited.* Apparently, there had been no second session. Five days later, there was another notation in Stark's writing. *Dr. Brian Gitter called to tell me that Anna Gorman had a stroke, and is confined at Cedars Sinai, Room 1107.* Just under a month later: *Anna Gorman has been moved to Hillside Golden Age Apartments.* An address and phone number, both underlined, followed.

Cerezzi was still mulling over the reports when Brenda Goldstein slipped back in.

"What'd you find?" he demanded, looking up at her flushed face.

"Just what I suspected. I knew those names, Grant and Gorman, didn't sound familiar." She tapped the two files on the lieutenant's desk. "The originals of these were not among the files we brought back from Stark's office."

"Jesus! It's only six now, so maybe Pelayo can still catch Gorman tonight. She sounds like a weak old lady. Maybe it'd be a good idea for you to be there too. In the meantime, I'm going to have a little talk right now with our senatorial candidate."

"Can I listen in, Joe?"

"Be my guest," Cerezzi grinned.

Brenda waited while Cerezzi checked the Washington phone number in Stark's file and dialed. Almost immediately, an answering machine came on: "You have reached the office of Congressman Russell . . ."

"Shit," he called out, hanging up, "I forgot, it's night-time back East." He checked the file again. " 'In case of emergency, private number . . .' "

He dialed the alternate number.

A moment later, a hearty "Hello!" boomed over the line. Cerezzi flipped on the intercom and nodded at Brenda.

"Is this Congressman Grant?"

"It is," the voice said, more cautious now. "And you are?"

"Lieutenant Joseph Cerezzi. LAPD, homicide."

"What's on your mind, Lieutenant?"

No reason to beat about the bush. "Did you know a Dr. Noah Stark?"

"Did I know a Dr. Noah Stark?"

Cerezzi recognized the trick—repeating a question was the oldest stalling technique known to cops.

"May I ask the reason for your inquiry, Lieutenant?"

"Dr. Stark died yesterday afternoon. And we want to speak with people who knew him. We have reason to believe you were one of them."

"I assure you, Lieutenant, that few people know better than I the importance of cooperating with police officials. I'm sure you're aware of the active role I played in the California legislature in pushing through increases for your department."

Jesus Christ, Cerezzi groaned mentally, *give me a break.*

"Let me thank *you,* Congressman. It's always a pleasure to speak with public officials who support police work as actively as you do." Cerezzi cleared his throat. "That's why I'm sure you'll want to be as helpful as you can in our investigation. So, I must ask you again, did you know Dr. Noah Stark?"

"Just one more thought, Lieutenant," the voice said crisply. "How do I know you're who you say you are?"

"Fair enough, Congressman. Why don't you hang up, dial the LAPD homicide division, and ask for Lieutenant Joseph Cerezzi. That's C-E-R-E-Z-Z-I."

The Final Analysis of Dr. Stark

"I'll do that, Lieutenant."

"But please get back to me right away, Congressman. If you cooperate with us, we will be most anxious to co-operate with you in minimizing any unnecessary publicity."

Cerezzi hung up.

"What's your take on him?" Cerezzi asked, looking up at Brenda.

"He sounds very self-controlled, but then he's used to difficult situations. Given what's in that file, I'm sure he's very frightened."

"He's got a lot at risk," Cerezzi conceded. "But plenty of Stark's files probably have much worse. God knows what these loonies have blabbed to the good doctor. So, the question is, why did Stark give that particular file to Daniel?"

Brenda shrugged helplessly. She went to the table near the window and poured herself some coffee, wincing at its taste.

A second later, the phone rang. Cerezzi scooped it up.

"I checked up on you, Lieutenant. Seems you're legit."

Cerezzi chuckled. "Thanks. Now, I—"

"Lieutenant," the man cut in seriously, "I want your word that you'll keep whatever I tell you in confidence."

"A blanket promise like that, Congressman—as I'm sure you know—is impossible for me to make. But I'll certainly do my best to hush things up if it's possible."

There was a pause, and Cerezzi heard a sigh at the other end. "May I ask how you got my name?"

"I'm sorry, I can't tell you that."

"Okay." Grant's voice betrayed his weariness. "Listen, Lieutenant, I'm going to level with you. Stark was my psychiatrist."

"Working with you out of Los Angeles?"

"Most of the time we'd have sessions over the phone. When I was out on the coast, I'd go in to see him."

"And the last time you saw Dr. Stark was when?"

For a fraction of a second, the congressman hesitated. "You're not going to start getting into what I was seeing him about, I hope?"

"Of course not. Your reasons for seeing Dr. Stark are

not the department's business." Cerezzi looked down at the open file in front of him and smiled grimly.

"I had a session with Dr. Stark two days ago."

"You mean on Monday, the day before he was killed?"

"Yes, that morning."

"Did you hear about the appeal the police department made, asking patients to come forward?"

A long pause. "I did."

"Is there a reason you didn't contact us?"

Grant drew a long breath. "Lieutenant, do you think it was easy for a man in my position to start seeing a shrink? Every time I saw Stark, I was scared there would be a leak and the media would get hold of it. Do you know what a field day they would have with that kind of information? They'd crucify me. It would be the end of my political career, everything I worked all my life to accomplish. You want to know something? I was so paranoid I used to put on a disguise when I went to see Stark. Then, when he was killed, I thought of contacting the police, but I realized there was nothing I could tell you. The last time I'd seen him was more than twenty-four hours before his death. I figured if the only thing that would come out was that I was Stark's patient, it wouldn't help you. And God knows, it wouldn't help me."

Cerezzi drummed a finger on his desk. He was tempted to ask Grant if he had any idea why Stark was hiding copies of his files. "So you didn't see him after Monday morning?" he asked instead.

"I told you that, Lieutenant."

"What sort of mood was Dr. Stark in?"

"I'm not sure I would know. He never talked about himself."

"Of course, but was there anything unusual about him, or about your session that day?"

"Excuse me, Lieutenant," Grant said dryly, "but are you on—what do lawyers call it—a fishing expedition?"

Cerezzi chuckled. "A little, I suppose."

"Well, you understand, Lieutenant, I'm uncomfortable speaking about something so private. . . ."

Twenty-five hundred miles away, Cerezzi nodded. *That's just how I'd feel.*

"But then again," Grant continued, "I don't want to sound coy. No, nothing special happened. Just a normal session . . . Anything else, Lieutenant?"

"Not at this time." Cerezzi paused. "But if necessary, Congressman, we'll be speaking again."

"If necessary," the man repeated without enthusiasm. A moment later, he hung up.

When Brenda glanced at the lieutenant, his fingers were massaging weary eyes.

"Didn't learn much, did we?" He smiled ruefully at her.

"So what do you think, Joe?"

Cerezzi flipped his palms. "He's probably okay."

"He did seem unusually jumpy that somebody might find out he was in therapy."

"If that caused him to bash Stark's head in, then I'm in danger now too." Cerezzi laughed sourly. "No. I don't think Grant's our man. For one thing, there's no shortage of crooks in Washington, but . . ."

"But what?"

"But when was the last time you heard of a congressman committing a murder?"

Maria Pelayo extended two fingers toward Willie King and grimaced. "Choose you for who digs in first." The two were standing in front of a long line of steel garbage cans in the cellar of 1350 Westwood, the office building where Noah Stark had practiced. According to the building's super, Bubba Talmadge, the garbage had last been collected Tuesday morning.

"Sure," Talmadge had answered their next question. "Anybody who can press C on an elevator button can come down here and dump anything they want."

Now King, ignoring Pelayo's challenge, rolled up his sleeves with a grunt and stepped over to the first can. He popped off the lid and untied the twist sealing the large plastic garbage bag. Then he made a sweeping bow in the petite policewoman's direction.

"After you, mademoiselle . . . I'll start at the other end."

"First one in's a rotten egg," Pelayo said bravely. She plunged her hand to the bottom of the bag and gingerly edged it from side to side.

A few minutes later she cried out. "Hey, Willie, I think I got something!"

Ten cans over, Willie King, his long arm covered with a dark, wet mass, jumped up and raced over.

Very slowly, one hand still in the bag, Pelayo rose to a standing position.

"Come on, let's see," King urged impatiently.

Finally, an impish smile on her face, Pelayo drew out a miniature grey plastic soldier, a likely discard from a Crackerjack box.

"So what do you think?" she said, laughing at his expression.

"I think," King replied glumly, "that it's going to be one helluva long night."

Daniel pulled back the brass knocker, then saw that the door was slightly ajar. He pushed it open, and walked in. The hallway mirror was draped with a white sheet. On a small table by the entrance to the living room, a pile of paper *yarmulkes* and prayerbooks stood available for visitors. He paused in the open doorway. Around the two low mourner's stools, a handful of visitors huddled on several armchairs and one long chintz-covered couch. Others stood near the card table filled with light refreshments.

The first person he recognized was Leslie Stark, seated on one of the wooden stools, her eyes bloodshot and dull. His heart went out to her. She looked so much like Noah —the same wide brown eyes, open expression, and curly blonde hair. Catching sight of him, the young woman started up from her seat, but Daniel motioned her downward. Jewish tradition stated that mourners need not rise to greet visitors. Probably no area of Jewish life, he thought, as he took a seat on the sofa opposite Stark's sister, was more heavily regulated than this one. Mourners sat on low stools, the law regulated, as a way of symbolically acting out their despondent mood. Even the English language, it struck him now, expressed the same idea. "I'm feeling low," a depressed person might say. In biblical times, this symbolism was carried even further. Mourners actually sat on the earth.

Daniel looked around the room. In a house of mourning, a visitor must say nothing until the mourner speaks. An arriving guest has no way of knowing what the mourner most needs at that moment. He might think it best, for example, to speak about the deceased, but, at that moment, the bereaved person might desperately need to speak about something else. On the other hand, the guest might lead the conversation to something general, just when the mourner might need to speak about the lost relative. And then, too, the guest might just try and make conversation, when the only thing the mourner might crave is silence.

Daniel nodded a greeting at Jerome Steen, acknowledged a few faces from the funeral, then stared at the empty stool next to Leslie. He wondered where Jonah was. Finally, Leslie broke the silence.

"Your words this morning were very beautiful, Rabbi. I was just telling the doctor," and her head dipped toward Steen, "that Noah was lucky to have two such good friends. Lucky," she repeated, then wrapped her arms around herself as if she was cold.

Daniel remained quiet, this time not because of any Jewish law, but because he could think of nothing to say. No words could ease Leslie Stark's anguish.

"It was a very moving service," the middle-aged woman seated beside Daniel said.

"Yes," said the reedy man beside her, taking hold of the woman's hand. "And all those people there, it was a testament. A testament," he repeated, pleased with the phrase, "to Noah."

"Do you think I'll see my brother again, Rabbi?" Leslie asked in a low voice.

The silence became awkward. Funeral services were easy enough to speak about. But middle-class American Jews did not speak easily about afterlife.

"I do," Daniel told her. "I really do believe you will. Tell me, Leslie, do you believe in God?"

"Yes."

"And that He is just?"

Leslie bent her head to the side. "Sometimes."

"Well, if you do believe in God," Daniel went on, glad that finally he had some consolation to offer, "and that He is just, then of course there's an afterlife. The only possible explanation for all the suffering and injustice we see, the death of someone like Noah, is that this world is not the whole picture."

The woman next to Daniel perked up. "But the rabbi at our temple,"—Reform, Daniel noted automatically; Reform Jews went to temple, Conservative Jews to synagogue, and Orthodox Jews to *shul*—"he said that Jews didn't believe in an afterlife, that it's not even mentioned in the Bible."

"Listen," said Daniel, running his fingers through his thick dark hair, "I can't tell you for a fact why something's in the Torah and why it's not. But I do think I understand why the Torah's silent about afterlife. When was it written? Just after the Jews were brought out of Egypt. And during the centuries they were living there, they saw just how destructive an obsession with afterlife could be. The major achievement of many of the Egyptian pharaohs was the pyramids—enormous, expensive tombs they built for themselves. Do you know what the holy book of the Egyptians was called? *The Book of the Dead.* Maybe the Bible didn't raise the issue of afterlife because it realized that the moment the next world becomes the central issue in religion, it takes people's minds away from the real business of improving this one."

A wry smile flickered across Jerome Steen's face. He leaned forward in his armchair, opened his mouth to speak, then seemed to think better of it.

There was a sudden flurry at the living room entrance.

The Final Analysis of Dr. Stark

An elderly couple, the man stooped with arthritis, the woman with skin as white as her hair, shuffled in. Leslie sprang up from her stool. "Aunt Rose, Uncle Max—" Her voice broke. "You shouldn't have. It must have been so hard for you to get here."

Daniel strained to catch the old man's muffled reply, but he could make no sense of it. The voice was a strangled whisper.

"I'm going to get you two something," Leslie said firmly when Max had finished speaking.

The plump woman next to Daniel called out, "You stay here, Leslie dear. I'll take care of it."

"Nonsense," Leslie replied. "It'll keep me busy." She led the couple toward the kitchen, clearly glad to have something to distract her.

The remaining guests, most of them strangers to one another, gazed around the room or at the floor.

Daniel leaned toward Steen. "I have a suspicion," he said, "you're not a big fan of religion."

The psychiatrist smiled mockingly. "You know the origin of the word 'fan,' Rabbi?"

"No."

"Short for fanatic. In the final analysis, is that not what religion usually leads to? Fanaticism? I am a reasonable man, Rabbi. I do not believe God created the world in six days—"

"Religious people don't have to believe that," Daniel cut in.

"—and I do not believe there is some loving father up in the sky who is going to reward or punish us after we die. Or before, for that matter."

"What do you believe in, Doctor?"

"Human beings," Steen replied in his deliberate, resonant voice. "I believe in people. In their ultimate desire to be good. In their ability to deal with their problems, and not rely on blind superstition."

The bitterness in the doctor's last words, coupled with the trace of a European accent, suddenly sounded familiar.

"You went through the Holocaust, didn't you?" Daniel asked.

"Yes, but I don't see—"

"Are you perhaps angry with God because of what happened during the war?"

Daniel was conscious of seven pairs of eyes moving back and forth between him and Steen, like fascinated spectators at a tennis match.

"I prefer not to be angry," the doctor replied stiffly. "And I prefer not to hate. Because if there is a God, Rabbi, and He allowed that horror to happen, I would have to hate Him. It would be immoral not to. That is why I prefer not to believe in Him."

Daniel nodded. Convincing a Holocaust survivor why he should believe in God was something he knew from bitter experience was beyond his capabilities. Better let the whole matter drop. Unfortunately, Daniel's reedy neighbor was enjoying the debate immensely.

"That's a damn good point the doctor made, Rabbi, and you didn't answer him. How can you believe in God after something as horrendous as the Holocaust? Where was He then?"

There's no way out, Daniel thought. He turned to Steen.

"You tell me you don't believe in God, but you believe in human beings?"

"That is correct."

"I can't understand that. It wasn't God who built Auschwitz and the crematoria. It was men. It was men, not God, who are responsible for the Holocaust. So how can you believe in men?"

"I don't accept what you are saying, Rabbi." Steen's features twisted, accentuating the deep lines in his face. "People are good, and want to do good. Those who do not are sick. Or afraid. Like most of the Germans and Austrians during the war. I'll admit it, I have sometimes done things out of fear that I am not proud of. And I am sure every person in this room has too. But very few people make a conscious, rational decision to do evil. That is why I believe

The Final Analysis of Dr. Stark

in people—and why I have dedicated my life to treating the fears, the anxieties, the guilts that cause people to act badly. If you overcome those rationalizations for doing evil, people's goodness will come out. But your God does not have those excuses. He is powerful and just, as you put it. So He could have stopped the slaughter. But He didn't. Why?"

The thin man made no effort to conceal a triumphant smile.

"Because God gave man free will," Daniel answered slowly. "He can't intervene every time people misuse it. Free will is what makes us human. Maybe we'd prefer it if people had been created as robots who could do only good, rather than as human beings who can also choose evil. . . ."

Daniel caught himself sharply. Sitting in Leslie Stark's home, observing mourning for his dead friend, was not the place for a heated religious debate.

It was the heavy woman next to him who spoke next, in a deep, throaty voice. "Excuse me, Doctor, I also lost some of my father's family in the camps. Treblinka. Where were you, if I may ask?"

A shadow passed over Jerome Steen's face. "I don't—I find it too painful to speak about my war experiences."

"Anybody try this apple strudel?" a woman called out incongruously from the table. "It's incredible."

Relieved at the diversion, most of the group stood and headed for the refreshments. Daniel and Steen were left alone.

"I'm sorry if I offended you, Doctor."

"Not at all, Rabbi," Steen answered courteously. "To tell you the truth, I was concerned my more rational approach to religion might have offended you. Certainly, if you are comfortable with your faith, I do not wish to undermine it."

"Thank you," Daniel said, suppressing a smile at the man's gracious display of tolerance. "I was wondering, Doctor. If one of your patients believed in an afterlife, would you have spoken to him in the same way you spoke to me?"

"I am pretty much retired now," Steen said, withdrawing a fresh handkerchief and patting it against his nose, "so it is not likely to come up anymore. But, no, I would not. If a person wants to believe in an afterlife, that is his decision. But my responsibility as a psychoanalyst is to make sure that he knows the difference between belief and fact."

They spoke a few more minutes. Finally, Daniel excused himself and headed for the kitchen. Inside, Leslie was fussing over the elderly couple. Coffee, milk, sugar, cheeses, and rolls were spread on the table in front of them. She didn't notice Daniel's entrance.

"I'm sorry, I have to go now," he said gently, walking up to Leslie's side.

She looked up, startled.

"Thank you so much for everything, Rabbi," she said, her eyes suddenly liquid.

"I want to say good-bye to Jonah. Where is he?"

Leslie's mouth pulled into a tight line. "Jonah walked out about an hour before you came," she said, her voice taut. "He said he'd wasted enough time today on Noah and he wasn't going to waste seven more days in mourning." The last sentence was an effort, and when she finished, she could hardly suppress angry tears.

"It's okay," Daniel comforted her. "It's not your fault. . . . Leslie, what's behind Jonah's anger at Noah?"

She struggled to regain her composure, then answered his question, her eyes blazing. "Why don't you ask him?"

Joe Cerezzi was staring covetously at an unopened pack of cigarettes when the buzzer sounded on his desk. Shoving the cigarettes away, he stabbed the button down.

"Cerezzi!" he barked at Desk Sergeant Debbie Hall.

"Roger Levin is here to see you, Lieutenant."

"Come again?"

"Roger Levin. Says he's a reporter for the *LA Times*. I mean he is—he showed me his press card. Wants to speak to you about the Stark homicide."

Cerezzi groaned and glanced at his watch. "Goddamn," he said, "it's ten o'clock. I'd like to go home sometime this week. Don't these bastards ever quit? Look, Debbi, why

The Final Analysis of Dr. Stark

don't you tell this Levin that I've got nothing for him? We have a few promising leads, that's it. You get the picture."

"I already did, Lieutenant. Levin says he doesn't want information *from* you. Wants to *give* you information."

"That's a switch," Cerezzi said sourly. "Okay, send him up." He picked up the cigarettes, dumped the pack in his desk drawer, and firmly turned the key.

A moment later, the wiry Levin knocked and entered. His maroon necktie swung over his right shoulder, and his cuffed pants hung so close to the tips of his shoes that it seemed he could trip at any moment. He held a small manila envelope in his right hand.

"Have a seat, Mr. Levin."

"I'm too wound up, Lieutenant." The reporter had a high-pitched voice which immediately got on Cerezzi's nerves. "I'll just stand, okay?"

"Whatever," Cerezzi shrugged. "I understand you have some information for us."

"Lieutenant," Levin said with a triumphant smile, thrusting the envelope at him, "take a look at that photo."

Skeptically, Cerezzi withdrew the four-by-six print. It showed a mustached man emerging from an office building he immediately identified as 1350 Westwood.

"You know who that is, Lieutenant?" Levin demanded.

"Who?"

"Congressman Russell Grant!"

Cerezzi examined the print again. "I didn't know the congressman had grown a mustache. If that's him, it looks good on him."

"It's a disguise, Lieutenant. I've been following Grant around for more than a week now. He puts that mustache and sunglasses on whenever he goes to his shrink."

Cerezzi stood, his large bulk easily dwarfing the small figure of Levin, and let his eyes flick downward. "Didn't your mother ever tell you, Levin, that it's disgusting to creep around following a person seeing a psychiatrist? I know all that crap about the public's right to know every-thing. But I also know that somebody seeing a psychiatrist has a right to privacy."

Levin's back straightened and his thin arms went rigid. "This is not some goddamned symposium at UCLA Law School on media ethics, Cerezzi. A man's been murdered. Forgive my naiveté, Lieutenant, but I somehow got the stupid idea in my head that the LAPD might also have some faint interest in catching the killer."

"The murder was committed on Tuesday," Cerezzi barked. "Grant last saw Stark on Monday."

Beads of perspiration moistened Levin's forehead. "So he admitted to you he was seeing Stark?"

Cerezzi flushed. Foolishly, he'd let the reporter provoke him, and now, of course, he had said more than he wanted. He stuffed the picture in the manila envelope and shoved it across the desk toward Levin. "I think it's time for you to go get some sleep."

Levin seemed not to have heard him. "So Grant admitted to you he saw Stark on Monday?"

"And suppose he did?"

"It would just be very interesting, Cerezzi. But really quite irrelevant."

"What the hell's that supposed to mean?"

With a triumphant flourish that strained Cerezzi's thin patience, Levin pulled out the print from the envelope. "This picture," he declared with satisfaction, "was taken Tuesday afternoon at 2:40."

Chapter 10

Thursday Morning

"God Almighty," Pat Hastings exclaimed as she walked into Daniel's office at three minutes after nine. She took in the rabbi's tousled hair and pale, unshaven face. "You look awful."

"Thanks." Daniel pushed back in his chair and let his eyes close. "You know what I could use now, Pat, more than anything else?" He sighed. "Some good news. Got any for me?"

"*Hmm.* What would make you happy, Rabbi?"

He held out his forefinger. "First, to hear that the cops have arrested Noah's killer."

"Uh-huh." Pat nodded gravely.

"Second," he went on, "since I'm not too optimistic about that happening just yet, I'll settle for my whole schedule today being canceled. And third, well, maybe I'll be willing to take one emergency meeting at the health club, in the sauna. . . . So, how'm I doing?"

"You're one-half for three."

Daniel opened his eyes. "Which means?"

"Which means I have no messages from the police department, and no canceled appointments." Pat smiled wanly. "But I do have an emergency meeting for you. Unfortunately, it's not at the health club."

"What's the emergency?"

"John Goodman."

Daniel sat up. Goodman had been appointed to the Board some years earlier, during the fund-raising drive for the new sanctuary. As Wilbur Kantor put it, "Rain or shine, John Goodman is good for fifty thou." As it turned out, Kantor was wrong. Goodman had donated double that sum. Oddly enough, however, since his appointment, he seldom came to synagogue, and rarely attended Board meetings. For that matter, Daniel recalled, he hadn't even come to Sam Bornstein's house on Monday night.

"He phoned a half-hour ago. Seemed upset when I told him you weren't in yet. I told him you'd be here by nine." Pat glanced down at her watch. "He should be here by a quarter past."

"I don't have anything else right now, do I?"

"You're free. Don't worry, I checked. But even if you weren't, I think you'd have to cancel. To tell you the truth, Daniel, he sounded terribly rattled."

"Really?" From the few encounters he'd had with Goodman, Daniel had always been struck by the suave self-confidence of the middle-aged executive. A rattled John Goodman sounded like a violent contradiction in terms.

"When he gets here, show him right in. . . . Anything else?"

Pat handed him a copy of the morning *Times*, opened to the inside obituary page. The headline "Funeral for Murdered Psychiatrist" dominated the first four columns of the page. Accompanying the text, in descending order, were three small photographs: of Noah, Daniel, and Jerome Steen. Inside, the article quoted at length from both Daniel's and Steen's eulogies.

"The paper called up yesterday," Pat said, "and asked for a photo. So I gave them the one from the book jacket."

"Thanks, Pat," he answered, not looking up. Inevitably, his eyes went up a notch, back to Noah, to the wavy blond hair and clear, genial expression of his face. He shook his head. It had really happened. But it was still so difficult to accept.

The Final Analysis of Dr. Stark

"Remember," Pat reminded him gently, "there's The Remnant meeting tonight."

He nodded.

"And the radio show this afternoon."

"Got it," he said.

"It's going to be a debate, you know?"

"Bartley warned me." Daniel was the moderator of radio station KLAX's weekly "Religion and You." As a courtesy for Daniel's work at the station, Bartley Turner, the director of programming, had arranged for Daniel to be a guest on the Thursday afternoon "Book Hour." Each week, a recently published author would be interviewed for a few minutes, then listeners would phone in with questions. This past Monday morning, Turner—in a characteristic burst of enthusiasm—had telephoned Daniel with "great news."

"You know," Turner declared, "how deadly those book shows usually are? Bor . . . r . . . r . . . ing. So, you know what we decided to do, Danny Boy? Turn the whole show into a debate. You know, have somebody who disagrees with you on at the same time. Don't worry," he said smoothly, forestalling Daniel's protest, "whoever it is, I'm sure you'll wipe the floor with them. After a few more minutes of exuberant speculation on Turner's part about how fantastic the resulting program would be, Daniel acquiesced. Not that he had much choice—it was clear Turner was confronting him with a *fait accompli.*

"Do you know who's debating you?" Pat asked.

"Not a clue. And for the life of me, I can't imagine who they'll come up with. It's not like I wrote some controversial book—you know, favoring capital punishment, or pro-Israel, or something like that." He lifted the slender blue volume off his desk top. "It's a book against gossip, for God's sake. Can you imagine someone arguing on behalf of gossip?"

Pat laughed heartily. "This is Hollywood, Daniel, not the yeshiva. This city lives and breathes gossip. Turner will come up with somebody, don't worry."

Daniel groaned, and, laughing at his expression, Pat started for the door. Suddenly, she turned back. "Oh, and Brenda called."

"So there *was* good news, you killjoy. Where'd she call from?"

"Headquarters."

Daniel nodded and reached for the phone. "How you doing, copper?" he asked a moment later.

"Your files seem to have lit a fire under the lieutenant," Brenda replied, without bothering to greet him. "Something's up with the congressman, though Cerezzi's playing it very close to the vest." Daniel grinned at the jargon Brenda was increasingly picking up at homicide headquarters. *Close to the vest,* he almost repeated, chuckling. He wondered if she even realized that it was a poker phrase.

"What about that other patient?"

"Strikeout, I think. I went to see Anna Gorman with Maria Pelayo. She's a sweet woman, in her mid-seventies. An immigrant, with a heavy accent. We asked her about her meeting with Stark. It seems she'd been suffering from insomnia, so she went to see him for treatment. We kept on pushing her, at least as much as we felt we safely could—she's a pretty frail old lady, and the stroke's really disoriented her—on anything else she could remember. Zilch. Afterward, I called her doctor. He told me that she's on heavy medication, which also helps explain her vagueness. Anyway, we asked her, of course, about the picture —you remember what it says in her file about how that picture set it all off?"

"Of course; and what'd she say?"

"I don't even know if she knew what we were talking about. She dug into her purse and came up with a little plastic folder crammed with photographs of her family, nieces, nephews, even a great-nephew. I'd bet it was Maria Pelayo's first exposure to a Jewish mother." Brenda chuckled softly. "Anyway, *nada.* So Gorman's a probable scratch, but something's going on with Grant."

"A congressman?"

"Listen, I'm not saying Grant's involved. Maybe he saw something. I don't know. But—"

His intercom sounded. "Wait a second, Brenda." He depressed a button. "Yes?"

"John Goodman's here," Pat Hastings said in a low voice.

"Send him right in." He turned back to the phone. "Brenda, I gotta run."

"Daniel," she said quickly, "aside from all this police stuff, you and I have to talk."

"Of course. Are you okay?"

"Yes . . . No. It's important, Daniel. It's about us."

Puzzled by her urgency, Daniel wanted to pursue it, but John Goodman was standing in the doorway looking at him. His face was ominously anxious.

"Absolutely. But now's not good. I'm sorry. I'll get back to you."

"Daniel, I'm serious. I've been thinking about us all day."

"Nice thoughts, I hope. No, seriously, I just can't talk to you right now. . . . I'll get back to you."

Hanging up, Daniel looked at the tall, square-faced executive and motioned him gently to sit down. Goodman slid into the chair opposite, his hands clutching its arms. Goodman's shirt was a casual Perry Ellis design, but this morning, nothing else about him seemed casual. There were dark circles under his deep gray eyes.

"I don't think I slept an hour altogether last night," Goodman began miserably. "It was my wife who insisted I had to speak with you.

Daniel looked at him, bewildered. Until this moment, neither John nor Joyce Goodman had ever struck him as the sort of people whose moods of desperation would drive them to a rabbi.

"All last night, I was thinking about my mother, of blessed memory. She also would have told me to speak to a rabbi. Maybe that's what Joyce gave the idea. You know, when I was a kid, I remember a story my mother once told me, about the old country. I must have been twelve. Two guys in the shtetl she came from, Jewish guys, had clothing stores just opposite each other. Anyway, one of them had found some trick to get out of paying taxes, some way of hiding his income. His competitor figured out what he was doing, told the police, and got the guy closed down and locked away. I remember when my mother told me that, I said, 'Boy, he must have cleaned up then, being the only clothing store in town.' But she said no, that he went bankrupt within two months. Because the whole community excommunicated him. The rabbi ruled that it was forbidden to buy from his store, or even to talk to him. They wouldn't even let him set foot in the synagogue. And everybody just went along with it."

Goodman rubbed his haggard face. "Tell me something, Rabbi. All last night I was lying in bed thinking about that story. What do you think, was it one of my mother's *bubba maysahs*"—Goodman gave a small smile, but his eyes were miserable—"or do you think it really happened?"

"It could have happened." Daniel was struggling to figure out why a story John Goodman heard at least thirty-five years ago was suddenly giving him insomnia. "In Jewish life, an informer is called a *moser*, and informing is one of the worst crimes a Jew can commit."

"It's even in the prayer service, isn't it?" Goodman asked hoarsely.

"Three times a day, *Ve-la-malshinim al tehi tikvah*, and let there be no hope—no salvation would be a better translation—for informers. Of course, Mr. Goodman, the prayer refers to a very specific type of informer. It was written when the Romans occupied Israel and were doing terrible things to the Jews. Stealing property. Making Torah study a capital offense. There were informers who used to betray the locations of the underground Jewish schools to the Roman officials. Your mother's story also has to be understood within a certain context. In Czarist Russia they used to have discriminatory laws and taxes against Jews, so of course Jews didn't feel obligated to obey all the laws.

That's why they hated informers so much. In Russia, the police and the government were the enemy." He smiled ruefully. "Of course it hasn't changed much under the Communists. Remember the Shcharansky trial? The KGB schlepped in that informer—what's his name, Sonya Lipavsky?"

Goodman hardly seemed to have heard him. "So it's wrong to inform on a Jew?"

Daniel tapped his pen on *Sticks and Stones*. "You want to tell me, Mr. Goodman, why you couldn't sleep last night?"

Hollow eyes stared back at him. John Goodman was suffering. "I think I know who murdered Noah Stark."

A chill shot through Daniel. "Who, for God's sake?"

"An employee of mine. Andrew Perl."

Briefly, Goodman reviewed the circumstances under which he had sent Perl into treatment with Stark.

"Then Tuesday, it must have been about one in the afternoon, I called Perl into my office. I told him that we were on to him again, and this time he was fired. I had given him a second chance, I said. There wasn't going to be a third. He stormed out. But the last thing he said to me was, 'I'm going to get that head-shrinking son-of-a-bitch.' I should have known there would be trouble.

"Let me understand something, Mr. Goodman. You've been holding on to this information for the last two days?"

"Only since last night. Tuesday afternoon I flew to Denver on business. I only got back yesterday, pretty late, and that's when I heard Stark had been murdered."

"Did anybody other than you hear this threat?"

"Nobody else. Owen Mortimer, our accountant, was in the room when I first confronted Andy, but then he left."

Daniel's mind was racing. "Is Perl paranoid?"

"How do you mean?"

"I mean thinking that Noah was filling you in on his sessions.

The man laughed, but his eyes did not meet Daniel's.

"I hope that's not your definition of paranoia, Rabbi. How else do you think I found out what I was going on?"

Daniel stared at him, suddenly speechless. It wasn't possible. Noah wouldn't violate a patient's confidence. Why was Goodman lying?

"Look," Goodman answered quickly, "the first time I caught Andy stealing I could have gone straight to the cops. But I didn't. I didn't want to be an informer. Besides, Perl is some sort of cousin. Not that close. A second cousin. But still and all, mishpocha. That's why I decided to send him to a shrink instead of dumping him in jail for embezzlement. Which is probably where he belonged. Even if I say so myself, I think that was pretty generous of me."

"Uh-huh," Daniel murmured noncommittally.

"But you got to understand, I didn't want to get ripped off again. I had to know that about Perl. Did he mean what he said when he swore it wouldn't happen again? Am I making my position clear, Rabbi?"

"Go on."

"Well, I used to see Stark occasionally. You know, socially. So I asked him, what's the story, Noah, once a thief, always a thief, or can I trust the guy? You know Stark. He'd give me one of those, I don't know what you'd call it, enigmatic smiles—isn't that what they always write in novels? Said he couldn't talk to me about a patient. Well, damned if I was going to accept that. I told Stark straight out, if I can't trust the guy, cousin or no cousin, I'm gonna have to can him. And then you, I said to Stark, can wave goodbye to those fat fees you're getting from me to treat him. So finally, Stark and I worked out a little system. When I'd see him, or call him—it didn't happen often, you understand—I'd ask him: 'Look, on a scale of one to ten, how much can I trust this guy?' I must have done it five, six times. And Stark would always say, nine, once even ten. I felt very encouraged about Perl. Then, this past Sunday night, I invited Stark out with me to the West LA Country Club for dinner. Joyce was with me, and the doctor had this pretty girl with him, Jenny something. Anyway, at one point, the two ladies went to the john, you know the way women always go together. And we were just sitting there, the two of us. Suddenly Stark says to me, 'Aren't you going to ask me your usual question?' For a second I didn't even know what he was talking about. Then I realized what he meant, and I got like a jolt in my stomach. I said, 'What the hell's going on, Noah?'—excuse me, Rabbi, but that's just what I said. And he just sat there with a little smile, and he said, 'Ask the question.' Okay, so I said, 'On a scale of one to ten, how much can I trust the guy?' And he brought his thumb and forefinger together and made a big zero.' Goodman imitated the gesture. 'Then he looked at me and said, 'Now I didn't say anything, remember.' Let me tell you something, Rabbi, I don't feel a damn bit guilty about what I've done. And Stark was one hundred percent right, too. Had I acted like a normal guy from the beginning, they would have locked Perl up and thrown away the key. And goddammit, my money was paying for his goddamned analysis. So I had every right to know the guy was backsliding. Right?'

Daniel shook his head dumbly.

Goodman nodded decisively, as if Daniel's astonishment justified his actions. 'Anyway, when that skunk left my office, I felt I should give Stark a ring. Warn him, maybe. Not that I really thought Perl would do anything violent, but just to be on the safe side. So I called up Stark's office and got his answering machine. I started leaving a message when Stark cut in. Apparently, he'd been monitoring the call. And he gave me hell. Said he thought I'd act with a little more subtlety. According to him, Perl had figured it out that Stark had told me. I felt bad, of course, and then I told him about Perl's threat.'

'And what did Noah say?'

'That he was going to watch his step. That Perl was capable of a lot worse than he had realized at first.'

'That was it?'

'That's not enough?'

'What time did you speak to Stark?'

'Right after Perl left my office. One forty-five, two o'clock the latest.'

For a moment all that could be heard was the clatter of Pat's typewriter in the next room. Then, Daniel's voice rang out. "Mr. Goodman, I hope you're planning to go right over to the police department."

"And all that business about informing? My mother used to quote some Jewish saying, 'The only way to handle an informer is to throw him into a sack, weigh it down with heavy stones, and dump him in the river.'"

"All that stuff is irrelevant. One hundred percent irrelevant. The laws against informing made sense—a lot of sense—when Jews didn't have a chance in gentile courts. When the informers were telling the Spanish Inquisition about some poor soul who was secretly keeping the Sabbath, or the Russian police about some Jew who was liable for induction at a time when the Czar's armies were swallowing up Jews for twenty-five years at a stretch. That's the kind of informers your mother was talking about. That has nothing to do with a country like America, where Jews have equal rights. And it certainly has nothing to do with murder. No, Mr. Goodman, we have no tradition of omerta. Not here."

"So, as a rabbi, you're telling me I should go to the cops and tell them about Perl?"

"Exactly. Tell them just what you told me. Remember, if you don't want to press charges on the stealing, don't. And don't exaggerate. You don't have to describe your cousin's facial reactions or other gestures when he yelled his threat. Just tell them what he said and about your call to Noah."

The man stood. Despite the coolness in the air-conditioned room, sweat beaded his forehead.

"This has been a revelation to me, Rabbi. Thank you. You've been a great help."

"Good." For the first time, Daniel smiled, but his eyes remained worried. "Maybe we'll see you here a bit more often. But first,"—he picked up his pen, wrote down Cerezzi's name and number, and pushed the paper forward—"go see this guy."

"Congressman," Joe Cerezzi began, cradling his hands and looking through them at the seated Russell Grant, "this

The Final Analysis of Dr. Stark

morning we're going to start all over. With only one difference. Today, we're going to be telling the truth. Okay?"
Cerezzi had spent a long time deciding what approach
to use with Grant. He started out with only one given.
Politeness and courtesy—his manner the night before—
would only encourage the congressman to bullshit him.
Therefore, no more nice-cop routine, Cerezzi had concluded. From now on, it's hard-ass—calm, but hard-ass—
all the way.

"Don't push me, Cerezzi," the congressman snapped.
"I'm not some two-bit hooker on Sunset." He massaged
weary eyes with the knuckles of his right hand. "I don't
appreciate being roustled out of bed and onto an airplane
in the middle of the night. And when some of my friends
hear about it, they're not going to appreciate it either."

"Is that some sort of a threat, Congressman?"

"The only one who's been making threats around here,
Lieutenant, is you. That was a cheap trick, Cerezzi, threatening me with arrest. You know how vulnerable we public
figures are to adverse publicity. The media tears us to shreds
the second they smell blood. But I'm not the only vulnerable one, big shot. It just so happens Ron Toth is a good
friend of mine. I don't think he's going to be impressed
with what he hears from me about you."

Casually, Cerezzi lifted the black phone off the cradle
on his desk. "You want me to dial Chief Toth for you?"

"Don't tempt me, Cerezzi."

"Oh, I'm perfectly serious, Congressman," Cerezzi went
on, well aware that the calmer he acted, the more upset
Grant became. Which is exactly what he wanted. It requires
a hell of a lot more calm to string a consistent pattern of
lies than to tell the truth. Because it's only when you're
telling lies that you have to remember things. "If you feel
I, or anybody else in this department, has mistreated you,
you should notify the Chief immediately."

Grant said nothing.

"Do I take it then, Congressman, that you do not wish
to speak with Chief Toth at this time?"

"Has anybody ever told you you're a wise-ass, Cerezzi?"

"Yup," he said. "Generally, it was people who were lying to me." Out of habit, Cerezzi reached for a cigarette, swore softly, then took out a few sticks of chewing gum. He worked them into a wad at the side of his mouth, then swiveled back toward Grant.

"I'm going to give you one last chance to tell the truth, Congressman."

"I told you the truth."

"Okay, if that's the way you want to play it. When was the last time you saw Noah Stark?"

"I told you. I left his office Monday just before noon."

"That's what you told me yesterday."

"Well, I haven't seen him at any seances since then."

Cerezzi disregarded the sarcasm. "And you'd be willing to swear under oath that you didn't see him after that?"

Grant nodded.

"What would you say, Congressman, if I told you we have an eyewitness who saw you walking out of Stark's office building at 2:40 P.M. Tuesday afternoon?"

"I'd say you have a witness with a vivid imagination. I'm willing to stand up to him, my word against his."

"Are you also willing to stand up against the photograph he took of you coming out of Stark's office at that time?" He withdrew the picture from a manila envelope and handed it to Grant. The congressman studied it carefully, wincing at the telltale sunglasses and brown mustache, then dropped it back onto the lieutenant's desk.

"I don't see anything in this picture indicating when it was taken."

"So you're willing to swear this picture was not taken on Tuesday?"

"Are you willing to swear it was?"

"Congressman, the person who took this picture has no reason to lie about when he took it. You, on the other hand, do. Who do you think the jury's going to believe?"

Silence.

The Final Analysis of Dr. Stark

"You want to tell me the real story now? What happened when you went to Stark's office Tuesday afternoon? Why you bashed his head in?"

Grant's voice came out as a strangled cry. "That's a lie!"

"Is it, Congressman? Then why did you go to Stark's office on Tuesday? Why did you lie about it?"

Grant ran his palm over his ashen forehead. He kicked at a small paper clip on the battered rug. The eyes that now stared down at the floor were hollow. "I want to speak to my lawyer."

Chapter 11

Thursday Afternoon

Daniel Winter stepped into the guest room at radio station KLAX and gulped. A familiar face, capped by an overflowing head of impossibly yellow curls, stared back at him, smiling at his startled gaze.

"Do you know each other?" "Book News" host Larry Korn jumped to his feet, eager to perform introductions.

"Not exactly," Daniel answered. He turned to the woman. "You're Joan Reider, aren't you?"

"Indeed I am," drawled the lazy voice. She lifted a copy of *Sticks and Stones* from the coffee table. "Considering what you write here, Rabbi, I'm surprised—pleasantly surprised I might add—that you watch my show."

"Well, I've seen you on TV. I wouldn't exactly call myself a loyal fan."

"Listen, you two," Korn broke in nervously, gesturing to the overhead clock. "The debate starts in six minutes. On the air, not here."

"Oh, don't you worry, Larry," Joan Reider murmured, flashing the host a look at a full set of gleaming white teeth between crimson lips. "I know the rabbi doesn't approve of me. I hear he even wants to stop me from speaking at his synagogue." She pouted mockingly. "That's why I accepted the challenge to debate him today. You see, Rabbi, unlike you, I'm a believer in free speech."

"So am I, thank you."

The Final Analysis of Dr. Stark

"Really? I'm impressed. Then why are you trying so hard to get your sisterhood to disinvite me?"

"Because I don't think your message is appropriate for a synagogue."

Joan Reider shrugged expressively. "Because *you* don't think something is appropriate, you try to get it canceled. Precisely what I'm saying; you don't believe in free speech."

"Ms. Reider, the reason I don't want you speaking at B'nai Zion is because of your values. Of course I believe in free speech. In a similar vein, I also believe Christian missionaries have a right to proselytize. In their churches or, if they want, on street corners. But I don't intend to invite them into my synagogue to make their case."

"That's a cheap debater's trick, Rabbi. Nobody in your congregation is inviting any missionaries. But they do want to hear me. And you're trying to prevent them from doing so."

"From hearing you?" Daniel asked, his voice affecting a slightly startled quality.

"Yes," she answered. A bright red spot appeared on each cheek. "From hearing me."

"Really? To tell you the truth, Ms. Reider, I think everyone in my congregation has more opportunity to hear you than to hear me. I'm in the pulpit once a week; you're on television every night. I just don't want them to hear you in my synagogue."

"Even though they want me?"

Daniel struggled to remain patient. "Listen, my obligation as a rabbi isn't to win popularity contests. It's to try and enforce Judaism's values—one of which is its laws against *lashon hara*, gossip. Your problems are with Judaism, not me. You're a gossip columnist, Ms. Reider. You spend your life prying into the intimate details of people's lives and broadcasting the most embarrassing morsels you pick up to millions of people."

"And every word I broadcast is true." Reider's voice had lost its drawl and was becoming slightly shrill. She nibbled her lip, then resumed in a lower tone. "I've never had to retract a single item."

"Congratulations. All that means is that you can't be sued for libel. It still doesn't make what you broadcast anybody else's business. According to Jewish law, the only time a person's allowed to transmit negative information about other people is when the person they're speaking to *needs* the information. And I truly wonder, Ms. Reider, the last time anybody needed to know anything about the scandals you broadcast."

"You are impossible. You are the most self-righteous—"

"Hold it, Joan," Korn cut in, his voice exuberant. "This is great stuff, you and the rabbi both." The host kissed the tips of his fingers, then blew the kiss at them. "You're both fantastic. I can feel the electricity. It's incredible. I just know it, I can feel it, this is going to be the best show we've ever done!"

Brenda's Volvo turned onto the 9800 block on Whitworth, just north of Pico.

"That's it, across the street." Maria Pelayo pointed to a pink stucco apartment building.

Brenda glided easily into an open space and parked.

"How we going to handle it?" Pelayo asked as they stepped out onto the sidewalk. Brenda's hair flew back in the warm breeze.

"You're the cop. That's what's going to get us inside. I'll just follow you in. Then we'll play it by ear."

As they crossed the street, a man on a bicycle stopped suddenly and followed the two women admiringly with his eyes as they strode toward the building. Oblivious to his approval, they stepped inside and checked the register. Apt. 214. A. Stark. Pelayo buzzed.

A throaty female voice quickly came on the intercom. "Who is it?"

"It's Officer Pelayo of the twenty-ninth precinct, Mrs. Stark. We'd like to ask you some questions."

"Oh . . . Very well," Arlette Stark responded with cold formality. "I do hope it will be brief."

It was a two-bedroom West LA apartment, thickly

The Final Analysis of Dr. Stark

carpeted and nicely furnished. Twelve, thirteen hundred dollars a month, Brenda figured.

Noah's ex-wife escorted them into a living room tastefully decorated in shades of pale blue. "Can I offer you something—Perrier, orange juice?"

"No, thank you," Pelayo answered. "We're fine."

Arlette Stark turned to Brenda. "You sat near me at the funeral, didn't you?"

"Yes. My name is Brenda Goldstein."

"Didn't I realize you were a cop."

"I'm not, actually. To be precise, Mrs. Stark, I'm working with the homicide division as a psychologist."

The woman gave a sour laugh. "So much for my feminine intuition. I figured you for one of Noah's old girl-friends. He had a thing for redheads."

"We have a few questions," Pelayo, scenting dangerous territory, broke in.

Arlette glanced pointedly at her watch. "I do hope the emphasis is on *jeu*, officer."

"You came to Dr. Stark's funeral in a *Van Gogh's* van, correct?"

"Very observant. And you, Officer Pelayo, came to my apartment in a police car, correct?"

"As a matter of fact, no," Brenda answered. "We came in my Volvo."

"Touché," Arlette said with a thin smile. "In that case, forgive my sarcasm. Yes, I've been working with *Van Gogh's* for several years."

"And they provide you with a company vehicle?" Pelayo asked.

"No. But my car's in for repairs right now. Vanessa Caron—she's the owner of *Van Gogh's*—lent me the van for a few days. Till I get my car back."

"So we can assume, then, that you knew your husband had just bought a replica from *Van Gogh's*."

" *La Joie de Vivre.* Of course. Noah was not the world's greatest art aficionado. Who do you think sold it to him?"

"And when was that?"

"Three months ago, maybe even a little less. During one of our truces."

"But it was only delivered Tuesday?"

"There were only a few replicas of the work available. Unfortunately, the first one was chipped in shipment. And it took a while till this one was ready."

"Mrs. Stark," Brenda asked, "how would you characterize your relations with your ex-husband?"

"It depended."

Brenda waited for her to go on, but she didn't. "On what?" she prodded.

Arlette leaned back in her chair, withdrew a long, brown cigarette, and lit it. She took one long draw, then exhaled smoke out slowly. "About three times a year," she began dispassionately, "Noah would start raving to me about some extraordinarily warm woman he had met. That was always the way he put it. *Warm*, passionate, giving. His own charming little dig. My maiden name was Goldberg. When we'd fight, he'd tell me it should have been Iceberg."

"So it would be fair to say that your relations with your ex-husband were generally tense?"

"Wait. I was telling you about the three times a year he was in love. Most of the time he wasn't. Then he'd start remembering how he had once loved me. Start wondering aloud, sometimes, whether we could ever get back together."

"And these last weeks, how were you getting along?"

"He'd met someone *warm*." Her voice dripped acid.

"More than met," Brenda said, knowing how cruel her words would be if Arlette had not been informed of Noah's plans. "Dr. Stark was engaged to Jennifer Steen."

"So I heard at the funeral."

"Had he told you he was getting married?"

"No."

"But you knew he was involved with someone?"

"Yes."

"So was this a tense period?"

With deliberate motions the woman crushed out her half-smoked cigarette. "You don't have to play games with me, Ms. Goldstein. We're both well aware of the message I left on Noah's answering machine Tuesday morning. I assume that's what all your oh-so polite questions have been getting at."

Brenda glanced down at her notes. "You threatened to come over to his office, and make a scandal. . . . Did you?"

"Make a scandal?"

"Come over to his office, Mrs. Stark."

"No."

"Why not, after saying you would?"

"I thought the threat would be sufficient."

"For what?"

"To stimulate some renewed interest in Adam. Our son. Noah could be a great father when it mattered to him. But it sometimes seemed like he could only love one person at a time. Whenever he was hot and bothered about a woman, Adam was the one who paid."

"Did Noah phone you back?"

"I have no idea."

"What do you mean?"

"I waited at home for awhile after I made the call, but then I was out the rest of the day—and I have no answering machine. I hate coming home and having to return fifteen calls."

"Where were you?"

"Venice."

"The Boardwalk?"

"Uh-huh."

"What about your job at *Van Gogh's*—do you go in only when you want?"

"I'd made a number of very substantial sales this last month. Vanessa was pleased. She told me to take a couple of days off. You can check with her if you wish."

"Anyone with you in Venice?"

"I met a friend there."

"When?"

"For lunch. From about twelve to one-thirty."

"And then?"

"I wandered around. Even played some Skeet-Ball at

the Santa Monica Pier. I needed some time alone. It can be hard finding that spare time when you're a single mother."

"And you returned home when?"

"About four. Adam was going to a friend's after school, so I was in no rush."

"Where is Adam now, by the way?"

"With my parents, in Riverside. They came and picked him up Tuesday night. I didn't want him around for all this."

"So, between one-thirty and four, did you see anybody who could identify you?"

"Unless the boy at that Skeet-Ball dive is a lot brighter than he struck me as being, probably not."

"Do you know Tom Kahn, Mrs. Stark?"

"That son-of-a-bitch."

"Why do you say that?"

"You mean Noah's lawyer, right?"

Brenda nodded.

"Kahn represented Noah in our divorce. Let me give you a good general axiom about life, Ms. Goldstein. Every divorce lawyer in the United States is a son-of-a-bitch. Except maybe for the one who's representing you."

"Kahn represented Noah on other matters as well."

"And what does that have to do with me?"

"Are you familiar with the provisions of your late husband's will?"

"I know there was money in there for Adam."

"Do you know how much?"

"No idea. I never figured it was terribly relevant. Noah was only thirty-seven and healthy as a horse." She shrugged.

"Your ex-husband, Mrs. Stark, had recently made a few very successful real estate investments. Kahn estimates that, when probated, his estate is going to come to something over three-quarters of a million dollars. Most of it in a trust for Adam. Which you manage. And another hundred thousand dollars for you."

Arlette whistled. "My God. I had no idea."

"Were you nervous, Mrs. Stark, about Noah's relationship with Jennifer Steen?"

The Final Analysis of Dr. Stark

"Nervous? Why?"

"That he was going to marry her?"

"I think she was about the fifteenth candidate since we got divorced."

"That's what you've been telling us. But apparently she was the first to whom he publicly announced an engagement?"

"So? I wasn't exactly counting on our getting back together."

"But surely it entered your mind that if a marriage occurred there might be some changes in Noah's will?"

Arlette Stark met Brenda's even gaze calmly. She checked her watch again, then stood. "I have no intention of continuing this discussion without an attorney present. I do thank you, though, for the news about the $750,000."

She headed for the front door and pulled it open. "It's certainly been a pleasure. Let's not do it again."

"Rabbi," Larry Korn said, opening *Sticks and Stones* to a page marked with a paper clip, "you say here on page seventy-four that Judaism compares gossip to murder. With all due respect, that's going a little overboard, isn't it?"

Daniel cleared his throat. "First of all, Larry, the rabbis of the Talmud weren't planning to execute anyone for gossip."

"Thank God for little things," Joan Reider called out.

"It's more like the expression we use in English," Daniel continued steadily, "character assassination. It—"

"Precisely," Reider broke in. "That's an expression. Like a proverb. And like most proverbs, its opposite is just as true. Because what you choose to call character assassination, Rabbi," she said, her face creasing into what an unknowing spectator might have mistaken for a congenial smile, "I call character analysis."

"Well, Ms. Reider," Daniel said smoothly, "there we disagree. I think assassination comes closer to the truth. There's a Jewish folktale about a man in a small town who went around slandering the rabbi. One day he realized what a terrible thing he had done. So he went to the rabbi and begged for forgiveness. The rabbi told him to go home, cut open a feather pillow, scatter the feathers to the winds, and then return. He went home, ecstatic that he had been let off so easily, took a feather pillow, cut it open, and scattered the feathers. Then he came back to the rabbi. 'Am I forgiven now?' he asked. 'One last thing,' the rabbi said. 'Go and gather all the feathers.' 'But that's impossible, the wind has scattered them,' the man exclaimed. 'Exactly,' the rabbi answered. 'And though you really want to correct the evil you've done, it is as impossible to repair the damage done by your words as it is to recover the feathers.' "

"That's beautiful, Rabbi, just beautiful," Larry Korn enthused. He turned to the show-biz columnist. "Care to comment, Joan?"

"It's a wonderful story, and I agree with it one hundred percent."

"You do?" Korn asked, cocking an eyebrow.

"Of course. What the man in the story did—spreading slanderous, *untrue* stories—was disgusting. That's why any news I air has to be verified by at least two sources."

"It's still not right," Daniel insisted.

"Why is that, Rabbi?" Korn asked.

"Because not all truths ought to be revealed either."

"It's a good thing for America you're not on the Supreme Court, Rabbi," Joan Reider mocked with a light laugh.

"Look, according to Jewish law, people should not spread nasty gossip, *even if it's true*, about other people, unless the person they're speaking to needs the information. I'm not saying that should be government policy. I'm not naive. I know a president could use that standard to censor any newspaper article he didn't like. . . . Of course the public had the right to know about Watergate. When a public official acts illegally, that's exactly the sort of information people need. But does everybody have to know that, during the crisis, President Nixon got down on his hands and knees and asked Henry Kissinger to pray with him, or that an aide to President Johnson was once arrested in some Washington bar for an act of homosexual solicitation? Besides,

The Final Analysis of Dr. Stark

this law isn't directed at the government. It's directed at individuals. To you, Larry, to me, and to you, too, Ms. Reider. Just because something's true doesn't mean a million other people have the *right* to know about it. Haven't you ever done anything in your life, Ms. Reider, that you'd prefer would remain unknown?"

The woman shook her thick mass of curls. "My life, Rabbi, is an open book."

"Sounds to me, Joan," Larry Korn said, a faint smile softening his words, "like either you've got a poor memory or you've led a very boring existence."

"Not at all, Larry. Sounds to me like the rabbi's the one with the secrets to hide."

"And even if I was, Ms. Reider, what gives you the right to publicize them?"

"Look. I don't invade private people's lives. I report news—*news*, Rabbi, not gossip—about actors, actresses, politicians, people in the public eye. *What gives me the right to publicize it?* The public's right, the public's desire to know, that's what gives me the right."

"I'm not talking about legal rights—I'm talking about moral rights. Human beings, even if they're famous, have the moral right to observe their griefs privately—without you or one of your colleagues sticking a microphone in front of their face and asking how they felt when their child died of an overdose. They have the right to love in private, and to divorce in private. And the fact that plenty of people desire to hear all the intimate details doesn't mean a thing. It's still wrong."

"But isn't it just human nature, Rabbi, to be curious about other people?" Korn asked.

"If the only reason people gossiped was curiosity, then they would be as curious about their maid's private life as about their next-door neighbor's. But they're not. They only gossip about their social equals or superiors. That's the way they elevate themselves. By lowering others."

"You're a very cynical man," Reider said. "Everybody has disgusting motives—except for you, I suppose?"

"Oh, I'm as curious about people as anyone. I just try

and curb my inclination to snoop into other people's secrets, just as I hope they'll try and curb their inclination to snoop into mine."

"I wonder what you're hiding, Rabbi," Reider said sweetly.

"If there really is something, Ms. Reider, I suspect you'll be the last person I'll tell."

"You amaze me." Her manicured fingers tightened around the microphone. "I can't get over it. You really believe I'm doing something evil, don't you?"

"There's a statement in the Talmud that gossip ends up killing three: the gossiper, the one who listens to the gossip, and the victim."

"Did you say *kills*, Rabbi?"

"Yes. The Talmud means destroys. The victim—"

"Kills! Destroys!" Reider broke in shrilly. "Are you some sort of a nut? You know, this is appalling, Larry. If this man wasn't a rabbi, I'd say he was threatening me!"

There was an awkward pause. Korn looked desperately at Daniel for a response, but Daniel said nothing.

"Rabbi," Korn prompted.

Silence. Suddenly Joan Reider, Larry Korn, the whole program, seemed very remote to Daniel. It was Noah he was thinking of now. *Gossip kills three: the gossiper. . . .* He thought back to what John Goodman had told him that morning about Noah. Snatches of conversations he'd had with Noah over the years came back. Noah's comment about Cheryl Bornstein on Monday night. His comments about Bornstein's threat to Daniel.

"Rabbi," Korn prompted again, gesturing frantically for a response.

Daniel looked around blankly, then coughed to gain a few seconds. "There are different kinds of destruction, Ms. Reider," he began slowly. "In regard to the victim, the rabbis meant it quite literally. Having your name destroyed can be a little bit like being murdered. They're both irrevocable. Regarding the gossiper, I suppose they meant it damages his,"—and he met Joan Reider's icy gray eyes unflinchingly—"or *her* soul."

The Final Analysis of Dr. Stark

"My soul, Rabbi, is *my* business."

"Just as other people's private lives are *theirs*."

Larry Korn's gaze shifted quickly between Joan Reider's furious face and Daniel's set expression. Korn beamed. No doubt about it. Best show they'd ever done.

Chapter 12

Attorney Leonard Korman, his bright red bow tie contrasting sharply with the grave expression in his eyes, led an even grimmer-faced Russell Grant into Cerezzi's office at three o'clock that afternoon. Only an hour earlier, Korman had negotiated with Cerezzi—after a short, sometimes loud, series of phone conversations—that the lieutenant would be the only police official present at this round of questioning.

"If you're planning to arrest my client, Lieutenant," Korman—the man the LA press loved to label a real-life Perry Mason—had said, "you'll have plenty of time to show everybody how brilliant you were. But, on the other hand, when my client turns out to be innocent, *you*, Lieutenant Cerezzi, are going to thank me for saving you from the embarrassment of charging an innocent congressman—*congressman*, Lieutenant—with murder."

"Thanks for your concern," Cerezzi had snapped, but he finally acceded to Korman's demand, making it clear, however, that the whole proceeding would be taped. He had tangled with the high-priced lawyer before, at two murder trials, and the experience had convinced him that it was always worth giving in to Korman on nonessential issues—before the lawyer had the chance to blow them up in the media. Courthouse scuttlebutt had it that Korman had a large P.R. firm on permanent retainer to ensure that

134

The Final Analysis of Dr. Stark

his clients got the right headlines. Like "Police Lieutenant Harasses Congressman." One thing Cerezzi was sure of: whatever publicity the lawyer or his publicists might generate would not hasten his own advancement in the department.

Now the short, bald Korman guided his silent client to a seat and, still standing, turned to Cerezzi.

"Congressman Grant has a statement to read you, Lieutenant."

Nodding, Cerezzi kept his eyes fixed on Grant. He saw no reason to challenge Korman just yet.

Grant cleared his throat and shifted in the armchair. A muscle on the side of his cheek twitched spasmodically.

"I would like to clarify some of my earlier statements to you," he began. "I might have inadvertently given the impression that the last time I had seen Dr. Stark was Monday morning." A slight smile of triumph twisted the corners of Cerezzi's mouth. *Given the impression, my ass.*

"In actuality, Dr. Stark and I had one subsequent meeting. On Tuesday afternoon, I went to the doctor's office. I told Dr. Stark that I felt his consultations with me over the past several months had been helpful, but that the arduous responsibilities I was now assuming made it necessary that we temporarily terminate our professional relationship. We then shook hands, wished each other well, and I left at about 2:40 P.M. At that time, Dr. Stark was sitting at his desk, in—as far as I could tell—perfect health."

"As you can see, Lieutenant," Korman began, his voice so smooth that for a brief moment it sounded as if he was continuing the reading of the statement, "I have advised my client to be totally forthright with you in your investigation."

Cerezzi nodded curtly, his eyes on Grant. "Are you assuring me then, Congressman, that from now on all answers you give me will be true?"

"Yes."

"Good. I'm delighted at your change in attitude." Cerezzi pinched his pen between thumb and forefinger and jabbed it downward. He stared at Grant. "There are a few things that are still puzzling me. To begin with, what happened between Monday morning and Tuesday at 2:30 P.M. that caused you to suddenly terminate your relationship with Stark?"

Grant's response was colorless. "It was not sudden at all, Lieutenant. Following the announcement of my candidacy for the senate, I realized that my life would become too hectic to enable me to profit from my conversations with the doctor."

"But you knew that on Monday?"

"Of course. But, like all serious decisions, I didn't want to act hastily. When I discussed this matter with Dr. Stark on Monday morning, he told me to go home and think about it. And I did. Which is why I returned Tuesday, to tell him of my decision."

"During the course of your therapy, did you confide things to Stark that would have damaged you if they had become widely known?"

"Lieutenant," Korman interjected, "the conversations between a patient and a psychiatrist constitute privileged communication. I'm advising my client not to answer."

"Mr. Korman, all I want is an answer to a very broad question. Were there things he confided to Stark that would have damaged him if they had become widely known?"

"You want to explain the reason for your question?"

"It's all right, Lenny," Grant broke in. He turned to Cerezzi with an ingratiating smile that did not reach his eyes. "Lieutenant, I realize that the only way I'm going to allay your suspicions is if I am fully forthcoming. So, despite the advice of counsel," he patted Korman's arm, "I'm going to answer your question. Yes, like anybody who's been in therapy, I told my doctor secrets. And yes, some of those secrets would be embarrassing to me if they became known to others."

"Thank you. Now, how many people knew you were Stark's patient?"

Grant glanced uncertainly at his attorney, who gave a small nod. "I did not tell anyone about it."

"No one at all?"

"No one."

"Were you afraid that Dr. Stark might talk to others about what you told him?"

"Oh, for heaven's sake, Lieutenant," Korman interrupted, "this is unbelievable. Is this the ace up your sleeve—that Congressman Grant murdered Stark because he was afraid the doctor might gossip about him? What are you doing here—playing games or trying to solve a murder?"

"Thank you, counselor, for your assessment. Now, Congressman," Cerezzi went on, unperturbed. "So far, we've established two things: you told no one you were in therapy, and you told Stark things you wanted kept secret."

"So what else is new?" Korman snapped. "That's true of every person who sets foot inside a pyschiatrist's office."

"Perhaps. But there are other things true only of your client."

"Such as?"

"Such as the fact that Congressman Grant's file was missing from Stark's office after the murder. And—"

"Oh, come on," the attorney sneered.

"—and that in this picture," Cerezzi continued evenly, extending the photograph of Grant to Korman, "which I suspect you've heard about, your client is coming out of Stark's office building at about the time the coroner says he was murdered. Now, a couple of hours ago, I held this photo under a magnifier, and picked up something very interesting." Cerezzi's broad finger ran down the photograph, stopping at Grant's right arm. "That, counselor, looks very much like a folder in your client's hand." The lieutenant's eyes panned from Korman's puzzled expression to Grant. The congressman sat motionless. "All this might not seem very relevant to you, counselor, but if you look at your client, I think you'll see it's not so irrelevant after all. We're going to enlarge this picture, and when we do"—the lieutenant returned to his desk and extracted a manila folder from the top drawer—"I suspect the folder in Congressman Grant's hand will look remarkably similar to these others we picked up at Dr. Stark's office. That's exactly what we're going to find out, Congressman, isn't it?"

Grant's nervous twitch was now painfully conspicuous. His eyes sought Korman's, and the lawyer shook his head vigorously.

"Then let me tell you, Congressman," Cerezzi resumed, "what I think happened. For some reason, you became terrified that Stark would betray you. And you panicked. After all, you're a prominent man. Any embarrassing revelations about you at this time would receive the widest publicity. And that was always your fear. Isn't that why you took such extreme precautions to make certain no one ever knew you were in therapy—to the point where you even assumed a disguise? No, Mr. Grant, despite what your lawyer says, your desperate need for secrecy, particularly now that you were running for office, was greater than the average person's. That's why on Tuesday afternoon you decided to guarantee that no one would ever know what Stark knew." Grant's face was ashen. "So you killed him, Mr. Grant, and stole your file out of his office, figuring no one could ever prove he was your doctor." Cerezzi bent over the visibly shaken congressman. "Isn't that what happened?"

A muffled sound emerged from the shaken Grant.

"For God's sake, man, keep quiet!" Korman rasped.

But the demoralized congressman ignored him. "I . . . I . . . I swear to you, it's not true. I never touched him. . . ."

Cerezzi raised the photograph. "Is that your file?"

Grant nodded dumbly.

"Lieutenant," Korman protested. "I want to confer with my client. Now."

"No, Lenny," Grant said. "I have something to say."

"Stop letting him intimidate you, Russell. All he's got is speculation—"

"I've got to tell him what really happened."

"As your attorney," Korman raged, "I am telling you to keep quiet."

Grant jerked to his feet and looked down at his lawyer.

"The only reason you want me to keep quiet, Lenny, is because you think I'm guilty. But I'm not!" He turned to the lieutenant. "Yes, I went back to Stark's office Tuesday. To get the file. That part you had right. But you know *why* I did it? Because some blabbermouth reporter named Levin was planning to interview Stark about me. I was at Stark's office Monday. I heard a message on his answering machine from Levin. And all Monday night, I was sweating, worrying about what Stark was going to tell that bast . . . guy. So Tuesday, I decided. Enough. I went to Stark's office and told him flat out that if he so much as breathed a word to Levin, I'd sue him for every penny he was worth. I'd ruin him. He'd never practice again. If he let Levin take me down, I'd take Stark down with me. Stark acted very conciliatory. Mr. Nice Guy. Tried to convince me it must have been somebody in my office who squealed to Levin about me. But I wasn't buying. We were through. I told him. I didn't trust him anymore. And he agreed and—"

"He agreed?"

"I mean, he said if there's no trust, there can't be a therapeutic relationship. He said he hoped I would recon-sider . . . you know, that sort of stuff. And then I told him I wanted any files he had about me. You see, he often took notes during the sessions. And I wanted them. I didn't really know what the story was with him. But I couldn't have those notes falling into Levin's hands. Stark refused. So I told him I'd haul him before the Ethics Committee, or whatever those godda . . . shrinks have. And tell them about Levin. Well, he denied telling Levin again, but I guess lie didn't like the threat I'd made, because he opened up a file cabinet and took out a folder with my name on it. 'That's it. I swear. That's all that happened. I never touched a hair of Stark.' "

A police siren sounded from the street. Grant shivered.

"I don't believe you, Congressman."

"Why not?" Korman thundered. "The man's pouring out—"

Cerezzi ignored Korman. "I don't believe you. Just getting the file back wouldn't make you feel safe. At all.

Stark still carried the contents of that file in his head. And you yourself admit that you were afraid of what he might say to Levin. No, Congressman. You needed two things to feel secure: Stark dead, and the file in your hands."

"That's absurd. . . ."

The jangle of the phone silenced Grant's protest. The last light started pulsating on Cerezzi's desk phone—the emergency line, the only line Desk Sergeant Hall had been instructed to let through. The lieutenant scooped up the receiver. "Cerezzi here."

"Rick Adams, Lieutenant. I've got two of your people, Willie King and something Pelayo, down here in my lab. They just brought in some damn statue, and they're going on about how this must be the weapon in that loonytune's murder. They're telling me to drop everything and get to work on it. Lieutenant, why don't you tell this pair they don't carry enough weight to go around giving me orders? You want it done right now, fine. But I need the request direct from you."

"Well, you've got it," Cerezzi said brusquely. "That stat . . ." He halted, his eyes on Grant. "I want everything they brought you analyzed, pronto. In every which way. I'll be right down."

He slammed down the receiver and pressed a button. Seconds later, a dusty blonde with large, unfeminine muscles stepped in.

"I want you to show these gentlemen to the conference room."

"Just a minute, Lieutenant," Korman blustered. "Are you placing my client under arrest?"

"Not at this moment."

"Then I gather we are free to leave."

"Technically, you are. But if you ask me, counselor, I'd strongly advise you not to set foot out of this building until I get back."

"But we're not asking you, are we?" Korman lifted his snakeskin attaché case and motioned to Grant. "Come on, Congressman."

"Just a minute, fella." Cerezzi turned to Grant. "You

make your own mind up, Congressman, about whose advice you want to take. But if you are not here when I get back, I am going to personally give every reporter in LA the most interesting backgrounder they've ever gotten from a police official. And it's gonna be one hundred percent about you." He snatched up the pack of cigarettes and tucked it in his pocket. "Now you just brood about that." The door slammed behind him.

Chapter 13

Thursday Late Afternoon

"You didn't want to say Kaddish when we buried your brother."

Daniel paused, hoping the bluntness of his statement would prompt a response. Stroking his dark mustache, Jonah Stark regarded him levelly. He was silent.

"Why?" Daniel pressed.

The deep creases around his forehead made him look prematurely aged. "Maybe I don't believe in God, Rabbi."

"Maybe," Daniel conceded. "But somehow I suspect God had nothing to do with it."

Stark took a long puff on a briar pipe and slowly blew the smoke out. Then, still looking at Daniel, he rested the still-smoldering pipe in an ashtray.

"My brother was a piece of *shit*, Rabbi," he said evenly. "Does Judaism ordain prayers to God over pieces of shit?"

"Are you crazy? Your brother was an extraordinary human being. Everybody who knew him thought that." Daniel's mind drifted to his conversation Monday night with Sam Bornstein, but he suppressed the memory. "I loved him."

"I know you loved him, Rabbi. Everybody loved Noah Stark. He had the greatest Act 1 of anyone I've ever met. It was his Act 2 that stank. Till the day they died, my parents thought Noah was the cat's meow. He was their hero, *herr doctor*, an enlightened man. Me? I was a nice boy. Not that much up here, maybe"—Stark tapped his forehead—"but a good boy. Only you should know this, Rabbi. Five years before he died, my father went broke. And who do you think supported him and my mom? *This* nice boy." He thumped his chest. "Leslie was too young, and wonderful Noah didn't give a red cent."

"Maybe he was short of money?"

"Who are you, my mother? Mom had a million excuses why good ol' Noah never chipped in. Short of money?" Stark snorted contemptuously. "A hundred and something dollars an hour, six, eight patients a day—what are you talking about? If Noah Stark was ever short of money, it was only because he was shelling out four thousand a month on his mortgage in Bel Air, and God knows what on that place in Mammoth. Short of money? You knew my brother, what car did he drive?"

"A Jaguar," Daniel said softly. A dull flush spread over his neck.

"I went to Noah," the embittered Stark said. "'Help me,' I said to him. 'I got a wife, three kids—bills up to here. I can't take care of Mom and Dad alone. For God's sake, help me, help them.' He took my hand in his and patted it, you know, the way he would always do.' 'I know what you're going through, Jonah, and you're just great. And I'm gonna help out. Soon. I'm involved in something very big now, and when it comes through, you can bet I'm gonna take care of Mom and Dad. And you, too. For four years—until Mom died last spring—he handed me that crap." Stark leaned back and stared moodily around his office. "But that wasn't the end of my big-hearted brother's generosity. I'm in a bit of a spot now with my business. About twenty thousand dollars short, and I've worn out my welcome at the bank. So I went to Noah with the figures, what I'd given Mom and Dad those last years. If he'd just cover his share, I told him, I'd be all right. And you know what he kicked in?" Stark held up his hand and formed a zero, his dark eyes glittering. "My wonderful brother's always been like that. All talk, no action. Then, on Passover, he'd come over for the seder. Bring a necklace for my mother, a beautiful sweater for Dad. Oh, yes, his gifts were always perfect. My mother would just glow for days when she got them."

Daniel shifted uncomfortably in his chair. He knew he should stop this fierce flow of words, that he should just get up and walk out. This bile pouring out, he didn't need to—didn't want to know about it. The jealousy of an older brother toward his more brilliant, more successful younger sibling. It was common, Daniel knew. People would be shocked at the bitter rantings against the dead he had often heard in houses of mourning. Daniel thought of the cliché, "They loved each other like brothers." Which brothers, he thought? Aaron and Moses? Or maybe Cain and Abel? He examined Stark's twisted face. Was there any truth in what the man was saying? How could he ever know? Noah was dead, and the parents were too. Only Jonah remained, a seeming testament to the staying power of hatred.

"Did my brother ever tell you about the first time he almost got married?"

"Is it relevant, Mr. Stark?"

If Stark picked up on Daniel's reproof, he gave no indication. "Nancy Wilcox. Nice girl—a nurse over at University Hospital, where Noah was interning. They were going out almost a year. Then Nancy got pregnant, and she didn't want an abortion. Said she became a nurse because she wanted to prolong life, not end it. Besides, Noah had told her he wanted to marry her. . . . Only it seems my brother didn't see things that way. Said he couldn't marry her. . . . You know why? Because Nancy wasn't a Jew. . . . That goddamn hypocrite. Judaism meant nothing to him. It was a sham, Rabbi. A month later, Nancy had a miscarriage, then a breakdown. Last I heard, she was still in Camarillo."

"I don't know that that's Noah's fault, Mr. Stark."

"You know what, Rabbi? Nancy had even offered to convert, but Noah told her he'd never allow her to do that just for marriage. He was a good Jew, my brother, wasn't he?"

"Better than you think. In the last two years he had

become one of the most active members of the congregation. In fact—"

"You sap." Stark's voice was soft with malice. "Tell me
something, Rabbi. Your congregation, is it wealthy?"

Daniel cleared his throat. "There are some people who
are—"

"Your Board . . . how many people are on it?"

"Thirty-five."

"Are they rich?"

"They're comfortable."

The brittle voice was relentless. "How comfortable?
Of those thirty-five, how many have a net worth of under
a million dollars?"

Daniel was silent.

"How many, Rabbi?"

"Very few."

"You know why Noah got so active in your congregation? Because he saw dollar signs there. He used to brag
to me about who he was rubbing shoulders with at B'nai
Zion. And referrals? I'm sure he got them by the bucket.
Rich people are a blessing to psychiatrists. When rich people get problems, they think nothing of pissing away a
hundred, who knows, a hundred twenty-five bucks an hour
to talk about it. Your congregation was a gold mine to my
brother." Stark gleefully watched the discomfited look on
the rabbi's face. "You probably gave him referrals, too,
didn't you?"

"You're a very cynical man, Mr. Stark," Daniel said,
reluctantly meeting his eyes. "But before I leave, there's
only one other thing I want to know—"

Stark held up a palm, and a sly smile crept over his
gaunt face. "Where I was when Noah was killed, right? I've
got nothing to hide. I'll tell you exactly what I told that
Italian cop. Between three and five P.M. Tuesday I was in
my car, driving back from a business meeting in San Diego."

"What time did you leave San Diego?"

"Noon."

"Then you should have been back in L.A. by three?"

"I took a long lunch en route."

"Where?"

The smile returned. "Well, I'm sort of ashamed to tell you, Rabbi; the restaurant wasn't kosher."

"Where?" Daniel persisted, ignoring the jibe.

"You know what, Rabbi? Suddenly I'm not in the mood to answer any more questions from you."

"Were there any witnesses?"

"As a matter of fact, none that I can think of. So what do you think, Rabbi—did I do it? Did I bump off my beloved brother?"

Daniel stood. "One thing makes me think you didn't."

"What's that?" Stark spoke with exaggerated casualness.

"If you had, I don't think you would be foolish enough to go around declaring your hatred so openly. Tell me, Mr. Stark, why do you want me to believe you murdered your brother?"

Stark's reply came with savage promptness. "Because I'm ashamed of myself, Rabbi."

"Ashamed of what?"

"That I never had the guts to kill him."

Chapter 14

Thursday Evening

With three easy strides Leonard Korman crossed to Cerezzi's desk. He eyed the bronze statue on the top of it. Then he gave Cerezzi a look of infinite compassion.

"And this, I suppose, is the damning evidence you've been detaining us here for?"

Cerezzi leaned back in his chair and made a mental note to have it oiled one of these days. "Does your client have a statement to make?"

"My client already made his statement, Lieutenant."

"I mean a truthful statement."

"You never cease to amaze me, Cerezzi. You still think the congressman is guilty?"

"Look, counselor. We've established motive. We've established opportunity." Cerezzi's blunt finger poked the statue. "Now we have the weapon."

Korman was unruffled. "And what's that going to prove?"

"For starters, we have prints on it; we'll check them against the congressman's. But forget prints. I suspect just looking at this little beauty might have a sobering effect on your client."

In the corner, Grant made a choked sound.

Korman pivoted. "Keep your mouth shut," he roared.

"I—"

"No! N-O. With all due respect, Russell, every time you open your mouth, you just get yourself in deeper."

You're paying me good money. So why don't you just let me earn it, okay?" Without waiting for an acknowledgment from Grant, Korman turned back to Cerezzi. "Mind if I lift this thing up?"

"Suit yourself. The lab boys are through with it."

Grimacing, Korman heaved up the statue, then made an awkward downward motion. "Can't see killing someone like this, Lieutenant."

"Obviously not, counsellor. You're holding it with only one hand. You have to use both hands."

"You really think so, Lieutenant?"

"I do," Cerezzi said, clearly bored with Korman's theatrics. "Now, Mr. Korman—"

"And you still believe my client murdered Stark?"

Cerezzi blew out wearily, and said nothing.

"Congressman." Korman's deep bass voice filled the small room theatrically. "Could you please stand up and come forward?" He kept his piercing glance on Cerezzi as the silent Grant obeyed. "So you still think my client murdered Stark, Cerezzi?"

"Yes."

Korman waited till Grant reached the desk. Then, dramatically, he eased off the congressman's tan sport jacket. Underneath, Grant wore a short-sleeved white shirt, the collar an incongruous dark blue. Only that wasn't what caught Cerezzi's eye. It was the left arm hanging useless at Grant's side that attracted all his attention.

Using *both* hands now, Korman lifted the statue from Cerezzi's desk.

"Now, Lieutenant, you want to tell me *how* my client murdered that shrink?"

Aaron Baum, the Jerusalem Talmud scholar and philosopher, had been flown in as the guest speaker for The Remnant Holocaust Survivor's dinner.

"Ten grand we're paying him, Rabbi, plus expenses," Sam Bornstein had bragged to Daniel. "Every cent out of my own pocket. And it's worth every penny. We're going to have five hundred people there, two hundred of them survivors. I bought five tables myself. Anybody from the synagogue wants to come, it's on me. Nobody goes second class when they honor Sam Bornstein."

The truth was, Baum's presentation, "Rabbi Akiva: What a Second Century Martyr Can Teach to Twentieth Century Martyrs," was the one thing about the evening Daniel was anticipating. Just a few days earlier, Pat Hastings had computed that in the past year he had gone to precisely sixty-three luncheons, dinners and banquets. And somehow it seemed that every affair had identical food, and identical guests on the dais. He thought of something Bernie Rabin, the Los Angeles Jewish Federation President, had said to him when they found themselves next to each other on a banquet dais for the third time in as many weeks. "Jewish communal life in Los Angeles is composed of 150 people, Rabbi, all of whom are on a first-name basis." That's why he had flirted with the idea of taking Brenda to the dinner. To break the monotony. But finally, reluctantly, he decided against it. A public appearance tonight—only three days after their coming-out at Bornstein's—and he might as well bring along the wedding invitations.

The obligatory fresh fruit cup had just been set in front of him when an olive-skinned, mustached waiter tapped him lightly on the shoulder. "Rabbi Winter?"

"Yes."

The man handed him a folded sheet, then motioned toward a portly, tuxedoed gentleman at the opposite end of the dais. It was Sam Bornstein, anxiously watching the transaction. *Meet me outside,* the scribbled note read. Daniel looked up, and Bornstein gestured leftward with his thumb. Nodding, Daniel found himself following Bornstein out the entrance of the resplendent Beverly-Olympic Hotel. Daniel started to speak, but Bornstein put a finger to his lips and kept walking. Moments later, standing in a dark and solitary alley at the side of the hotel, Bornstein finally halted.

"I've been looking around for you, Rabbi, all evening," he began accusingly.

"I'm sorry, Sam. I got here as soon as I could. And

every time I tried to come over and say hello, there was a crowd around you." The president nodded mechanically. "Anyway, why all the secrecy, Sam?"

Bornstein made an impatient downward sweep with his arm. "You saw yourself. If I had tried to get a word in with you there, it would have been crazy. Every two seconds some lady coming over—" his voice broke into a mimicking falsetto—" 'Mazal tov, Sam, mazal tov, Sam.' I wouldn't have gotten anywhere."

"The truth is, that's exactly what I wanted to tell you. Mazal tov."

"Mazal tov, my ass," Bornstein snapped. "Look, excuse me, Rabbi, that was out of line. I shouldn't have said that." He scrutinized Daniel's face, waiting for an acknowledgment that his apology to the rabbi and the Hebrew language had been accepted. "I suppose you noticed who didn't come here tonight to see me honored?"

Daniel said nothing.

Bornstein pulled at his chin. His voice was hoarse. "Rabbi, I'm worried sick about Cheryl. Ever since Stark was killed . . . it's been terrible. She just stays by herself. She wishes she was dead, that's what she says. Hilda and I are terrified. You know, after Stark got himself murdered, Cheryl went down to the cops—they made that broadcast that all of his patients should come in. Then when she came back and I asked her what happened, she ran into her room and slammed the door. Now she stays there all day. She hasn't come out. Not once. Would you believe it? We bring food in, and she hollers us right out. . . . I was thinking, Rabbi, maybe you could speak with her."

"If you think it'll help."

"Maybe she'll listen to you—you were Stark's friend. Talk some sense into her. Tell her—I don't know—tell her I'm sure he wouldn't have wanted her to act like this."

"I'll come home with you right after the dinner."

"Bless you, Rabbi," Bornstein said feelingly, and put a heavy hand on Daniel's shoulder. There was a flash of car headlights in the distance.

The Final Analysis of Dr. Stark

"Dr. Baum will be speaking soon, Sam. We better get back inside."

"Sure." The synagogue president gave a bitter smile. "I don't want to miss any more mazal tovs, do I?"

Brenda was half out the office door, briefcase in hand, when the insistent buzz of the phone brought her to a halt. She paused, silently praying that the call be picked up downstairs. Four rings later, her prayers unanswered, she sighed and stepped back into the office. She tossed the case onto her armchair and reached for the extension.

"This is Jennifer Steen," a dull voice said.

Quick, contradictory images ran through Brenda's mind—of the perfectly groomed brunette she'd met at the Bornstein's, of the dishevelled, hysterical woman she had comforted yesterday at Noah Stark's funeral.

"Jennifer," she said impulsively. "I've been worrying about you. How are you?"

"Do you want me to say okay, or do you want the truth?"

"The truth."

"I'm horrible. Half of the time I'm crying, the other half I feel like I can't breathe. I was speaking to a girlfriend yesterday, and suddenly I couldn't get a word out."

Brenda murmured sympathy. She knew exactly what Jennifer Steen was talking about. Two and a half years earlier, Brenda's own parents had been murdered while she was away on a trip to Europe. When she finally returned to LA, she had spent long days wandering through her parents' empty home. She remembered the bouts of sobbing, the voice suddenly reduced to a strangled whisper, the endless nights.

"Is there anything I can do?" she asked softly.

"I need to speak to you."

"Anytime, Jennifer."

"No, not like that. I mean officially."

"You mean about the murder?"

"Yes."

"Do you have some information you think is relevant?"
For a second there was silence. "Possibly."

"Look, Jennifer, I just want to make sure you understand something. I'm not a policewoman. I'm a psychologist who works for the homicide division."

"I know that."

"I'll be glad to meet with you, but it sounds to me like the person you really need to speak to is Lieutenant Cerezzi. He's heading the investigation."

"No," the girl said emphatically. "Not him."

"Why not?"

"I promised my father . . . Look, I'll explain everything when we meet."

"Okay. How's your schedule for tomorrow?"

"I can be in your office in an hour," the girl countered.

Brenda checked her watch—7:45 P.M.—and stifled a groan. She had just been setting out for a final briefing at Cerezzi's. Then home. Now, it looked like it was going to be the third time this week her twelve-year-old daughter Jessica was going to be spending the night at a friend's. Brenda had so wanted to get out of the office, pick Jessica up, and spend some relaxed time together. Not just for Jessica's sake. Hers, too. Recently, her job seemed to be consuming everything. Time with Jessica. Time with herself. And dammit, she thought, feeling a flicker of anger, Daniel hadn't gotten back to her yet either.

"Fine," Brenda said, hoping her weariness could not be heard. "Don't rush. I'll be here."

She waited for the click. Then she slammed the receiver back into its cradle.

"Some of you are familiar, perhaps," Aaron Baum said, his thin, angular body bent over the podium, "with a debate the Talmud records—apparently a theoretical debate—between Rabbi Akiva and his contemporary, Bar Petura." Baum, nudging his thick, black-rimmed glasses back up the bridge of his nose, peered shortsightedly down at a sheet in front of him. "Two men, the passage begins, are traveling on a journey far from civilization, and one of them has a pitcher

The Final Analysis of Dr. Stark

of water. If they share the water, they will die, but if one drinks all the water himself, he can reach civilization." Baum paused and gazed up at the audience. "So what are they to do?" he called out, his high-pitched voice a Talmudic sing-song. "Bar Petura teaches: 'It is better that both should drink and die, rather than that one should behold his companion's death.' " As if the very words made him thirsty, Baum raised a glass of water and took a sip. "And, in fact, that was the accepted ruling. Until Rabbi Akiva came and taught, 'No, the Torah teaches that your life takes precedence over your brother's. The man with the water has the right to drink it. He is not required to share it, to sacrifice his own life.' "

Baum rested his long arms on the podium. "I have often thought," he resumed, his voice softening, "that Rabbi Akiva was very hard. He was very hard on the survivor."

A collective gasp escaped the audience. Daniel, his mind bedazzled for the preceding forty-five minutes by the subtle brilliance of the Jerusalem scholar's intellect, looked quickly around the hall, startled by the intense reactions the last sentence had provoked. Across the dais, he could see tears unashamedly trailing down Sam Bornstein's plump face. And throughout the banquet room, sobs could be heard. He stared at the scene, uncomprehending. He thought back to the passage Baum had cited, a theoretical dispute if there ever was one. But looking at the grieving faces around him, he suddenly understood. For the two hundred alumni from Auschwitz, Bergen-Belsen and the other Nazi hells gathered that night, there was nothing theoretical about the Talmud's debate. All of them had spent World War II as exiles from civilization with only one pitcher of water. And all of them, disciples of Rabbi Akiva, had not shared their last drops of water and final scraps of food. If they had, they would all have died, along with the recipients of their charity. And so they drank, and beheld their companions' deaths. And for the rest of their lives, they, the purest victims of Hitler and the Nazis, were condemned to a guilt that few Germans ever experienced, and that few allies who had turned ships of refugees back to the Nazis ever felt. Yes, he thought, Baum was right. Akiva was very hard on the survivors.

A moment later, the scholar finished to an eerie silence. Only after Baum sat down did the clapping start, swelling into a thunderous, cathartic applause. Finally, it subsided. Myron Steele, the chairman of the evening, rose and thanked the speaker, his own voice raw with emotion.

"Before we present the plaque to tonight's honoree," Steele said, "just a few announcements." He elaborated on a few upcoming events, and Daniel's mind drifted. Suddenly, however, his attention riveted on Steele's words.

". . . Anna Gorman, an active member of the Remnant since she moved here from New York just a year ago, has suffered a cerebral hemorrhage. She is currently being cared for at the home of our beloved member, Sadie Rosen. Anna can talk, but she is paralyzed on her left side. Any of you who would like to visit Anna—and I needn't remind you of what a mitzvah that would be—please call Sadie."

Strange, Daniel thought, how often the many different worlds one inhabited merged. Anna Gorman, the mystery lady whose unexplained file Noah had deposited with him, staying at Sadie Rosen's house, the house he had stopped Lester Schonfeld from repossessing only three days before. He thought back to the entry in Anna Gorman's file. Before turning the pages over to Cerezzi, Daniel had copied down most of their contents in tiny handwriting on a small piece of paper, and then folded the sheet into his wallet. Now, as Steele droned on, he drew out the paper. *Extraordinary revelations. Martin Reisman. Dr. G. Simon. Hannah Weiler. Bierman. Patient said it was all brought out by that picture. Tried to calm her down, convince her that everything she was telling me had nothing to do with her reality now. Started her on Valium. I am very excited.* But if it had nothing to do with her reality now, Daniel thought—and it was so traumatic—then it must have had something to do with this reality, the Holocaust. By why had Stark been so excited by what Anna Gorman had told him? It couldn't be some breakthrough he had made with Gorman—after all, it was her first visit to him. What extraordinary reve-

The Final Analysis of Dr. Stark

lations could this elderly woman have offered Noah, rev-elations that had driven him to hide the notes he had taken of their meeting? Daniel brooded.

Suddenly, he became acutely conscious of many eyes focused in his direction. The woman on his right poked him gently. He turned and saw Myron Steele watching him, a bemused smile on his narrow face. "Once again," Steele said, motioning him forward with his hand. "I'd like to invite Sam Bornstein's spiritual leader, Rabbi Daniel Winter, to join us for the presentation of The Hemmatt's Man of the Year Award."

A red-faced Daniel Winter jumped up and quickly started toward the podium.

"I want to thank you, Brenda, for yesterday," Jennifer Steen began. She was dressed simply in a black skirt and gray blouse. Her luxuriant hair was pulled back in a tight knot. She wore no makeup to relieve the extraordinary pallor of her face.

"I'm just happy I was able to help."

There was a long pause. The two women looked at each other—Jennifer Steen with undisguised suffering, Brenda with sympathy for the girl's grief.

"Look," Jennifer continued, crossing and uncrossing her legs. "Now that I'm here, I don't even know why. I suppose I feel sort of close to you after yesterday. You were the only one. . . . And when I thought about it, you seemed like the right person. . . . My father would be furious."

"Wait a second," Brenda said softly. "I don't understand—furious about what?"

"You haven't caught Noah's killer yet, have you?"

"No."

"Have you made any progress at all?"

"We have some promising leads."

"Really?" the girl asked eagerly.

Brenda felt an immediate pang of guilt. "We have some promising leads," as Cerezzi had once put it in his inimitable style, was a police euphemism for, "We don't know shit from Cheyenne." After two years with the department, Brenda had no compunctions about fobbing off persistent reporters with the formula, but Jennifer Steen had been Noah Stark's fiancee. She deserved better.

"No, Jennifer. That's just police jargon. I'm sorry, but we don't know very much just yet."

"But I heard something on the radio. A rumor you'd brought somebody in for questioning."

"It came to nothing."

"Who was it?"

"He was innocent."

"Please, Brenda," Jennifer whispered hoarsely, "I have to know what's happening."

For a second, Brenda regretted not having stuck with the "promising lead" line. She looked down at the page of tiny, neat script on her desk, notes she'd taken earlier during what had turned out to be an unexpectedly comprehensive briefing at Cerezzi's office.

Grant—Out!!!" were the first words she'd written on the pad, *unless he hired someone to do it. Perpetrator definitely needed both hands—and Grant's left arm paralyzed.* Brenda recalled her own shock at the revelation. She had seen the congressman on TV often, had even seen him once when he was campaigning, and never noticed his disability. Unfortunately, she remembered thinking—as she looked sympathetically at the lieutenant's deep scowl—neither had Cerezzi.

Pelayo and King had reported next. Under instructions from the lieutenant—responding to John Goodman's visit —they'd gone to see Perl. Perl had "gone white as a ghost," Pelayo reported, when they'd confronted him with his threatening statements about Stark. But the bottom line was that he'd reached into his wallet and withdrawn losing stubs from the second, third, fourth, fifth and seventh races at the race track for Tuesday. King had already checked the times out—the second race had taken off 1:47, the third 2:15, the fourth 2:45, the fifth 3:13, the seventh 4:11. "We asked him why he had no stub for the sixth," King said.

The Final Analysis of Dr. Stark

"Told us he had the winner in that one—Pearl Necklace. Figured the name would bring him luck. Claimed he always held on to losing stubs in case he ever hit it big, you know, for tax purposes . . . So what do you think, Lou?" King had continued, lapsing into the patrolman's universal nickname for all police lieutenants. "Perl could have arranged for somebody else to go to the track and buy those tickets, couldn't he?"

"Possibly," Cerezzi answered unenthusiastically, "but that means a collaborator and a lot of planning. Nope. Don't buy it," he said moodily.

They sat in silence, King scratching his head, then Cerezzi had struck his palm against his desk. "What are we, a bunch of assholes? Perl bought those tickets all right, but who says he bought 'em right before each race? That second race," he went on, "that was at 1:47, that's what you said, right? How about if he bought all his tickets then, ducked out of the track, and headed straight for Stark's office?"

"We thought of that," Marie Pelayo replied quietly. "In fact, that's why Willie and I were so late getting back here. We got hold of the head cashier at the track—Brian Ryan, no joke, that's his name. You know with these computers, they can tell what time each ticket was punched out at. Anyway, Ryan met us down at the track, and he checked it out." She looked at her notepad. "1:41, 2:12, 2:37, 2:48. And 4:06."

"Which means there was an hour and eighteen minute gap between the last two purchases. Did you clock it?"

"Thirty-one minutes from the track to Stark's building," King said. "And that's at night—with no traffic. But at three P.M., there's no way he could make it that quick. It would take him at least fifty minutes." He shook his head.

"What if he was on a motorcycle?"

"Didn't think of that," the patrolman answered. "Does Perl have one?"

"I don't know. But let's think it through. Thirty-one minutes to Stark's office each way. Total of sixty-two. Plus getting from the ticket window to his vehicle. Figure another four minutes each way, total of eight. That gives him no more than eight minutes at the building."

"Barely seems enough time, Lieutenant," Brenda said, "to go up to Stark's office, manage to somehow get him across that couch, and kill him."

Cerezzi's palm crashed down again on the desk. "Let's go back a minute to that idea of somebody else buying the tickets."

"I thought you were ruling out a collaborator," Pelayo said.

"Not a collaborator. More like a Good Samaritan. Listen. A man meets another man at the track. They sit next to each other for two, maybe even three races. Talk a little. Exchange names—given that it's the track, probably just first names. Then one says he needs to go out for awhile—if he left some money, would the other guy bet it for him? He'd be coming back later. Even sets up a place to meet."

"Do people at the track trust each other enough to do that sort of thing?" Brenda asked.

Cerezzi turned to King. "Did you guys get the size of the bets on those stubs?"

King looked down at his pad. "Twenty dollar tickets for the first two races. Then he dropped down to five. But the seventh race he was back up to twenty."

Cerezzi nodded shrewdly. "Did you ask him about it?"

"Told us he was losing at the beginning, so he cut back. Then, when he won in the sixth, he felt lucky again."

The lieutenant smiled sourly. "Anything's possible, I suppose. But doesn't it make sense that if he was leaving the money for someone to bet, he'd leave smaller bets? Wouldn't want the guy running off with the money—and his alibi. Now, when was the ticket for the third race bought?"

"2:37, Lieutenant," King contributed excitedly.

Cerezzi grinned. "Yes, sir," he said. "We're going to bring our friend Mr. Perl back in here tomorrow. He's gonna be sweating pearl necklaces till we're sure we're getting the truth."

He paused, then grimaced. "On the other hand, this

The Final Analysis of Dr. Stark

time we're going to be circumspect. Remember, at this stage, all we have on Perl is totally speculative. Which is the problem with this whole damn case. Too many god-damned people wanted this guy dead. . . . So, let's move on." He checked the legal-size yellow pad on his desk. "Jonah Stark. Two things in particular strike me about the guy. First, he was angry as hell at his brother."

"I'm not surprised," Brenda said. "You saw how he acted at the funeral. He wouldn't even say Kaddish."

"Precisely. And he makes no bones about his hostility. Told me straight out he'd supported his parents for years with no help from his brother. Anyway, Jonah Stark recently needed money, and the very day he was iced, brother Noah told him nyet. Claimed he was strapped for money himself."

"Grudge killing, you're thinking, Lieutenant?" Pelayo asked.

"There's more. It turns out Stark had left a bequest for both Jonah and Leslie of a hundred thousand each. After things fell apart tonight with Grant, I called Jonah and asked him about it. Said it was news to him."

"He's bullshitting, Lieutenant."

"Probably," Cerezzi mused. "Since I then called the sister and she did know about it. Noah had told her."

"This is getting good," King smiled toothily.

"Second, Jonah has an alibi, but it doesn't mean crap. I checked out the meeting he had in San Diego Tuesday morning. The guy he met with says he was through with Jonah by 11:30. And Jonah himself admits that he started back for LA before noon."

"So he had plenty of time to get back and bump off his brother by four."

"Exactly. Jonah claims that he stopped off for a long lunch. Only the poor man doesn't remember where." King chuckled. "Says he just saw some sign on the Number Five freeway and pulled off the road. Let's check it out. To-morrow morning, you two," Cerezzi cocked the trigger fin-gers of both his hands at King and Pelayo, "are taking Mr. Jonah Stark for a ride to San Diego and back. Let's see if that restaurant exists."

"Gotcha, Lieutenant."

"Now, I want to go back to that will for a minute. Most of Stark's money is tied up in a trust for the boy, Adam. And as I said, Leslie's also in for one hundred thousand. But her alibi's airtight. She teaches English at Pali High. Had classes straight through from two-thirty to four, then was with two teacher friends in the faculty lounge till after five, grading papers. On the other hand, there's that one big fat surprise in Noah's last will and testament—that one hundred K for his ex, Arlette. What'd you ladies find out about her?"

"She's a tough cookie," Pelayo answered promptly. "Very much in control. Cold too. And she knows it. Stark nicknamed her the Iceberg."

"A hard, cold bitch. Enough to kill, you figure?"

"Maybe," Brenda answered. "She's angry enough, I can tell you that. A lot of suppressed rage. At Stark. At the world. And, of course, she's the one who sold him the statue—who knows, it could be part of some macabre plan she hatched? Also, they were married five years, so she may not have had too much trouble getting him onto that couch. And she doesn't have a ghost of an alibi. Says she spent the day shooting Skeet-Ball and wandering around the Santa Monica Pier and Venice Boardwalk. Even if it's true, she could very easily have slipped away for an hour. It's a nothing hop from there to Westwood."

Cerezzi turned to Pelayo. "So what do you think, Miss Police Academy Honor Student?"

The young woman's cheeks turned pink, but she met his mocking eyes steadily. "She's got one hell of a motive, Lieutenant. Stark left all that money for the boy, and another hundred thou for her. Now all of a sudden he announces he's getting married. If I was Arlette, I'd be worrying about the next edition of that will."

"Exactly," Cerezzi nodded. "Then again, we're talking about a thirty-seven-year-old guy. Even before the girlfriend came into the picture, Arlette had no reason to think she'd be collecting any time soon. But she's got a strong

The Final Analysis of Dr. Stark

motive, no denying that. Tomorrow morning, I'm paying a visit to Mrs. Arlette Stark's bank. I want to find out exactly what sort of financial shape the lady's in before I try breaking the iceberg."

Brenda was frowning. "But Jennifer, of course, isn't in the will, Lieutenant, is she?"

Cerezzi shook his head.

"What's your take on the fiancée, Lou?" King asked.

"The way she was carrying on at the funeral—a little melo-dramatic, wasn't it?"

"Maybe. But carrying on's no motive. And unless you come up with one, all I can tell you from my experience is that most women don't kill their fiances the day after they announce their engagement."

"What about her old man?" Willie King went on doggedly. "He was treating Stark, I mean, look, he was with him that day. Jennifer's his only kid. Maybe Steen knew some disgusting things about Stark—and didn't want to let the marriage go through?"

"So he picked up that statue and smashed his pro-spective son-in-law's skull in? Not likely. You've seen the guy. He hardly seems the physical type. Even if Steen had some bad dope on Stark, all he'd have to do is tell his daughter, or even just threaten Stark he'd tell her. That alone would probably have scared Stark off. By the way, Brenda, how have your meetings with Doc Steen been going? Is he cooperating?"

"As much as his scruples permit. He has been opening up a bit, though. And we've narrowed the files down to about twenty that seem current."

"Any of them look promising?"

"Hard to say. Three or four of them, I think, have potential for violence."

"Peril one of them?"

"Unclear."

Cerezzi gave a tight smile and threw down the packet of Kents he'd been playing with the whole session. "A few more helpful leads like that and I'm back to two packs a day." He drew a long breath. "What about that patient who saw Stark Tuesday; what does the shrink say about that Bornstein girl?"

"Oddly enough, Steen's very familiar with her case. It seems Noah had discussed it with him. Steen had even met with her."

"Really. When?"

"I'm sorry, Lieutenant." A faint blush crept into Brenda's cheeks. "I didn't think to ask."

"And what does he say about her?"

She flipped open her pad. "Quote, depressed and self-destructive, unquote. With a heavy emphasis on *self*-destructive. But he did say he'd stake his forty years of work and reputation on this: that the only one Cheryl Bornstein is capable of hurting is herself."

"Okay," Cerezzi blew out wearily. "I suppose that's about it. With Grant out of the picture, we're pretty much back to square one. . . . Everybody clear on what they're doing tomorrow?"

"I don't know, Lieutenant." Willie King shook his head. "The more facts we uncover, the more balled up I get. Every scenario seems to make less sense than the one before it."

Cerezzi crushed the pack of Kents in his huge hand. "When you have eliminated the impossible, whatever remains, however improbable, must be the truth, Conan Doyle. All we gotta do is eliminate a few more impossibilities. After all, look how easily we eliminated Russell Grant." The lieutenant gave a rueful laugh. "But don't get discouraged. Conan Doyle was right. Once we get rid of all the impossibilities, we'll be left with our murderer. And we're going to get him, don't worry."

It had been an oddly upbeat ending, Brenda thought, to what had fundamentally been a very discouraging meeting. Two days after Noah Stark's murder, they seemed no closer to tracing his killer. But she knew if she told Jennifer any more than she already had, the girl would only grow more disheartened.

The Final Analysis of Dr. Stark

"Jennifer," she said instead, "we're working on so many different fronts at once, I can't even begin to summarize them for you. Trust me. You came here to tell me something. So why don't you just tell me? Who knows, maybe it'll be the piece that helps?"

The girl looked dazedly around the tiny room. "I don't know how much it means, and I hope I'm not just being vindictive. . . ." Shuddering, she took a deep breath. "Remember when we met Monday night?"

"Of course."

"Didn't it . . . strike you as odd that Noah took me to Sam Bornstein's to announce our engagement?"

"I thought he went there to see Daniel."

"I know that's what he said, but that was only a part of it. You see, Cheryl Bornstein was his patient. Did you know she had a crush on him the whole time she was in treatment? She always fantasized that one day he'd marry her."

"How do you know that?"

"Noah told me."

"He *told* you what went on in Cheryl Bornstein's therapy?"

"He had to," the girl answered, her tone suddenly defensive. "He wanted to protect me."

"Protect you?"

"From Cheryl. From things she might say. You see, Noah was trying to get Cheryl to understand that it was all in her head. That there wasn't anything between them. He was just her doctor. He even told her about me. I mean, I don't think he told her my name. Just that he was seriously involved with someone. But Cheryl refused to accept it. That's why he wanted to announce the engagement at Bornstein's. He knew Cheryl was going to be there, and he figured if she heard it announced, if she saw us together with her own eyes, she'd stop fantasizing. At least that's what he hoped. Only what happened was, when Daniel made the toast, Cheryl ran out of the room. Later that night, after we left, Noah was very upset. That's why I called him the next morning. I knew Cheryl had a ten A.M. appointment, and I wanted to find out how it went. He told me it had been awful. She had stormed out, saying all sorts of terrible things."

"Terrible things? Like threats? This is important, Jennifer. Did Noah tell you exactly what Cheryl Bornstein said?"

"Not in exact words. You know, at the time, I didn't think he meant threats like that. But he was worried. I felt it. . . ."

Brenda regarded her levelly. "Is that it?"

"Well, you can imagine how I felt. I knew Cheryl's father was a big shot in the community. Who knew what sort of trouble she could make? I was jumpy as a cat. That's why I called Noah again, it must have been a little after twelve; I knew he didn't take any patients Tuesday afternoon, so I thought maybe we could get together for lunch. And he told me he had just gotten off the phone with Cheryl. She was out of control, he said, going on about how she had to speak with him. He couldn't calm her down. He had finally told her to come over at four."

"That's four P.M. Tuesday? Did Noah tell you anything more at lunch?"

"No. We didn't have lunch. Noah told me that everything was going to be okay, but that I should be prepared, Cheryl might say all sorts of awful things. Which is exactly what I was afraid of. When I got off the phone, I was pacing my house, biting my nails—you know—imagining all sorts of things. Finally, around three-thirty, I decided to talk to my father about it, get his advice. But he wasn't in. Then, by the time we finally did speak, it was too late; Noah was dead. It wasn't even till the next day that I was in enough control to tell him the whole story. The funny thing is, my father wasn't even surprised. Apparently Noah had already told him everything. So I told him I was going to the police. And he was really opposed. I mean, he knew Cheryl Bornstein's psychological profile. He claims the only person she is dangerous to is herself. Noah said the same thing. But if I went to the police with my story, they'd question her,

The Final Analysis of Dr. Stark

my father said, and that could just destroy her, without getting us one step nearer to catching Noah's killer."

Brenda nodded. "So why did you decide to come to me now?"

"Because I can't get that four o'clock meeting out of my head. For my father, I sometimes think the only thing that matters is the patient's well-being." Jennifer made no effort to disguise the bitterness in her voice. "But I don't give a good goddamn about Cheryl Bornstein. . . . You see, if you had told me you had a suspect, or at least a sense of who it might be, maybe I'd have kept my mouth shut. But Noah's been dead two days now. And you don't know any-thing, do you?"

Brenda shook her head mutely.

"Okay, well, that's why I'm here."

Chapter 15

Sam Bornstein tossed the golden plaque onto an ornate chair by the front door. "This way, Rabbi," he said thickly, not even looking back.

Daniel followed him down a long plushly carpeted hallway. Bornstein paused in front of a thick oak door and gave a cautious rap.

"Go away," a voice responded coldly.

"Stop that, Cheryl. Rabbi Winter's here with me. He wants to speak with you."

"I don't want to speak to anybody."

"You're embarrassing me," Bornstein said, struggling to keep his voice, if not his tone, even. "The rabbi made a special trip here just to see you. So please open that door. Now."

After a moment of silence, the lock clicked. The door eased open a fraction.

Bornstein gave a hard shove, and the door flew open. He barreled in, an embarrassed Daniel a few steps behind. Cheryl had retreated to her white, gilt-framed bed. She was wearing dark red stretch pants and a cotton balloon shirt with an elastic band that hugged her thighs. The thick pink carpet in her room perfectly matched the hue of the silk venetian blinds. Daniel was startled to see how pinched the girl's face had grown since he last saw her on the night of the party for *Sticks and Stones*.

166

"I want you to talk to the rabbi."

"And if I do, will you leave?" Cheryl's voice was raw with unconcealed hostility.

Bornstein's dark eyes smoldered, but he nodded without speaking. He turned and slammed the door behind him. Daniel sat down on the chair opposite the bed, sinking into the soft cushion. He carefully folded his hands in his lap, and remained silent.

The girl regarded him with mocking eyes. "Did my father make you come?"

"More or less."

"Well, at least you're honest. I wonder what miracle he thinks you're going to accomplish."

"To get you out of this room, for one thing. But then again, since I don't know why you're here, maybe you should tell me, to help me understand."

The girl was silent. She pushed her golden hair off her sullen face with both hands.

"Tell me, Rabbi, do you believe in God?"

"Yes, Cheryl, I do, but . . ."

"What about Jewish laws, do you believe in them too?"

Again, Daniel nodded.

"Always believe in them, in God, the whole thing?"

He said nothing. "C'mon, Rabbi," she scoffed. "Tell the truth. Do you?"

"I've had moments of doubt. Like any person."

"Noah told me you hated God."

"What!"

"After your wife died, he told me you said that religion was nothing but a farce, a sham. He said you told him you hated God."

"That's not true. . . . I had moments of anger, but I never said that, nothing even like it." He bit his lip to keep from adding—*And I'm certain Noah never said anything like that to you.*

The girl laughed mirthlessly and pulled at an invisible thread in the gleaming satin quilt that covered her bed.

"Remember that retreat we had, when I told you I was going to start keeping kosher? Noah warned me that I should be very careful about getting into religion. I told him you were encouraging me. Noah said that, if your faith was so shaky, maybe you weren't the best role model."

There had been a time, Daniel remembered, when Cheryl had been going to two of his classes at the synagogue every week, and showing up at his office to chat regularly. Then it had stopped, very suddenly, and she had subsequently spurned every effort he had made to speak with her.

"You said he told you a lot of things," he prodded gently.

"He said he loved me." She paused. "He never told you he loved me, did he?"

"No."

"Of course not. It was our secret. Noah told me that in another year or so I'd be all better. And then we could start going out in public."

"He told you that?" Daniel's mind was reeling. The tortured girl was spinning out detail after detail, each one more fantastic than the preceding. Now he realized why Noah had given him so stern a warning on Monday evening. Cheryl Bornstein was much more disturbed than he had ever realized.

"Oh, not once," Cheryl went on. "Many times. Until a couple of months ago. Probably when he met that girl." Cheryl glared at Daniel, her stiff tone starting to show faint glimmers of emotion. "You know why I think he said it, Rabbi? Because he wanted to sleep with me."

Daniel kept his voice impassive. "And did he?"

"About twice a week for most of the time I was in treatment. Usually in his office . . . Do you believe me?"

Daniel hesitated. If he told Cheryl what he really believed—that the part of her mind that seemed to be functioning best was her imagination—she would shut him out of her life as completely as she had shut out her parents. And something told him that, even in her sickness, the girl held the key to Noah's murder. "I think," he finally responded cautiously, "that *you* believe everything you're

The Final Analysis of Dr. Stark

telling me. But I'm not sure that it all happened exactly the way you're saying."

The girl scrutinized Daniel's face. "Tell me, Rabbi. When you were married, did you go through a period of several months when you were impotent?"

Daniel's mouth flew open involuntarily. His face became bloodless.

"Noah told me."

Daniel felt as if the girl had struck him a physical blow. This time it was no fantasy Cheryl was weaving. He had told Noah that, all right. And nobody else.

"Noah said you were always giving people advice on love and marriage, and that you weren't so perfect yourself. Now, Rabbi," she said, her face white with fury, "now do you believe me?"

Daniel remained motionless, his eyes focused unseeingly on the plush carpet. There was a subtle, burning sensation deep inside his brain. He felt like he had just been injected with poison. "Go on," he said, in a voice that sounded foreign in his ears.

"You know what I think Noah's genius was? He made me feel that I had big problems, really serious. But that he alone knew the real me, knew how beautiful I really was. Do you follow what I'm saying? That he was the only one who saw all my potential greatness, and that he was going to use it to make me all better. I suppose he did that with everyone. I mean, you were in therapy with him, so you know, right?"

Something else Cheryl could only know through Noah. Daniel's vision blurred. Until a few moments ago, he had dismissed all of Cheryl's vicious claims about Noah as delusions. Just as he had earlier dismissed Jonah as an envious malcontent. But the deluded one, it now appeared, was he. Twice a week for four months he had spilled his life out to a sieve. Under the guise of professional integrity and warm friendship, Noah Stark had pulled secret after secret out of him, and then dispersed them whenever and to whomever he thought appropriate. And along with the secrets, Stark had added his own embellishments, apparently when he felt the truth wasn't damning enough. But why? Why poison Cheryl against him? And why—Daniel's mind reeled back to Monday evening, remembering Noah's cautionary words about Bornstein—had Noah tried to poison him against Sam?

"He could make you feel he was the only one who knew the real you, couldn't he, Rabbi?"

Daniel made no response. He was remembering Noah's amazing ability to make you realize that he knew how special you were. And that he alone was going to get you through.

For a while, like two mourners, they sat together in devastated silence. Cheryl continued to pick at the white quilt; Daniel stared blankly ahead. "He was a genius with words," the girl said finally. "Just a few weeks ago, my father wanted to pull me out of treatment altogether. He was mad and he said there was nothing wrong with me, that the whole thing was a giant waste of money. So Noah called him up and had us both down for a joint session. He told my father I was a schizophrenic. Right in front of me. Scared the hell out of both of us. By the time my dad left, he was willing for me to go four times a week. He would have gladly forked over the money for Noah to have a session with me daily by the time Noah finished with him. Then, the next day, when I went to see Noah, he asked why I was so depressed. I told him I had gone home and looked up schizophrenic. The whole time I was with him, I thought I'd been getting better. Now I found out I was psychotic, with all sorts of personality disintegration. When I told him that, Noah just sat there and laughed."

"He what?" Daniel realized with a shock that there was now quite literally nothing Cheryl could tell him about Noah that would seem impossible.

"He laughed. He told me to go over to his bookcase and take down this certain book. I even remember the name. *Mental Disorders*. It was by some big psychiatrist,

The Final Analysis of Dr. Stark

Insel or something. And he told me to open up to page 187, or whatever, and read aloud some lines he had underlined. I memorized them. . . . 'Schizophrenia is one of the most overused terms among American analysts and therapists. In many instances, to designate a person as schizophrenic is about as meaningful as designating a person as a person. Because to one degree or another, all of us are schizophrenic.' Can you believe it, Rabbi, that's what the book said?"

Daniel's heart went out to her, to the cruel damage Noah had so deliberately, so maliciously wrought.

"I wanted to tell him he was a bastard, but I couldn't even speak. 'Do you know what you did to me yesterday,' I wanted to scream at him, 'what you did to my father?' . . . But you know Noah. Screaming wouldn't have helped. You could shout all you wanted, he'd be as calm as ever. So I just told him what had happened the night before. That I'd overheard my father almost crying, telling my mother, 'I don't know if Cheryl's ever going to get better.' And Noah came over and put his arms around me. 'But I'm not your father,' he said. 'I do know you're going to get better. And part of the reason you're going to get better is because I upset your father so much.' And he gave me this whole megillah how if he had told my father about all the wonderful progress I really was making, he would have cut down on my sessions, or pulled me out of therapy altogether. And then, of course, I would have gotten worse. So instead, he deliberately frightened my father. And that's why my father ended up agreeing to four sessions a week. 'You see,' Noah said, 'now you'll be getting better so much faster. . . .' " A shudder convulsed the girl's slender body.

"You know, Rabbi, the most amazing thing about Noah Stark?"

"What's that?"

"That I believed every word he said. I always did. And you know when I finally stopped believing him? Monday night."

"When you found out about Jennifer?"

"That's when I saw what a phoney he was. Can you believe it? All those months telling me how much he loved me. And me paying a hundred and twenty dollars an hour to hear it. I was a meal ticket to him. And a good lay. When I came in Tuesday morning, I finally gave it to him. And you should have seen him. Telling me how he had been preparing me for weeks to realize he was involved with someone else. Trying to convince me it was all in my head. That I was simply projecting all my fantasies onto him. That he had never given me any reason to think he loved me. But that's a lie, Rabbi. . . . I could have killed him. But I didn't, Rabbi. Instead, I ran out of his office, and you know where I went? To Dr. Steen. I remember everybody was so impressed the night before that Jennifer was his daughter. So I looked him up in the phone book and went right there. I wanted to make sure he knew what a prize he was getting for a son-in-law."

"How did he react?"

"Very polite. Very sympathetic."

"Do you think he believed you?"

Cheryl's right hand chopped the air. "Who the hell knows what shrinks think about anything? Their whole point is to never tell you what they're thinking. He kept asking me questions." She laughed bitterly. "Reminded me of Noah, with all his stupid questions. They're all alike. Then, after Noah was killed, Steen called here. Asked me straight out if I had done it. And I told him no. I wanted to, I told him. I even thought about how I'd do it, but I didn't. I couldn't. And Steen said he believed me, and that's why I shouldn't tell anyone the story about Noah."

"I don't understand. Why not?"

"Steen said it would just make the police suspect me. He's right, Rabbi, isn't he? They're going to suspect me!" she shrilled. "Aren't they? You've got to answer me, Rabbi." She clasped her hands together, and then suddenly, in a strangely calm voice, said, "Steen said he was asking me, as a father, to be quiet. He said it would break Jennifer's heart if an ugly thing like that came out about Noah."

"And you listened to him?"

"Well, I did go to the police, told them I had seen Noah Tuesday morning, but I didn't say anything more. I couldn't hurt her too. Noah has done enough damage."

The minutes ticked by, agonizingly. Daniel looked at her with a painful mixture of compassion and pity. He felt ashamed as he sat before her—ashamed for himself and ashamed for her. In the background, a doorbell rang, unnaturally loud in the cavernous house. At the sound, Daniel spoke.

"There's one thing I must ask you, Cheryl."

She met his gaze unflinchingly. "No, Rabbi, what I told you is the truth. Maybe he deserved it, but I didn't kill him."

"No, not that. I want to know why you're hiding out in this room. I understand the betrayal you're feeling. God knows, I'm feeling it too. But why torture yourself in here, particularly given what you know now about Noah?"

A look of fear fleetingly crossed the girl's strained face. She looked past him, absorbed in her own world. Outside the sanctuary of her room Daniel heard quick footsteps.

"It's definite that he was killed by that statue, isn't it?" Cheryl asked dully.

"Yes, but—"

A rap sounded on the door.

"Go away, Daddy!"

"Cheryl," Sam Bornstein called shakily. "There's a Lieutenant Cerezzi here. Please, honey. You're going to have to see him."

Cheryl swayed. Daniel rushed over and put his arms around her trembling body.

The door opened, and Cerezzi, followed by Brenda and Sam Bornstein, entered. Brenda swiftly took in the scene, and quickly looked away. The lieutenant nodded a greeting at Daniel, then tapped his breast pocket. "I'm carrying a warrant here, Ms. Bornstein, to bring

you in for questioning in the murder of Dr. Noah Stark."
Cerezzi pulled out a card and brusquely read through the
Miranda warning. "Why don't you pack a few items?" he
said when he finished. "Just in case you're with us for some
time."

Chapter 16

Friday Morning 3:00 A.M.

It was only a few hours before dawn, and he was still in Cerezzi's office. To Daniel, these last hours—since Cerezzi had come into Cheryl's room—had been interminable.

He and Bornstein had followed the lieutenant and Brenda back to headquarters in Sam's car. There, the aggrieved father stridently insisted that Cerezzi engage in no questioning of Cheryl without his lawyer present. Cerezzi, well aware of the girl's tenuous mental state, readily consented. Daniel knew that he had no intention of jeopardizing his case on any procedural technicalities. But, Cerezzi informed Bornstein firmly as two female officers escorted Cheryl to a cell, she would be spending the night downtown. "We're not charging her with anything at this minute. And if your man wants to, he can file a writ of habeas corpus. That is, if he thinks there's a point to it." Finally, realizing he would accomplish nothing more till the morning, the distraught Bornstein left.

"It's madness," Daniel told Cerezzi and Brenda as the latter passed each a mug of steaming coffee. "That girl didn't kill Noah Stark any more than I did." Daniel selectively outlined what the girl had told him—the specifics of what he had so recently found out about Noah and himself were still too painful to mention.

When he'd finished, Cerezzi nodded skeptically.

"Hmm . . . Sounds to me like you don't *want* to think

175

she did it, Daniel. Now, that might be a very commendable attitude for a rabbi to take about a member of his congregation, but the fact is, everything you told me only makes me more sure that she's guilty."

"What did I say?" Daniel challenged, already worrying that he had spoken too freely.

"Well, for one thing, it makes her motive one hundred percent clear. I mean, Jennifer Steen told us about the rejected lover angle, but it helps that the Bornstein girl herself owns up to it." Cerezzi held out a restraining palm as Daniel rose from his chair. "Don't get me wrong, Daniel. If she's telling the truth, then Stark acted disgustingly. And any jury in the world's going to take that into account. Cheryl Bornstein's not going to walk, but we're not talking life sentence here either. Five years, maybe six and she's out. But . . ." He shrugged fatalistically.

"Oh, that's really wonderful," Daniel said bitingly. His blue eyes blazed. "I'll call up Sam and tell him to pop open the champagne. Maybe it'll become a family tradition. First, the father spends his youth in Auschwitz, and now the daughter will spend her's in prison!" Out of the corner of his eye, he felt Brenda go rigid, but he didn't take his furious gaze off the policeman.

"You're not in your pulpit here, Rabbi," Cerezzi warned gently. "And you're not the only person in the world who's concerned with justice." He stopped and drained his coffee. "Look, I'm tired, I suppose you are too. . . . We've both had a rough couple of days. But I don't like your making it sound like I pulled Cheryl Bornstein's name out of a hat. . . . I told you that what that girl told you makes me more convinced of her guilt. Now, do you want to hear why?"

"You told me already," Daniel said, his voice still brittle. "Motive."

"That's only a part of it. What really interested me was what she *didn't* tell you."

"Cut out the riddles, Joe."

"Will you stop snapping at me and use your head for a minute?"

Daniel ran his fingers over the stubble on his chin and struggled to control his anger. Cerezzi was right; they were all exhausted. "Go on."

"First, her fingerprints were all over the statue that killed Stark. But she didn't say a word to you about how they got there, did she?"

"No, and she also didn't tell me what she had for lunch that day either. Come on, that's ridiculous. Big deal. I'm sure a hundred people touched it."

"No, Daniel," Brenda broke in. Her face was drawn, and there were dark smudges under her eyes. She hadn't touched her coffee. "The statue had only been delivered that morning. There were three sets of prints on it—Noah's, the delivery boy's, and Cheryl's. That's it."

"So what? The murderer could have used gloves or wiped off his fingerprints."

"True," Cerezzi conceded. "Which, of course, is exactly what we assumed. And that's why, even when we found Cheryl's prints on the statue—and contrary to your current assessment of my abilities—I didn't go jumping to any conclusions. But then your girlfriend here found out a second thing young Cheryl didn't think was important enough to tell you. She had a four o'clock appointment with Stark the day he died."

"How do you know?" Daniel demanded harshly, turning to Brenda.

She winced, then scanned Cerezzi's face, her eyes pleading. The lieutenant sucked in air, then breathed out hard. "Okay, tell him," he said, grudgingly. Brenda quickly filled Daniel in on her late night session with Jennifer.

"So you see," she ended, "Cheryl had every reason to assume that no one else knew about that second meeting. I don't know if she premeditated killing Noah. Maybe she didn't. Maybe—"

"All you have," Daniel began in as reasonable a voice as he could manage, "is Jennifer's saying that Noah said that Cheryl said she was coming in at four. That's hearsay, isn't it?"

"It is," Cerezzi shrugged, then began piling up the papers on his desk and putting them in his attaché case. "But it's also damned suggestive. It also explains a lot."

"Explains what?"

"The goddamn missing appointment book, for one thing. I'll lay you any odds that when we get our paws on it, we'll find Cheryl Bornstein's name down there for four P.M. That is, if she hasn't thrown it away or burned it."

"Oh, that's just great. Guilty until proven innocent. You've convicted the girl already."

Cerezzi sighed and banged his case down on the desk.

"No, Daniel, she's convicted herself. I'll tell you something else. Before we went to Bornstein's tonight, I went down to the lab to check on one final thing. The last person to enter Stark's office Tuesday was you. At about twenty after five. So naturally your fingerprints were on the doorknob of his private office. But they only partially obliterated someone else's prints. And *lo and behold*, guess whose prints they turned out to be?"

"Maybe Cheryl showed up at four, saw Noah's body, and ran the hell out of there."

"And didn't tell you about it tonight, and didn't tell us about it when we questioned her yesterday. C'mon, Daniel."

"She was scared. That doesn't mean she's a murderer. When you really analyze it, all you've got on Cheryl is some fingerprints that I'm sure can be explained, and some suspicious behavior. That doesn't exactly make her unique."

Cerezzi looked at his watch and made no effort to suppress a yawn. "You've got something to say? You've got three minutes."

"Okay." Daniel rubbed his throbbing forehead. "What about Steen, for one? Did he tell you that Cheryl had gone to see him? Did he tell you what he had found out about Noah?"

"No. But the guy's so close-mouthed about his precious patients and their precious therapy that it doesn't exactly send me into shock."

The Final Analysis of Dr. Stark

"Oh, I see. It's only when Cheryl holds back information that it's suspicious."

"Steen's fingerprints weren't where they weren't supposed to be."

"And you don't find it odd, Lieutenant, that he told Cheryl to keep quiet about their meeting?"

"You're grasping at straws, Daniel. If you have a basis for making an accusation against Steen, make it. Just give me the material now, tomorrow morning if you like. I'll look into it."

"I'm not accusing anyone of anything!" Daniel shouted, gripping the back of the chair. "You're telling me what's suspicious about Cheryl's behavior, so I'm telling you what's suspicious about Steen's. And he's not the only one. That man I sent to see you—John Goodman. I know what he told you about Perl. Are you going to tell me that Andrew Perl doesn't have a motive?"

"Perl doesn't only have a motive, Daniel, he at least has a glimmer of an alibi. Of course we're going to check his story out further, but I wouldn't get my hopes up."

"And what about Jonah?" Daniel went on doggedly. "He hated his brother. And you know as well as I how flimsy his alibi is."

"That we do, thank you. And we're checking it out."

Daniel stopped. He had pushed Cerezzi as far as he could. Instinct told him it was time to back down, or he could permanently destroy his friendship with him. And, having lost one friendship—Noah's—so brutally that day, Daniel knew he could not face the loss of another.

"You don't have your car?" Brenda asked, when the door closed on Cerezzi.

"No. I came down in Bornstein's."

"I suppose I should take you home then."

"I'd like that."

As they waited by the elevator, he reached for her hand, but she pulled it back. He reached for it again as they walked through the empty parking lot. Once again she evaded him.

"It's three-thirty in the morning, Daniel. I'm really knocked out."

"I'm not challenging you to a marathon," he said, forcing a smile. "I just wanted to hold your hand."

She did not answer, but as they reached her silver Volvo, she busied herself twisting the key. Then, easing herself in, she leaned over and unlocked the passenger's side.

"I've been wanting to speak to you for days," she said, staring out of the windshield when he settled in. She stuck the key in the ignition, but then sighed and turned to him. Hurt glittered in her green eyes. "Why didn't you get back to me?"

"My God, Brenda," he said, taking hold of her hand now. "I feel terrible. I had no idea it was so important. And you know the pressure I've been under. I haven't had time for anything."

"You had time for Cheryl Bornstein," she declared, her voice dangerously even.

Of all things, he hadn't expected that.

"What's that supposed to mean?"

"That Sam Bornstein doesn't need a lawyer with you around. It doesn't matter what Cerezzi showed you. You're gung ho for that girl, aren't you?"

"Brenda, don't you understand? I'm the one who first sent Cheryl to Noah . . . I feel responsible."

"Is that *all* you're feeling?"

He released her hand and dug both of his in his pockets. "Okay, get to the point."

"Noah told me about you and Cheryl."

He stared at her, his heart pounding. Again, he felt the poison spreading through his system. "Noah told you what about Cheryl and me?"

"When we were at Bornstein's Monday night, you remember, he took me into the library. Telling me all the time how much he loved you, but that he felt"—she gave a clipped laugh—"morally obligated to warn me. To warn me that I shouldn't rely on your ever making a commitment, because you were still in love with Cheryl Bornstein."

The Final Analysis of Dr. Stark

Daniel regarded her speechlessly.

"He told me how, whenever her name came up, you became very self-conscious. Then, as soon as we got back to you, Noah mentioned her, and next thing I knew you asked me to get lost.

"Brenda, that's ridiculous. I wanted to be alone because I had to speak to Noah confidentially, as a rabbi to a psychiatrist. . . . You didn't believe him, did you?"

"Well . . ."

"Why in heaven's name didn't you say anything to me?"

"He claimed you didn't even know it yourself."

"Oh, come on, Brenda. I can't believe you bought that?"

"Then Noah was killed. That night in your house, you were so sad, so vulnerable. And it looked like you were finally opening up to me. I was waiting, Daniel, I'm telling you, I was waiting for you to say something to me."

"About Cheryl?"

She nodded.

"*There was nothing to say!*"

"Then tonight when we came into her room, you were there, your arms around her."

"For God's sake, Brenda, the girl was about to faint. What was I supposed to do, run to the opposite side of the room—

"Noah was your friend. If it wasn't true, why would he have told me that?"

Daniel looked away from her, at the deserted parking lot. It was a long time before he spoke.

"Noah Stark was not my friend."

"Daniel—"

"Please, Brenda. I know it sounds nuts, even to me. But I think deep down, part—maybe even a big part—of Noah hated me. I found out tonight that he told Cheryl that I hated God, that I thought religion was all a sham. A lie, of course. And then, for good measure, he told her she shouldn't listen to my advice on marriage and dating because I had been impotent while I was married. That, by the way, is true. I was. For the first couple of months after

I found out Rebecca had cancer. Noah learned that when he was my therapist."

Brenda gasped. "How could he have told Cheryl that?"

"Well," Daniel said flatly, leaning his head back against the seat, "it just so happens that what he told you, Brenda, was a lie from beginning to end. I've never had the slightest romantic involvement with Cheryl Bornstein. But when Noah started telling you that story, you didn't stop him. You didn't say, 'Hey, Doctor, you're breaking confidentiality.'"

"It's not the same thing. I didn't know then that he'd been your therapist."

"Oh, and then you would have told him to shut up?"

"I would have stopped him, yes."

"You mean it's all right as long as it's not a professional confidence. As long as it's just nice, simple gossip."

"I love you, Daniel, damn it! What do you expect me to do, when somebody who *you yourself* tells me is such a great friend starts talking about you? Of course I listened. You would have too!"

Daniel's whole body ached from the tension of the day's events. He could never recall being so tired. "You know what Noah's genius was?" he said now, remembering the question Cheryl Bornstein had thrown at him earlier. A horn blew and he was silent, letting the sound fade. "He could break every ethic of confidentiality in the book. And make whoever gave him an ear feel that they were special, that they had a *right* to know. You, because you're my girlfriend. Cheryl, for her own health, so that she wouldn't fall too far under my influence. And me. Yeah, me too." He grimaced. "The great crusader against gossip. Listening to him tell me what was going on in Cheryl's therapy. I mean, I really needed to have her psychiatrist's approval before I could ask her to chair a synagogue event, didn't I? Of course. Sure. We all had rights. Everybody. Except Noah's patients. The only right they had was to be gossiped about."

"But why did he do it, Daniel?"

"That's more than your area than mine. But I think I'm starting to understand. It gave Noah power. He knew things about people, and understood them better than they understood themselves. His knowledge made them dependent on him. You see, it was only when Cheryl started going to my classes, telling him she was thinking of becoming kosher, that he started tearing me down to her. And he did it by telling her things that made me look like a hypocrite. And a pathetic one at that. That way, he knew she wouldn't check back with me—in fact, she wouldn't want to have anything to do with me at all. On Monday night, he saw how close you and I had become. And to top it off, you were a psychologist. Maybe he saw you as a competitor. Maybe he started worrying that he'd lose me as a friend. Certainly as a dependent. And he was so smart. He understood immediately when he spoke to you that he couldn't attack me frontally, like he did with Cheryl. You would have seen through it. And then told me about it. So instead he seeded a doubt in your mind on precisely the sort of issue you'd be uncomfortable confronting me about. He was brilliant at it—every story tailor-made for its own recipient. All I had to do on Monday night was mention what good relations I had with Sam Bornstein, and next thing I know he's warning me that Sam's out to get me. It was wrong of me to believe him, of course. And half of me didn't. But after the fights I'd had when Wilbur Kantor was president—and three guesses who was one of the people I consulted with about how to handle *that* situation—I suppose it seemed possible. . . . Noah relied on his knowledge of people, of their weaknesses, their vulnerabilities. Half of the time he made up the stories. The other half he didn't have to. He already knew so much. In my case," he said, turning to Brenda, "he claimed to know things about me I didn't even know."

A flush stained Brenda's cheeks. "I'm sorry, Daniel. I'm so sorry. But . . . that's exactly how he made it sound so real. You see, it's what goes on all the time in therapy. The therapist sees something the patient hasn't yet realized," and guides them to that realization. And the reason we can see the pattern, and know where to guide them, is because they're so open with us."

"Yeah. And in the hands of an ethical, sensitive therapist, I suppose that's great. But look at the power it gives you. I don't mean just therapists. Look at the power someone like Joan Reider has. Just from knowing things about people. I could feel it at the show—she was looking me over, just dying to get her hands on some juicy scandal about me, something she could use."

"We had a name for doctors like Noah in graduate school. Loose-lips."

"And if a psychiatric ethics committee catches a loose-lips, do they take away his license?"

"I suppose. I've never heard of them actually doing it."

"The patients are probably too afraid to press charges. After all, the therapist has too much on them, he knows their secrets better than anyone."

"Don't get carried away, Daniel. There are very few psychiatrists like that. Noah was a rare, rare exception to the rule, a rotten apple."

He leaned his elbow on the car window, conscious for the first time of the coolness of the night air. "I was once staying at a hotel in Saint Louis, I was lecturing there for the Jewish Federation. And when I went down to breakfast in the morning, I saw a rabbi there—a guy I knew. Of course, I went over to his table. He was very uncomfortable to see me, I could sense it immediately. Then, when the waiter started over with his order, he jumped up, even before the man reached our table, and started yelling, 'I didn't order that.' You know what was on the waiter's tray?"

"I can guess," Brenda smiled.

"Ham and eggs." Daniel smiled back at her. "It's like that in every field. . . . But listen, Brenda, I want to take this loose-lips factor a step further. You see, Cerezzi's so sure Cheryl killed Noah because he rejected her—"

"That's not the only reason."

"Okay, okay. And her fingerprints on the statue, and

that four o'clock appointment. But that's really all he's got. And you have to admit, it's all circumstantial as hell. There are too many things his theory doesn't explain."

She hugged her thin jacket closer to her throat. "I'm listening."

"How did Cheryl get Noah to the couch in order to hit him with the statue?"

"We thought of that. Cerezzi's getting a search warrant for the Bornstein house. He's guessing she had a gun. She was probably afraid to use it because it could have been heard in other offices. Eventually, we'll get to the bottom of it. But it's always like that, Daniel. When you bring somebody in, it's because the overwhelming evidence points toward them. You never know every detail in advance."

"Two," Daniel went on stubbornly, "I was in therapy with Noah. I know his style. He was always extremely formal. Tie always in place, shirt buttoned to the top. But when I found him that day, his whole appearance was very casual. If he was meeting with Cheryl, he never would have looked like that."

Brenda leaned back and laughed softly.

"You want to fill me in on the joke?" Daniel asked coldly.

"You yourself told me they'd been sleeping together. How did you expect him to greet her—in a top hat?"

"And most important," Daniel continued firmly, "you've ignored the Anna Gorman file."

"I know what's in it."

"And you don't want to know what the extraordinary revelations were—"

"I'm very curious, Daniel. That's why I went out to see her. But now, after that Grant file fiasco, I think Joe's gonna be a little cautious. As he said to me, 'Your boyfriend'—actually that's not what he said, whenever he's annoyed with you, Daniel, he calls you the yarmulke— 'Your friend the yarmulke,' that's what he said to me, 'might have just gotten me into the most embarrassing incident in my twenty-eight years on the force.'"

"That's not my fault," Daniel snapped.

"Don't be so sensitive. He was joking. By the way, Rabbi Yarmulke," Brenda said, a dimple appearing on her cheek, "I saw this absolutely gorgeous man in the paper." She twisted around and pulled the *LA Times* from the back seat, open to the article about Stark's funeral.

Daniel stared down at his picture, wedged between Stark and Steen. He felt a sudden chill. "The guy in the middle is definitely the most attractive man I've seen in a long time," Brenda teased. Her hand rose and gently smoothed the lapels of his pale blue shirt. "Daniel, do you forgive me?"

He looked up at her, unhearing.

"Do you forgive me?"

"For not trusting me or for being jealous?"

"Both."

"For being jealous, no problem. Makes me feel wanted."

"And for not trusting you?"

"Can I have one more day to sulk?" He saw a muscle quiver at her jaw, and he pulled her toward him, pressing his lips firmly against hers in answer. Afterwards, their foreheads touching, he murmured, "Do you trust my love now?"

She gazed up at him, nodded, and tilted her head back, her eyes very bright.

They sat for a good while longer. Daniel stroked her cheek, then slowly combed through her thick, gleaming hair with the tips of his fingers. "Then, my tough copper, you're forgiven."

She threw her head back and laughed, sounding for the first time in days like the woman he had fallen in love with, then she turned the ignition and pulled into reverse. The streets were deserted, and the trip to Daniel's apartment in West LA went very fast. The whole time, Brenda kept stealing glances at Daniel, even though he could not help staring down at the paper in his lap.

"Hey, aren't you becoming the little narcissist," she said, smiling, as they pulled up in front of his building.

"Huh?" he mumbled, still frowning.

"Nothing."

The Final Analysis of Dr. Stark

He kissed her abstractedly, then popped open the door. "By the way, darling, I'm borrowing this," he said, holding up the paper.

She looked at him quizzically. "Sure. . . . Daniel? You really believe Cheryl's innocent?"

"More than ever."

"So what are you planning now?"

"*Bikur Cholim.*"

"What?"

"In precisely five hours," he said, consulting his watch, "I'm paying a sick call on Anna Gorman."

Chapter 17

Sadie Rosen, seventy-six years young, clapped her hands in front of her gentle, crumpled face when she saw Daniel from her front window. Shuffling forward, she quickly unlatched the door chain.

"Rabbi," she cried, rising on her toes to deposit a large, wet kiss on his cheek. "How can I ever thank you?"

For just a second, Daniel stared in puzzlement at her, then he remembered. Only four days had passed since his visit to Lester Schonfeld at the bank, but it seemed like an eternity.

"Mr. Schonfeld was very happy to help out, Sadie," he assured her, smiling.

"I'm sure, Rabbi. I could tell from the way he spoke to me on the phone how anxious he was. No, don't be modest, it was you who did it. . . . When I was a young girl, my father used to tell me stories about Hasidic rebbes, 'the miracle men' he'd call them." She clasped Daniel's hand in her own wrinkled one and beamed up at him, her gray eyes bright with tears. "I didn't know we still had them."

Daniel stooped and kissed her cheek. "My pleasure, Sadie."

"Anyway, Rabbi, I'm happy you're here now. You saved me a trip." Sadie disappeared into the kitchen, and came back quickly with a large package wrapped in wax paper.

The Final Analysis of Dr. Stark

"Honey cake," she said. "I made it special for you. I was going to bring it to the shul today."

"Thank you, Sadie. It will be the highlight of my Shabbat dinner." He looked down at her fragile frame. "By the way, are you going to be okay now financially?"

"Financially, shme-nancially," Sadie said gaily, waving her arms. "Who has time to think about money? Tuesday, a sick friend came to stay with me. That's what I'm worried about."

"I heard," Daniel said. "Last night at the Remnant dinner they made an announcement. How is Mrs. Gorman doing?"

Sadie sighed and shook her head. "Not good, Rabbi. The stroke left her so bad she can't move her whole left side. She lies in bed from morning till night. If we could at least get her into her wheelchair. But that means somebody has to lift her." With a shrug, Sadie lifted her right arm and flexed a gaunt muscle Daniel could have easily encircled with thumb and forefinger. "I can't do it. . . . Anna hasn't been out of bed in five days."

"I'll lift her."

"Bless you, Rabbi."

"Can she speak?"

"Almost as well as ever. The doctor at University told me that's not so strange; on the left side it's better to lose, you can still talk."

"And her mind, it's functioning properly?"

She flipped her hand from side to side. "Sometimes, Rabbi, she's clear like a bell. Remembers things from fifty years ago like from yesterday. Then, ten minutes later, she'll ask me the time, I'll tell her, and two seconds later she's asking me again."

Daniel nodded. He had visited the bedsides of many stroke victims. The pattern Sadie was describing was common.

"I understand the police were here to speak with her?"

"You really are a miracle man, Rabbi. How could you know such a thing?"

"How was Mrs. Gorman when they questioned her?"

Sadie shook her head and tut-tutted. "It was not good. They scared her."

"They questioned her roughly?"

"No . . . nothing like that. But you see, Anna's like me. A survivor from the camps. When the police came, one of them was a redhead, she was okay, but the Chicano girl was in a uniform with a gun hanging down. Now you'll tell me that's how all police go around, and I know you're right. But for people like Anna and me, it makes no difference. The police can speak English, and say please and thank you and ma'am at the end of every question, but it doesn't help. They bring back memories."

Daniel nodded sympathetically. Growing up in New York—he must have been about ten—he remembered when the city health department had purchased new ambulances. The sirens affixed to them had a distinctive ring, one that effectively steered away all other traffic. Unfortunately, however, the sound was a replica of the one that had been made by Nazy police cars. Throughout the city, Holocaust survivors had reacted with terror. The sirens had quickly been replaced.

"Were you in the room when they questioned her?"

"That redheaded one, she asked me to leave. Nothing doing, I told her. I wasn't going to let Anna alone."

Daniel stifled a smile. He could imagine Brenda having her hands full dealing with Sadie Rosen.

"And how did the questioning go?"

"Anna was all mixed-up that day. More than usual. And they were throwing questions at her about this Stark. Half the time, I'm sure Anna didn't know what they were talking about."

"They asked her something about a photo, didn't they?"

The diminutive Sadie shook her head angrily. "The whole thing is ridiculous. Asking a lady like Anna questions like that. I mean, take one look at her, and you tell me what she could possibly have to do with a *murder*?"

A minute later and Daniel indeed had the chance to take a look. A frail lady, whose gray head seemed too large for her wasted frame, lay in an old style four-poster bed.

The Final Analysis of Dr. Stark

A knitted afghan covered her, and three pillows propped up her head.

"I'm cold," Anna Gorman complained with the querulousness of the ill, refusing to acknowledge Daniel's presence. Sadie picked up a folded blanket at the foot of the bed, spread it out over the comforter, and assiduously tucked it around the sick woman's body.

"Is that better, darling?"

Anna Gorman's nod was weak. "I hope."

"This is Rabbi Wintor from the shul, Anna. He came here special to visit you."

Slowly and painfully, the old lady craned her head to regard Daniel. "Do I know you?" she asked in a thin voice, her face moving spasmodically.

"We haven't met," Daniel answered gently, moving forward to sit at her bedside, "but you're a friend of Sadie Rosen's, and Sadie's my friend."

"He's the one who spoke to that Schonfeld at the bank," Sadie put in. But Anna Gorman regarded her vaguely. Sadie looked knowingly at Daniel. "It's what I told you," she warned in a low voice, shaking her head. "Something that happened fifty years ago, and she could give you the name of the bank. . . . I must have told her about what you did with Schonfeld five times."

Rising, Daniel motioned Sadie to the side of the room. "Do you think it would be all right if I asked her a few questions?"

"What questions?" Sadie's eyes were glowing with curiosity.

"Questions connected to that murder."

"My God, Rabbi!"

"Trust me, Sadie. Anna has nothing to do with Dr. Stark's murder, but she might know something that could be helpful."

She looked up at him skeptically. "What could Anna possibly know about a murder?"

"Sadie, remember *you* called me a miracle man," Daniel teased. "Doesn't that entitle *me* to a little trust?"

She laughed like a young girl, and reached up to pat

him on the shoulder. "You're a wise guy, Rabbi. Okay, I suppose it wouldn't hurt. But I'm not leaving."

"Good." Daniel stepped up to the bed. He reached into his pocket and took out a pile of photographs, some of them pictures he had cut out from a book just an hour earlier. "Mrs. Gorman, I have a few pictures I want to show you. Please tell me if any of the people in them look familiar." The old woman made impatient noises, and Sadie hurried over with a pair of reading glasses and adjusted them on her face. Daniel held the first picture up. "Does this man look familiar, Mrs. Gorman?"

She puzzled over it, her sunken, parchmentlike cheeks creasing. "Is it somebody I'm supposed to know?" she demanded in a cracked voice.

"Probably not," Daniel said. He put the photo down. It was a classic Alfred Eisenstadt shot of the impressario Sol Hurok.

The old woman looked up from the picture to his face. "Then why are you showing it to me?" she demanded.

Daniel laughed. "Fair enough. In a sense, what I'm doing is testing your memory. There is no right or wrong answer. But some of the pictures might be familiar to you, and that would be a great help to me."

Anna Gorman nodded, but Daniel felt a stab of guilt. Adding more confusion to a mind already so confused was hardly an act of mercy.

He held up the second picture.

She stared at it a long while. "No," she finally said.

The third picture she shook away quickly.

It was Daniel's hand, though, that was shaking when he held up the fourth. He struggled to keep his voice even. "What about this one, Mrs. Gorman, does he look familiar?"

The old woman's dark eyes flicked over his face, then down to the photo. Then she gasped with far more power than Daniel would have thought possible. Sadie Rosen rushed over, picked up a glass of water from the night table, and passed it to Anna, placing an arm around her. But the old lady shook her off furiously, still panting. Daniel leaned

The Final Analysis of Dr. Stark

forward. "Please, Mrs. Gorman, I know you're trying to say something important, but I can't understand you."

Anna Gorman breathed as if she was fighting against a current. Then, painfully, her chest heaving, she lifted the forefinger on her right hand, and pointed to the picture. "Dr. Martin Reisman," she said clearly.

Friday Afternoon

Joe Cerezzi withdrew a key from a small envelope and fitted it into Stark's office door.

"Okay, Rabbi," he said as Daniel and Brenda followed him inside. "It's 1:57, and I've done everything you asked me. I gave instructions to hold off charging the girl until precisely 3 p.m. That gives you a whole hour to convince me otherwise."

"No problem," Daniel said, restlessly pacing the office. Dust had already begun to gather on Noah's books and framed diplomas. He remembered the hours he had spent here, his affection for Noah.

"Maybe you oughta get started then."

"I'm waiting for Dr. Steen." He turned to Brenda, hoping his face betrayed none of his underlying tension.

"He'll be here on time?"

Brenda's eyes crinkled. "Sure he will. He's a yekke."

"A what?" Cerezzi snapped.

"Jews from the area around Germany," Daniel answered. "Known for being very punctual. As opposed to East Europeans, like Brenda and me."

"In that case," Cerezzi said, inspecting his watch, "your yekke has got precisely twenty-four seconds to hold up his national honor . . . make that eighteen."

A knock. Daniel opened the door.

"Rabbi Winter?" Jerome Steen glanced around the room, acknowledged Cerezzi and Brenda unsmilingly, then turned back to Daniel. "Perhaps I misunderstood the nature of this meeting."

"As a matter of fact," Cerezzi boomed, "the rabbi's our

host. He called me this morning, said he had uncovered some angles he thought we'd overlooked. Insisted on a meeting with all three of us."

"You see," Daniel said, "I asked you and Dr. Goldstein because I think your psychological input will be helpful."

Steen nodded stiffly. "In that case, I am at your service."

They followed Daniel into Stark's inner office. Cerezzi motioned him to the seat behind the desk. "You're in charge," he said.

Daniel began abruptly. "I don't suppose any of you are familiar with the difference between *peshat* and *derash?*"

"Without the funny words again," Cerezzi said.

"If they had English equivalents, Lieutenant, I'd use them. Unfortunately, they only exist in Hebrew."

Cerezzi groaned. "And I suppose you're gonna tell me they have something to do with Stark's murder."

"With the murder, no. But with understanding it, very definitely yes."

Three pairs of eyes regarded him suspiciously.

Daniel went on. "You see *peshat* refers to the literal meaning of a biblical verse, *derash* to its homiletic or sermonic meaning."

"You want to run that by me again?" Cerezzi's confusion was almost comic.

"Better, I'll give you an example. There's a verse in Genesis—6:9. 'This is the story of Noah, Noah was a righteous and blameless man in his generation.' "

"That was the message you left for me with Doris?" Brenda cut in, leaning forward eagerly.

"That's right. You see, Brenda, at the time, I thought the reason you were upset was because you didn't like Noah. So I wanted to tell you how much I trusted him." He paused and turned to Steen. "Doctor, how would you explain that verse?"

Steen withdrew a handkerchief from his pocket and sneezed; then he looked up at Cerezzi, his eyes pinched behind the thick lenses. "Lieutenant," he began sharply, "I was called down here for what Dr. Goldstein led me to

The Final Analysis of Dr. Stark

believe would be an important conference about Dr. Stark's murder. Had she informed me that she was inviting me to a Sunday school lesson, I would have preferred to remain at home."

Cerezzi shrugged uncomfortably. "I'm sorry, Doctor, I think I understand your irritation, Rabbi, perhaps you could get to the point?"

"I give you my word that I'll tie it all together. In the meantime, Lieutenant, perhaps you could tell me what you think the verse means."

"C'mon, Rabbi. It's pretty clear. That Noah was a righteous man. The only saint in his time."

"Good. Pure, simple meaning. What we call *peshat*. The way most people would understand the verse. On the other hand, most of the rabbis in the Talmud would have disagreed with you. You see, they believed every word in the Bible was directly revealed by God. Not a single word was superfluous."

"So?"

"So let me repeat the verse: 'Noah was a righteous and blameless man *in his generation*.'

" *In his generation*," Brenda pondered. "Those words don't add anything, right?"

Daniel beamed. "Exactly. All the verse needed to say was that Noah was a righteous man. So the rabbis asked, what do those extra words 'in his generation' signify? And one of them answered that Noah probably wasn't so righteous after all. You see, it was only in his generation, a generation of terrible sinners, that he was judged righteous—as they put it, he was like a silver coin among copper coins. But had he lived in a moral society, he wouldn't have been anything special."

Despite himself, Cerezzi, an honors graduate of St. Francis Academy of Brooklyn, found himself intrigued. "Okay. But to me, though, it sounds like the rabbis had it in for the guy."

"Maybe a little." Daniel smiled. "But they had some other proofs. You see, when God told Abraham He was going to destroy Sodom and Gomorrah, Abraham argued with God, trying to convince Him not to. But when God told Noah He was going to destroy the world, Noah didn't put up any argument. Just started building an ark for himself and his family."

"This is ridiculous!" Steen's body was rigid with fury. "The three of you, adults, sitting around discussing fairy tales as if they were newspaper headlines. I am not a young man, my time is too precious for me to waste."

"Rabbi," Cerezzi said, "you're losing your audience. Better get to the point."

"Of course. To say, as you did, Lieutenant, that Noah was absolutely righteous, is *peshat*, understanding the text literally. But to say that he was righteous only by the standards of his own generation is *derash*, the sermonic meaning."

Brenda grinned. "I suppose I prefer *peshat*."

"Generally, I do too," Daniel answered solemnly. "Which is what occurred to me last night. You see, ever since Noah died, there's been one open question, and all our attempts to answer it have been *derash*."

Cerezzi cocked an eyebrow. "Meaning?"

"How did the murderer get Noah to the couch?"

"I'm betting the girl used a gun."

"But you know as well as I do the difficulties with that explanation, Lieutenant. Noah was twice as big as Cheryl. He would have had no problem jumping her before she crashed the statue down. How could she hold a gun and that heavy statue at the same time? And anyway, why should she bring him over to the couch at all? . . . Remember the discussion we had right after the murder? How every theory we offered gave a symbolic explanation, having to do with the patient getting the psychiatrist to the couch? Symbolism. *Derash*. But there's a different way to understand it. *Peshat*."

"Meaning?"

"If my understanding is correct, I think I can now construct a scenario of what happened on Tuesday. Cheryl Bornstein saw Noah at ten A.M. According to what she told me, she spent the session screaming at him, both about his

The Final Analysis of Dr. Stark

engagement to Jennifer and his affair with her. Then she stormed out and went to speak to you, Doctor."

"Is that true?" Cerezzi asked, suddenly alert.

Steen's eyes were on Daniel's grim face. "Yes, it is."

"How come you never told us about her visit?"

Steen cleared his throat. "As I have told you, Lieutenant, there are standards of professional confidentiality that all ethical psychiatrists abide by. One is that, unless there is an overriding reason, you don't go telling the police, or anybody for that matter, the names of those people who have consulted with you professionally. But in this instance it was even more than that. I was very familiar with Cheryl's case from things Noah had shared with me. He had, in fact, several times asked my advice on how to treat her. And since I believed her then—as I believe her now—to be incapable of killing another human being, I saw no reason to throw a troubled young woman into the middle of a police investigation.

"Let me go on," Daniel interposed. "Now, Tuesday, as we know, you had a session with Noah. Correct?"

Steen gave a barely perceptible nod.

"At those sessions, did Noah lie on the couch?"

"I am a traditional Freudian analyst. All my patients lie on the couch."

Daniel nodded. "Of course. And at that time did you raise the issue of Cheryl's visit to you with him?"

"I am not going to answer that."

"Any reason in particular, Doctor?" Cerezzi asked.

"Yes, a very particular reason. And I just gave it to you." Steen turned back to Daniel. "At such time, Rabbi, as you can show me how gossiping about my session with Noah will help catch his murderer, perhaps I will reconsider my position.

"Could you at least tell us then if you were concerned to learn that your daughter had just become engaged to a psychiatrist who stood accused of sleeping with one of his patients?"

Steen's face darkened. He did not answer.

"Let me put it to you a different way," Daniel countered diplomatically. "As a member of the Dittmyer Center for Psychoanalysis and Psychotherapy, could you tell me what action would be taken against a therapist found guilty of sleeping with a patient?"

"It would have been grounds for disciplinary procedure." Steen's reply was toneless.

"Including possible expulsion?"

"Possibly. Especially if we discovered other such cases."

"Did you believe Cheryl's story?"

Steen hesitated. He looked away from Daniel to Cerezzi. "I have always liked your American expression, 'let sleeping dogs lie.'" His cold gaze went around the room. "Noah Stark is dead. Can't we leave it at that? If you don't want to accept my hesitations as a pyschiatrist in discussing this matter with you, then let me ask you as a father. For my Jennie's sake. What good will bringing out a scandal do anyone?"

"Doctor, I'm impressed with your devotion to your daughter. I mean that sincerely. Which is exactly why I am sure you did confront Noah. But not at 12:30, as you so helpfully told the police was the time of your session with him. You saw Noah that day, no question. But later. I would guess it must have been around three. I'm sure that encounter with Cheryl horrified you. The things you learned about Noah must have shaken you deeply. Which is why I'm also sure you spoke to Noah about it, probably very sharply. You do get sharp, Doctor, when you're annoyed. You must have seriously questioned the wisdom of Noah's engagement to your daughter. You probably even raised the possibility of disciplinary action by the Center."

Steen remained in his seat, his eyes locked on Daniel's.

"Which now, Lieutenant," Daniel went on, "brings us to the *peshat*. You see, we all had fancy explanations for why a patient had murdered a psychiatrist on the couch. But in point of fact, there was a very simple reason for it all along." He fixed his eyes back on Steen. "Noah was having a session with you when you killed him."

Steen's face twisted, but he sat motionless. "You're a madman! What are you saying? That I murdered Noah to stop him from marrying my daughter? That's—"

"No," Daniel stopped him. "That is not why you killed Noah at all. You see, when you confronted Noah about Cheryl, I'm sure he acted very repentant. I knew him, Doctor, maybe not as well as you, but better than I knew him a week ago. I would guess Noah told you that you needed to understand him, that you were his psychiatrist, that you certainly shouldn't judge him without hearing him out. So that's why he went to the couch. Who knows, maybe he was uncomfortable looking you in the face when he spoke to you." Daniel pushed himself up from the chair and headed toward the couch. Still standing, he unbuttoned his shirt and loosened his tie. "Just as I'm sure Noah did." Slowly, Daniel stretched out on the couch and closed his eyes. "I'm no psychic, but Noah probably said something about how sad it would be if you started telling ugly stories about him, because then ugly stories would start coming out about other people as well. Like a man he knew, a very respected figure in the LA psychiatric community who, forty-five years ago, saved his own life by denouncing Anna and Michael Gorman and their hidden jewels to the Nazis?" Daniel sat up and his voice was dangerously gentle. "Isn't that more or less what he said, Martin Reisman?"

The psychiatrist gripped his chair and glared fiercely at Daniel.

"Wasn't it then, Doctor," said Daniel, now on his feet, "that you stepped over in back of him, slipped out a handkerchief from your ample supply, picked up the statue, and crashed it down on his head? And then proceeded deliberately to bring the statue down on his head, again and again. You knew very well that the police would believe it was one of Noah's patients, acting in a frenzy. And didn't you then, Doctor, go over to the desk and take Noah's appointment book, because it listed your session with him? Didn't you, in fact, murder Noah Stark because he threatened to expose you for crimes you committed under the Nazis?"

Jerome Steen sat motionless. He looked up at Daniel with a blank expression. "Noah promised me she was dead."

"No, Doctor," Daniel shook his head. "I showed Anna Gorman your picture just this morning. She identified you immediately. . . . You did kill Noah Stark, didn't you?"

Steen remained still. His smoky-gray eyes twisted into Daniel, as if pleading with him. Then he nodded.

Chapter 18

Friday Afternoon

*Transcript of Statement to Police of Rabbi
Daniel Winter*

I went to see Anna Gorman Friday morning,
May 8, at 10:00 A.M. At that time, I showed her
photographs of several people, one of them, Dr.
Jerome Steen. The picture was a small copy of a
photograph of Steen hanging in Noah Stark's office. While Mrs. Gorman could not identify any
of the other photographs, she became very upset
when she saw the picture of Dr. Steen. She identified the photograph as Martin Reisman—a name
I recognized from the file Noah had asked me to
safeguard the night before he was murdered. Before going on, I feel it imperative to emphasize
that though Mrs. Gorman is frail and easily confused about the present, Sadie Rosen—who takes
care of her and has known her for over forty
years—assures me that her memory for the past
has remained very accurate.

Mrs. Gorman told me that Martin Reisman
was her neighbor in Vienna. In the fall of 1941,
many Jews started receiving summonses to report
to the Community Center with twenty kilos of
luggage. The Nazis said it was for "resettlement

in the East." Among those receiving the summonses was Reisman, a young man in his early twenties, who lived next door to Anna and her husband Michael. During the preceding two years they had developed a close relationship with him. After receiving the summons, Reisman came to their house in despair. Michael Gorman, who, before the Nazis, had been a successful jewelry dealer, went to his hiding place—Mrs. Gorman emphasized that this was done in the presence of Reisman; indeed, he needed Reisman's help in getting to it—and took out two diamonds. "Maybe you'll be able to bribe them with these," he said, and gave Reisman the jewels. Two mornings later, a Nazi officer and two soldiers raided the Gorman house. After ordering the couple to a couch with a gun, they immediately pushed the dining room furniture to one side, lifted up the rug, and ripped out the fourth floorboard, under which was stored the cache of gold and diamonds which the Gormans had been hiding both for themselves and several other people—a Dr. Gerhard Simon, a widow named Hannah Weiler, and a third man whom Mrs. Gorman could only recall as either Bierman or Berman. These are, of course, the other three names mentioned in the file. As the Nazis started pulling up the jewels, Michael Gorman jumped up and cursed the soldiers, calling them "Nazi dogs." The officer knocked him to the ground with a club. "You mean Jewish dogs, don't you?" he taunted. He pointed with his club to Reisman's house next door. "My compliments to your young neighbor. His information was impeccable." That same day, the Gormans were deported. Michael Gorman was subsequently gassed in Auschwitz. Anna was sent to the "model" camp in Thereisenstadt, where she was one of the twelve hundred inmates released in February 1945.

After the war, Mrs. Gorman found herself

first in Poland, then Germany. It was during this period she found out about the death of her husband. She also made many efforts to trace Martin Reisman, including an affidavit she subsequently deposited with Nazi-hunter Simon Wiesenthal in Vienna. Nobody she spoke to had ever heard of him.

In 1950 she was admitted to the United States, and lived for the next thirty-five years in New York. She visited Los Angeles several times during this period, and always stayed with her friend and fellow survivor from Theresienstadt, Sadie Rosen— a woman whom I know as a member of my congregation. When Sadie's husband died last year, she invited Anna to Los Angeles. It was Sadie who insisted that Anna see someone about her increasingly severe problem of insomnia, and Sadie got the name of Noah Stark from the president of our synagogue, Sam Bornstein. As the date on Noah's file reveals, Mrs. Gorman went to see him just over three months ago. It was at Noah's office that she first saw the photograph of Jerome Steen. "The man, of course, was much older than Martin Reisman," she told me, "but I remembered the eyes, the same cold, gray eyes."

She had broken down in Noah's office when she saw the picture, and had told Noah the same story I have just recounted.

I asked Mrs. Gorman how Noah had reacted to what she said. He had assured her that the man whose picture had so provoked her was a psychiatrist he knew, a man who was American-born, and, in fact, not even Jewish. Needless to say, Noah's own files reveal that he must have immediately known that Jerome Steen and Martin Reisman were the same person. He wrote after the session, "Extraordinary revelations. . . . I am very excited," and underlined the name Martin Reisman—all of which would have made no sense if Mrs. Gorman's story was entirely unfamiliar to him. This also explains why he entrusted the document to me Monday night. He was preparing himself with material to use in case Dr. Steen reacted adversely to his engagement to Jennifer —and he wanted to take no chance on Steen, who was familiar with his office, finding and destroying the Anna Gorman file. While such behavior on Noah's part would previously have seemed inconceivable to me, things I have learned these past days have convinced me that Noah routinely used information about his patients when it was in his interest to do so.

One final point. I asked Mrs. Gorman if there were any distinguishing physical marks that characterized Martin Reisman. She could think of none, but then she finally said *der heuschnupfen*. When I realized that the word wasn't English, I asked Sadie Rosen for help. She knew the word immediately. "It's German for hay fever," she told me.

Written Statement and Confession of Dr. Jerome Steen

This statement is being offered voluntarily. The police have not coerced me, and have extended me no promises or offers of more lenient treatment.

Tuesday morning, Cheryl Bornstein came to my house. Though I had not previously met her, I was familiar with her case from several discussions I had had about her with Noah. He often consulted on his cases with me and solicited my advice. Miss Bornstein told me that she had learned of Noah's engagement to my daughter the previous night, and that there were certain facts of which she thought I should be aware. From almost the beginning of her therapy, a year and a half

The Final Analysis of Dr. Stark

earlier, Noah had been sleeping with her—often
during their sessions—and he had told her several
times that, at the completion of her treatment, he
expected to marry her. I questioned Miss Bornstein closely, and was drawn to the unhappy conclusion that she was telling the truth. In my capacity
as Chairman of the Ethics Committee of the Dittmyer Center for Psychoanalysis and Psychotherapy, several complaints had already come before
me concerning Noah. The first case, about three
years ago, was brought by a young woman who
told me that Noah had slept with her while she
was under his care. She, likewise, said he had
spoken of the possibility of marrying her. Noah
had vehemently denied the accusation, and the
young woman subsequently informed me that
she had decided against pressing charges. A year
later, during analysis, Noah inadvertently let it
slip that he had, in fact, slept with the woman.
He then swore to me that it was all at her insti-
gation, had never happened during a session—
rather, he was summoned to her house for a supposed emergency—and that it would never happen again. After much soul-searching, I concluded
that the matter should not be pursued. On two
other occasions, patients brought complaints to
me that they had heard from mutual acquaintances
that Noah had broken psychiatric confidentiality
and revealed that they were his patients, and even
details of their therapy. In both instances, the
accusations were denied by Noah, and were withdrawn before I could speak to the supposed recipients of Noah's gossip. I therefore concluded
that there was no grounds for disciplinary procedure, though it did raise a certain concern in me
about Noah's character and professional fitness.
When I gingerly tried to dissuade my daughter
Jennifer from forming a romantic attachment to
him, she reacted with great anger toward me, and

I felt duty-bound to not share with her the un-verified accusations that had been brought to my attention, and the admission Noah had made to me as his psychiatrist.

After the meeting with Miss Bornstein on Tuesday, I decided that I must confront Noah. While our sessions normally ran from 12:30 to 1:15, I had changed it that day to three, because I hoped to spend the day finishing an article for the *Psychoanalytic Review*.

When I arrived at the office, I immediately told Noah what I had learned. As I expected, Noah categorically denied all the accusations, claiming that Miss Bornstein had fixated on him during her treatment with him, and was now seeking revenge because of his engagement. I told Noah that I believed he was lying, and that I intended to raise the issue of his fitness to practice with the Board of the Center, and that—in addition to Miss Bornstein—I would invite the other three accusers to also meet with the Board. I further said that it should be obvious that this was no time for him to be involved in any romantic entanglements—and that I expected him to speak to Jennifer immediately. If not, I would feel compelled to do so.

Noah's reaction was almost precisely as Rabbi Winter depicted it. He pleaded with me as his patient to hear his side of the story, and told me it would be more comfortable for him if he could lie down on the couch—that was the only position in which he felt fully accustomed to speaking about himself with me. In retrospect, I believe it was simply that he did not have the nerve to look me in the face with the blackmail offer he was planning to propose. Noah stood up from behind his desk, and went over to the couch. It was at that point that I first noticed the statue on the small table

The Final Analysis of Dr. Stark

alongside it. When Noah spoke, he again firmly denied any inappropriate behavior, and swore that he was the victim of rumors. "Aren't rumors unfair?" he asked me.

"Sometimes they are, sometimes they aren't," I answered.

"Then tell me if this is a fair one," he said, and went on to detail allegations he had heard from a former patient of his—now deceased, he said—about a man named Martin Reisman who saved his life by denouncing other Jews to the Nazis. My heart froze. I saw that Noah intended to destroy me—to take the life that I had carefully built over the last forty years and destroy it because of a youthful indiscretion committed when I was twenty-two. What I had done in Vienna was wrong, I know that, and I have no intention of claiming that it wasn't. But nobody who was not there can understand the pressures under which all of us were then living. My whole life since the war has been devoted to helping people—Noah's, I now understood, was devoted to destroying lives. And yet the only way I could stop him from destroying mine would be to ignore Miss Bornstein's complaint, to allow him to go on practicing, and to let him marry my daughter, the most precious being on earth to me. I realized instantly that it would be self-serving and immoral for me to do so. I withdrew a handkerchief from my pocket and lifted the statue. Noah did not notice—his eyes were closed the whole time he was speaking—and I brought the statue down on his head twice. I checked his pulse. He was dead. I was shocked and frightened by all that had happened—some blood had even splattered onto my shirt—and sat down for a few moments to recover my composure. Then, I went back to the couch and slammed the statue on him several more times, taking care to avoid the blood. I wanted the killing to appear to be committed by what lay people would call a person insane with rage.

I knew the service elevator was next door to Noah's office. Until retirement, my office had been on the fourth floor of the same building. I quickly checked the hallway. It was empty. Then I stepped out with the statue, putting a matchbox under the outer door of Noah's office, so it wouldn't close against me. I went into the room where the service elevator is located, took it to the basement, and dumped the statue in a large can. Though I was quite sure my fingerprints were not on it, I feared I might have inadvertently touched the statue earlier. Also, I hoped it would be quickly carted away, and there would be maximum confusion concerning the weapon used. I returned to Noah's office for a final inspection—to see if I had left anything behind. It was at this point that I saw the appointment book on his desk. My session was listed there for three. I took the book—I subsequently tore up its pages and disposed of them in various public garbage cans—closed the office, and left via the service elevator, which I took to the parking level. I kept my briefcase in front of my bloodstained shirt. No one saw me. I then drove home.

I want it clearly understood, particularly by Jennifer and my colleagues at the Center, that since Tuesday, I have endeavored to ensure that no one else be charged with the crime. That is why I instructed Miss Bornstein to not tell the police about her unfortunate experiences with Noah, and her subsequent conversation with me. I feared that that would incline the police to suspect her. I likewise attempted to stop the police from confiscating Noah's files, and when I was forced to consent to their looking through them, I used whatever powers of persuasion were at my

The Final Analysis of Dr. Stark

command to influence Dr. Goldstein from focus-
ing on any one patient.

I know that, by conventional standards, what
I did will be considered wrong. And I am sorry
for the shame that this will bring down on Jennifer's head, and for any embarrassment that will
be caused to the Center. But only one thought
guided me—a sense of mission and responsibility
to the future patients that would otherwise have
entrusted themselves to Noah's care. It was I who
played so instrumental a role in certifying and
training Noah Stark. And, therefore, I would have
considered myself responsible for all the future
damage and evil he would have done in the name
of a profession I love and honor. Even in thinking
back over it, I do not believe I could have acted
in any other way.

Epilogue

Jerome Steen was convicted of voluntary manslaughter, and sentenced to six to ten years in prison. He is currently in the California state prison in Chino.

Congressman Russell Grant came in third in the Republican senatorial primary. He now practices law in Orange County, and periodically speaks with friends about running for his old seat in the House. Subsequent to the primary, Grant spent two months at the Betty Ford Clinic, and has not touched liquor since he got out.

Roger Levin has been shifted to the Washington office of the *Los Angeles Times*. In private conversations with fellow journalists, he has confided that the information about Grant was originally hinted at to him by Noah Stark. Over drinks at a cocktail party, Stark had bragged about a patient of his, a conservative congressman, who had dreams of running for the Senate, maybe the presidency someday. Levin figured out the rest.

Jennifer Steen left Los Angeles within days of her father's arrest and confession. She is currently assumed to be somewhere in the Pacific Northwest.

The Final Analysis of Dr. Stark

Anna Gorman died of complications from her stroke on August 23. Daniel Winter was the officiating rabbi at the funeral.

Jonah Stark's business was saved from bankruptcy by the timely arrival of his one hundred thousand dollar inheritance from Noah. Two months after the psychiatrist's death, Jonah showed up at Daniel's synagogue on a Saturday morning and recited the memorial prayer for the dead, the Kaddish. He subsequently continued doing so during the remaining nine months of mourning.

Arlette Stark married Ronald Kaplan, a successful Encino real estate developer. It was a second marriage for both partners. After an initially difficult period, Adam Stark now calls Kaplan "Daddy."

In September, *Cheryl Bornstein* moved out of her parents' house and took an apartment in West Los Angeles. She is currently undergoing a successful experience of therapy with LA psychiatrist Dr. Ronald Gray, and is enrolled in an M.A. program in Art History at the University of Southern California.

Four months after the events described in this book, *Gladys Perl* filed for divorce from her husband *Andrew* in Los Angeles Municipal Court. She was granted full custody of their two daughters. Perl is still unemployed.

Two libel suits were filed against *Joan Reider* in May and June; the first by actress Scarlett Payson after Reider had reported that she had undergone a secret abortion. Payson, a religious Catholic, argued that the report—which was false—caused her extreme mental anguish. The case was settled out of court for $150,000. A subsequent action against Reider was brought by the widow of actor Randolph Rich, who had committed suicide after Reider disclosed that ten years earlier—while still an unknown—he had supported himself in San Francisco as a homosexual gigolo. Reider brought affidavits confirming her allegation, and the case was dismissed. Two weeks later, the NBC network affiliate in Los Angeles chose not to renew Reider's contract.

Lt. Joe Cerezzi has now gone without a cigarette for six months. He has, however, gained fourteen pounds, and has been ordered to take off the excessive weight within sixty days by his superior at homicide, Capt. Robert Grier.

On August 28, seven months to the day they met, *Daniel Winter* sat over a candlelit dinner with *Brenda Goldstein*, and presented her with an elegant, dark velvet box. A flush crept over Brenda's cheeks. She looked up at Daniel, slowly opened the case, then threw back her head and burst out laughing. Inside was an enormous fake diamond, clearly purchased at the local five and dime. The plastic jewel was glued onto a painted gold band. It gleamed ostentatiously in the soft light.

"You once told me," Daniel said, when the laughter subsided, "that three months was not enough time to be certain. I wasn't sure if seven was either, so I figured I better be cautious before I bought real diamonds."

"Daniel, are you proposing to me?"

"Are you accepting?"

Their marriage is set for December 23 of this year.

ABOUT THE AUTHOR

JOSEPH TELUSHKIN, born in 1948, holds a rabbinic degree from Yeshiva University, and a graduate degree in history from Columbia University. Between 1977–83, Telushkin was education director of the Brandeis-Bardin Institute in California. He is author, with Dennis Prager, of *The Nine Questions People Ask About Judaism* and *Why the Jews*. His most recent book is *Uncommon Sense: The World's Fullest Compendium of Wisdom. The Final Analysis of Dr. Stark* is the second Rabbi Daniel Winter mystery in the series that commenced with *The Unorthodox Murder of Rabbi Wahl* and the author is currently at work on the third Rabbi Winter mystery, *An Eye for an Eye.*

NERO WOLFE STEPS OUT

Every Wolfe Watcher knows that the world's largest detective wouldn't dream of leaving the brownstone on 35th street, with Fritz's three star meals, his beloved orchids and the only chair that actually suits him. But when an ultra-conservative college professor winds up dead and Archie winds up in jail, Wolfe is forced to brave the wilds of upstate New York to find a murderer.

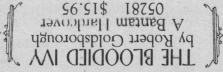

THE BLOODIED IVY
by Robert Goldsborough
A Bantam Hardcover
05281 $15.95

and don't miss these other Nero Wolfe mysteries by Robert Goldsborough: